SECOND TIME AROUND

LINDA KAY SILVA

Spinsters Ink
2009

Spinsters Ink
P.O. Box 242
Midway, Florida 32343

Printed in the United States of America on acid-free paper
First Edition

Editor: Katherine V. Forrest
Cover designer: Linda Callaghan

ISBN-10: 1-935226-03-7
ISBN-13: 978-1-935226-03-1

Thanks

Like Delta Stevens before her, Jessie Ferguson lives in the marrow of my bones...speaking to me in ancient riddles and whispering words of encouragement and wisdom in my ear. One of those conversations included thanking those who have buffeted us along this solitary path of writing. We are in this together, she and I, but we could not be successful without:

Lori: for giving me the gift of time to do what brings me so much joy.

Sandi: aka Bacon Saver. Thank you so much for saving mine. Invaluable and priceless.

All of those who picked up Jessie the first day.

My greatest true love, Lucy, who fills my heart and loves me unconditionally.

A Shout Out To

My...uh...peeps in the English Department at Maricopa High School. Let's face it...We ROCK! Thank you for welcoming me with so much laughter.

My sophomores and juniors at MHS who have managed to survive Miss' class and make her laugh in the meantime. You ROCK, too!

About the Author

This is Linda Kay's ninth published novel and the second in the Across Time series. She is currently working on the sixth of the series as well as another paranormal series starring an empath. Linda Kay works and resides in Arizona, where she teaches a crazy bunch of teenagers who keep her on her toes and make her laugh every day. Writing, teaching online and learning all there is to know about her new home state is keeping her plenty busy. She has a new motto on a banner in her classroom that she wants to share with all her readers in the hopes of inspiring them to follow their dreams:

It costs you nothing to dream and everything not to

So dream big.

Or go home.

Jessie Ferguson walked into the newly refurbished library and stood at the door staring. She and her father had finished the whole library by hand, creating ceiling to floor bookshelves, including a wheeled ladder for reaching the top shelves. The shelves contained over two thousand leather-bound books and another three thousand hardbound books purchased solely by her over the course of the three years she'd been living in the Inn. She'd spent her first two summers scouring the coastline estate sales, garage sales and library sales. Her third summer was spent cataloging and organizing her precious possessions. As a history major and a frequent flier through time, she'd found that the history books and thick tomes on philosophy and religion were like priceless relics to her and she cared for them as lovingly as anyone else might a puppy or kitten. This was her favorite place in the world; in this time period, of course.

When she'd returned from Wales, she announced that she, personally, wanted to contribute to the Inn's growth and well-being. The pronouncement had surprised and delighted her parents, who had thrown every penny and muscle into creating a

Grande Dame out of the ugly step sister Victorian, but they had never anticipated just how serious Jessie was about her books, the library or her studies. Now, her library was the talk of the town, and several of the town's antique dealers kept an eye out on the book trade in Portland, Salem and Eugene to help add to her growing collection.

She took in the smell of the dark woods and the leather wingback chairs, and admired the polished silver swords adorning the red wall on the far side of the library. A new window seat overlooked the majestic Pacific Ocean, and directly across from the window seat, thirty feet away, a stone fireplace loomed like a silent gargoyle. A huge mahogany desk balanced the room on the other side and held the one thing all the travelers of the twenty-first century would need: the Internet.

Her father had paid her for the work she'd done when they first moved here, and her contribution to the family's new life was to use that money to create her own special place in the Inn. She had works dating back to the sixteenth century, signed novels, and complete sets that were the envy of many a book collector. There were a handful of first editions, which she kept behind the only locked glass bookshelf. When no one was looking, she would open the glass door and just touch her first edition *Alice in Wonderland*. Maybe she felt a kinship to Alice because the rabbit hole was analogous to the portal she used when she traversed through time. Like Alice, she'd met fascinating characters, learned incredible lessons, and went places few would ever believe. She wondered about Lewis Carroll. The man, after all, also wrote the other first edition standing next to Alice, a book called *Symbolic Logic*, and though it wasn't fiction, it showed the kind of genius a man like Carroll possessed. Surely he had slipped through time as well.

Stepping into the library, she grabbed a stack of books and ensconced herself in the window seat to start reading up on pirates. She'd had a couple of odd flashes of pirates the last couple of nights, and that almost always meant that someone was trying to contact her. Someone was trying to come through. Cracking open a book that groaned as she turned the first page, she grinned. Pirates from two centuries—Irish pirates, Vikings,

English pirates, Spanish buccaneers—there were more pirates than she had imagined, but that didn't keep her from reading until she could barely keep her eyes open.

Just before nodding off, she glanced up at the clock and was surprised to see it was nearly ten o'clock. The dinner her mother had brought in for her lay cold and unappetizing on the desk. She had been too absorbed in the accounts of piracy and famous exploits of Bluebeard to stop and eat. Though her major in history had an emphasis in ancient civilizations, not one of her professors had given pirates so much as a passing glance. It was as if they had existed in some sort of vacuum which historians refused to acknowledge, perhaps due in part to the modern day British viewing their pirates much like Americans viewed their own shameful history of slavery.

Yawning and stretching, Jessie slid her Celtic bookmark into the book and rose unsteadily to her feet, her mind swirling with three-masted Spanish galleons, swashbuckling Errol Flynn types and booty galore. She was amazed at how rampant piracy was and even more surprised to discover that English piracy had been advocated by Queen Elizabeth I herself.

As she made her way to her room, she heard Daniel call her, so she stuck her head inside his room. "Hey, Sport, still awake?" Jessie sat on the edge of his bed and looked down at him. Gone were the X-Men and Spiderman posters of his childhood. Now, at age thirteen, Daniel had movie posters of old classics like *Poltergeist*, *Ghostbusters*, and, much to his family's surprise, *Ghost*. He'd found them all on eBay and bought them with his own money. Rick and Reena thought he was just going through weird boy adolescence, but Jessie knew better. Daniel was certain of the spiritual energies and powers within the house, and was determined to make contact with them. The posters weren't just posters…they represented his favorite movies. He belonged to three chat rooms about paranormal subjects, read everything he could get his hands on about psychic phenomena, and had even taken the bus on several occasions to "woo-woo" Eugene to listen to a renowned ghost hunter detail his experiences.

"I think I saw a man in the house this afternoon when you went out to lunch."

Hearing the spirits was one thing, but seeing them worried her. "A man? A real man or one of your—"

"A real man. I was outside watering the Japanese garden and I felt…I don't know…my hackles rise. So I turned around, looked up at the window, and there he was, staring at me."

"Maybe he was a worker or something."

Daniel shook his head. "Mom and Dad didn't have anyone scheduled. I checked."

Jessie felt her heart quicken. "Did he see you see him?"

"Yep. When I looked up, he stepped away from the window. The curtain moved. I saw him, Jess. I swear I did."

"I believe you, Sport. What did he look like?"

"Brownish-colored hair—that was really all I could see from down here. I went upstairs but he was gone."

"You say anything to Mom and Dad?"

Daniel rolled his eyes. "Yeah, right. They already think I'm cuckoo. That's all they need is to think I'm seeing things. I'd be sitting in a padded cell."

"Anything else you can remember about him?"

Daniel shook his head. "Just that he was looking down at me. It was kind of creepy."

"Which window was he looking out?"

"The library."

"Really? The south window?"

"Yeah."

Jessie nodded. "I'll check around town and see if there are any strangers in town. Maybe someone was lost or wandered in the wrong door. You're sure he wasn't someone just checking out the Inn?"

"I'm positive, Jess. There was something…not right about him looking at me. I felt…spied on. I know that sounds paranoid, but—"

"No, it doesn't. I'm glad you told me. For now, you get some sleep and don't worry so much." Rising, she tousled Daniel's hair.

"Hey Jess? Thanks a lot for believing me. That means a lot, you know?"

She nodded. "Get some sleep, okay?"

Walking into her room, Jessie exhaled loudly. Since coming to New Haven, she'd met a woman whose soul was over two thousand years old, hung out with a "bad boy" who was an empath, and her brother heard and was now seeing ghosts.

Suddenly, time travel didn't seem like such a strange concept after all.

***

21st Century

Jessie focused on her breathing before she held the ankh in her right hand. Closing her fist around it, she was surprised at how quickly it became hot; so hot, it felt as if it might burn her skin.

Falling deeper into the familiar embrace of the mists of the Otherworld, she found herself standing at the edge of a stone circle; the same circle where she'd met Cate and Maeve three years ago. The three squarish stones the size of hope chests made Jessie smile. She loved this circle and all it represented. Normally, when she arrived, Cate and Maeve were soon to follow.

Normally.

Odd how those fleeting moments with them had seemed so much longer. Like the ankh, those times were burned into her mind. Perhaps the greatest lesson she'd learned was that the quality of one's relationships had less to do with time spent together than with the manner in which it was spent.

In the background of the stone circle a mist dropped from the sky like a gray curtain. She had wondered if it were the fabled Mists of Avalon or merely the dividing line between her world and the Otherworld, for surely the Otherworld was where they had bridged the gap of two thousand years.

Taking her seat on the stone, she sighed. She felt so much more knowledgeable about this world than the last time she was here. It wasn't just college that had enlightened her. She'd read every book she could about Druidry, the ancient Celts, and the transmigration of souls. She'd scoured the Internet for chat rooms, usenet groups, and e-zines; anything she could get her hands on that would give her more information on where she'd been and where she might someday go. Nothing sated her curiosity about her Druid friends. There was only one thing she really wanted to know: Did they miss her as much as she missed them?

Watching the mist as she had done so many times in the last three years, she willed it to part. She had to see them this time. How could she help if she didn't know what was being asked of her?

Suddenly, the fog swirled around as if blown by a great wind. As it parted, Cate McEwen walked through it, her green robe gently caressed by the mist.

Jessie was on her feet in an instant. Three years she had pictured this moment, yet she still wasn't prepared for the flood of emotions washing over her.

"You came," she sighed, her voice sounding unlike itself.

Cate smiled and dropped the hood of her robe as she approached, revealing a shock of bright red hair cut short. "How could I not? You called and I answered. It only seems fair since you answered when I called." Wrapping her arms around Jessie, Cate hugged her tightly.

Jessie clung to her and tried not to cry. It had seemed so long, and she cared so much. Reluctantly pulling away, she stepped back and smiled at Cate. "You look wonderful, and I see you've moved up in rank."

Cate looked down at her robe. "Oh, yes. I finished my training earlier than anticipated. They gave me extra points for coming through the portal successfully. I see you've been studying your Druid lore. Are you remembering?"

"More and more each day." Jessie stepped further back. "Let me take a look at you. Oh, how I've missed you."

"And I, you. You look well, my friend. You must be happy." Cate gestured for Jessie to resume her seat.

She sat back down, but remained holding one of Cate's hands. "How's Maeve?"

"Quite well. She sends her love."

Inhaling deeply, Jessie said, "I have so many questions…"

Patting the back of Jessie's hand, Cate said softly, "I am sure you do, but they are not the reason for this visit, are they?"

Shaking her head, she replied, "I wish they were. Not a day has gone by that I haven't thought of you and Maeve. Not a single day in three years."

Cate wiped a tear from her eye. "As have I." She looked at the necklace around Jessie's neck. "I see you were able to dig up the ankh."

Jessie touched it. "Yes, thank you so much for burying it for me. It meant so much knowing you all made it out. I so wanted you to be safe. I don't know what I would have done if I had to live the rest of my life not knowing."

"Thanks to you, we managed to save so many more than we ever imagined. I cannot thank you enough…for saving not only my people, but the woman I love. Every day with her is a gift."

"It was my privilege. You…you've changed my life."

"Did Ceara help you figure out the ankh, or were you able to manage it on your own?"

Jessie blushed. "A little of both. I've been coming here… trying out my craft…hoping to find you, talk to you and see how you were. I know I promised—"

"You promised you would not use the portal. This is not that. To come here takes skill in the arts, a knowing that only comes with practice. I am glad that you have been practicing, and sorry that I have not been here. My time has been spent under the tutelage of Maeve and Lachlan, and they do not want me to get overly fond of this Dreamworld or the Otherworld. The Sidhe can be…dangerous."

"Dangerous?"

Cate nodded. "They enjoy a good joke, as many faery folk do, but they also have a power that can entrap a person. They are not to be trifled with."

"Then how come we never see any when we are here?"

"The Sidhe have left you alone because of Maeve."

"No kidding?"

Cate cocked her head. "No…I am not… kidding. Maeve has powers beyond anything I have ever imagined. Something happened in Gaul once, I do not know what, specifically, but she did something that put the Sidhe in her debt. They respect her.

She asked them to leave you be while you trained yourself, while you remembered that which is in you. The Sidhe have done so not only out of respect for her, but because people like you, in your time, have the power to bring the faery realm closer to the Land of the Living. They would really like that."

Jessie nodded. "That would be totally cool."

"Now then." Turning to the fire pit, Cate waved her hand and a huge fire rose. "Everything is magical in here, Jessie, but it is no place to linger."

"Not even for you?"

Cate grinned. "Not even for me. I respect it. I can move through it and around it, but it is not a place for either of us." She laid her hand over Jessie's. "Tell me, my friend, what is it that brings you here this day?"

Jessie sighed. It felt so good being with her again. She realized how lonely she had been. Spending so much time in her head, she had been neglecting her heart. Three years had gone by and she was no closer to finding her Anam Cara, or soul mate. Three years…she made a note to work on that part of her life.

"I had a visit from one of us," she told Cate.

Cate frowned. "A visit? From another?"

Jessie nodded. "He's a pirate."

"A pirate?"

"Yes. His name is Spencer. I think he lives in the fifteenth or sixteenth century, and he's looking for a box of some sort."

"A box? And what does he need you for?"

Shrugging, Jessie rose and warmed her backside by the fire. "That's just it. I don't know. I went through the portal to find—"

"You went to his time to find a…box?"

Jessie bowed her head. "I did. I'm sorry. I guess I was expecting to find a different you, another you, but I was wrong. I wasn't prepared for just how different."

"I see." Cate frowned and muttered something under her breath. "So, we are this Spencer the pirate in the fifteenth or sixteenth century looking for a box. Why on earth would he need you to help him find it? More importantly, how did he find you? Is he a Druid of some sort? Is he knowledgeable in the arts?"

Shaking her head, Jessie replied, "Far from it, I'm afraid. The man couldn't be more different from you."

Cate stared hard at her. "Once again, one of your past lives has come to you for help. You should not be so surprised, my friend. You have opened a door that any of us can come through now." Cate's eyes sparkled. "I cannot help you with this pirate and the box, because I know nothing about the time you speak of. Maeve and Lachlan have forbidden anyone from going through the portal again, though I have often thought about it."

"The portal? Did you all go back on Anglesey after the fire?"

"No. We are in Alba...Scotland... but Maeve found a portal in one of the rocky crags in a cavern near the shore. I am only now realizing how Maeve is tied to the portals in some strange manner. She appears to know where they all are." Cate rose and stood in front of the fire. Reaching into one of three leather pouches hanging around her waist, she withdrew a powder and threw it into the fire, which leapt and hissed. "I cannot help you with this, Jessie, because of my promise to Maeve to stay in my own time, but I do so long to hear about your life. You seem so whole, so alive, so full of energy. You are...happy."

Jessie looked into the fire and saw an image of herself laughing and hanging out with Tanner; Tanner, who had loved her as a friend from afar for three years, never asking her for anything more than that friendship. It wasn't until this moment, as she watched him looking at her that she realized just how deeply he cared. And she cared back. But, do you sacrifice a friendship in order to sate your loneliness, even though you know he isn't the one? Jessie sighed.

"I am happy, Cate. My life is finally moving in the right direction. I am in school, I have friends, and I have my Druid studies. I love my life."

"I can tell, and I am happy for you. You deserve it...but you need to fill that emptiness somehow, my friend. Who knows how long it will be before you find her again?" Cate peered into Jessie's eyes. "We have to take love where we find it. People come and go in our lives, dropping pieces of wisdom for us. Do not close yourself off because of this foreknowledge."

Resignedly, Jessie said, "There's a saying my friends have that gives me the creeps. They say, 'He may not be Mr. Right, but he's good enough to be Mr. Right Now.'"

Cate frowned. "And this gives you the creeps?"

Jessie stared at her. "Because it means you know this guy is only temporary and you don't care."

"I do not understand. Jessie, everyone in your life is temporary with the singular exception of Maeve. Do you not yet realize what that means? It means we must open our hearts to everyone who offers, and even to those we do not love." She gently laid her hand on Jessie's. "Open your heart to him, my friend...even if for only a little while."

Jessie closed her eyes and tried to imagine being close enough to Tanner to kiss him. They had only shared a New Year's kiss once, and it was that one kiss that let her know he cared for her as more than just a friend. "He does love me."

"Of course he does. Who could not? Just think about it, Jessie, and ask yourself what you would have done if you hadn't known she was coming. You must always conduct your life that way. By doing this, you will not inadvertently close any doors." Cate motioned to her. "Now, sit...please, and tell me what you have been doing."

For the next hour or so, Jessie shared her life with Cate, from the trip to Wales all the way to the Spanish galleon floating back and forth in her dreams for over a week. Cate listened, enrapt at the notion of flying in a plane to Wales. She asked dozens of questions she hadn't had time to ask before, from electricity to the Internet, and her eyes grew wide as Jessie told her about the university. When Jessie finished, Cate clapped her hands with delight.

"What wondrous ways you've spent your time, my friend. I can see the wisdom in your eyes and I hear it in your words. You have grown into a remarkable young woman, Jessie Ferguson."

Jessie reflected on this. How could she not become remarkable? She was Cate McEwen, a Druid priestess who had trained herself to remember who she was. She was a woman who wanted to continue on in time, to know the lessons she'd learned in other lives. Cate was who Jessie was, but she was so much more than that. Cate McEwen was also who Jessie wanted to be. Cate was Jessie's idol, her mentor, her hero. It was because of Cate that she had stopped being a stoner, that she stopped being rebellious for rebelliousness' sake. Cate made her want to be her best. So, she learned in her studies how important ancestors were to the Celts, and how the Druids always called up the spirits of the ancestors for guidance and wisdom. For a culture that believed they would see each other the next time around, staying connected to who you were and the people who bonded you to a particular time was essential to healthy spiritual growth.

Cate McEwen shared Jessie's soul, and in the twenty-first century, Jessie took Cate with her everywhere she went. When considering her first class schedule, she had thought about the courses that Cate would love. When thinking about the altar she created for her private rituals, she wondered how Cate would have set hers up. Cate was never far from the forefront of Jessie's mind or heart, and she loved her as she did a dear friend, even though she had been dead for over two thousand years.

"Now, it's your turn, Cate. What happened after Mona? There's so little in the history books, and what there is available is questionable as to authenticity."

Cate nodded. "Thanks to you and Boudicca's great sacrifice, we managed to get almost five dozen of us off the island before the Romans finished their massacre. We sailed to Eire, where we remained for two years before heading back."

"You went back to the mainland from Ireland?"

Cate shook her head. "Not to Britannia, but to Alba."

"Scotland."

"Yes. We felt the need to spread ourselves out in the event another such massacre took place. We left a dozen or so of us in Eire and took the rest with us to Alba. A handful made their way to Gaul. It was the only thing we could think of doing to save ourselves, to be able to create a future."

For Jessie, it was never easy knowing the fate of people she loved or the fate of the spiritual path she had adopted. Sometimes, it simply hurt knowing the painful outcome of a path that was not only beautiful, but powerful. "The good news, Cate, is that the Romans never reached Ireland...er Eire."

Cate nodded. "Too cold for them, I am sure."

"The Druids remained unmolested until Saint Patrick arrived at the beginning of the fifth century. He converted most of Ireland to Catholicism and, in the process, destroyed hundreds of ancient Druid and Celtic texts."

Cate nodded. "I have seen that man and the damage he incurred on our ways. So, he was successful after all? Eire no longer believes in the old ways?"

Feeling her heart constrict at the truth, she replied, "No. It does not. However, Druidry has started making a comeback because the Christian religion is too harsh and unforgiving. It has turned its back on a lot of people and they, in turn, are returning to the old ways."

Cate's eyes lit up as the fire danced as if in tune with her emotions. "You mean your people are beginning to believe again?"

"Yes, lots of people. The earth is in serious danger now and, as you know, when the Druids and the goddess religions ceased to be the most powerful religions, the earth was put in jeopardy. Only the nature religions can save it from the destruction at the hands of men."

Cate reached out and touched her cheek with her fingertips. "You really have become one of us, haven't you?"

"I try. It is a difficult place to be when the Christians are such a huge percentage of the world's religion. I am judged by people who do not know me or my path. They are very powerful, indeed."

"And destructive, from the sound of things."

"Maybe that's why you're spending your life trying to prepare your soul to remember. Maybe my memory will someday save the earth...or at least a small part of it. But enough about the future, that is what it is. What happened once you made it to Scotland?"

"We managed to make it safely to Alba, where we met many more like ourselves, but they were too frightened to come out of hiding, preferring to stay beneath the ground and in the groves in relative safety. Lachlan and Maeve have spent the last cycle teaching and training, hoping to lure the scared ones out into the open. A Druid who keeps her light to herself may as well live the rest of her life in a cave."

"Is Alba weird? I mean, different?"

"Yes, very much. They are a peculiar people who center their world around clans and tribes. Family ties are more important to them than the well-being of the whole, which makes their existence rather precarious."

Jessie nodded, knowing well her British history. The Scots were conquered because they couldn't bring their clans together to fight a common enemy. "Yeah, that clan allegiance is both the strength and the greatest weakness of the people."

"Still, I find them to be incredibly passionate, assertive, and full of fire. I like them, but."

"But?"

"Lachlan...well...he is not so sure. I think their passion frightens him."

"What does Maeve think?"

Cate laughed. "It is she who frightens them, so they tend to act more civilized around her. She is getting along quite well, actually, with her teaching and her healing. She is determined to keep the old ways alive and has instructed several women in the ways of herbal magic."

Looking up at Jessie, Cate smiled warmly. "I think of you every day, Jessie. I wonder what you are doing, what you are thinking. I wonder if you feel me within beckoning you to remember. Just the other evening, I was looking up at the stars and knew you could see the same stars. It was a wonderful thought."

Jessie felt her eyes brim with tears. "Some nights, when the moon is full and I am performing a ritual of thanks and blessing, I can practically feel you beside me."

"As I am."

Jessie rose again and walked over to the fire. It seemed alive, and she sensed that the walls between her world and this one were getting thinner. "I don't know what to do about the pirate, Spencer. That's why I came here first. Is there anything you can tell me that will help me decide what to do?"

Cate rose and reached into her pouch once more and tossed a different color powder into the flames. This time, they sizzled before parting into two separate flames. "Do nothing for now. I shall speak to Maeve and Lachlan on how best to proceed. It is entirely possible that my future selves continued to train our soul to remember, thereby allowing Spencer to know who we are. If I have done this, then the man you call Spencer could very well know me, and therefore, know you. It all depends on how much he can remember. It's all in the remembering Jessie."

Jessie stared into the fire. "He could remember you?"

Cate nodded. "And if he remembers me, he might also be able to access my memories of you and our encounters. That would give him an abundant amount of information. Who knows how many moments you and I will share together in our lifetime?"

Jessie blew a breath out and ran her hands through her hair. "What would life be like if we could truly remember our past lives?"

Taking Jessie's hands in hers, Cate held them tightly. "It would make us wise beyond our imagination. It would also make us yearn for that which we once had." Lowering her head, Cate closed her eyes and stood very, very still. Suddenly, the ankh began to heat up against Jessie's chest.

"You can remember that far back, can't you?"

Cate nodded once and released Jessie's hands. "I can remember as far back as the ankh, but not necessarily from whence the ankh is from. I have spent nearly every life recalling those lives from my past and training myself to remember them so I can do so in the next."

"Because of Maeve, isn't it? You remember so you can find Maeve in every life."

Cate looked deep into Jessie's eyes. "I wish to be wise, Jessie, but I have no desire to yearn. I have no need to wander half my life looking for that which I could find if only I could recognize it. Yes, Maeve and I will spend this life remembering, training, conditioning as it were, our souls so that we can recognize each other in the next life, and the life after that, and the life after that."

Jessie could only shake her head.

"People are empty vessels, Jessie, wandering about trying to figure out why they experience so much sorrow. They look, yet they do not know what they seek. Maeve and I wish not to feel those emotions of emptiness and sadness. We want to know that there is that being that completes us, who makes us whole, who is also out there looking for us."

Jessie gazed into the fire. The way its fingers moved was hypnotic. "Why did it take you this long to tell me?"

"We were a bit…busy when you first came. Time was not on our side then. I also wanted you to have a chance to work with your craft and gain some experience so that you could truly grasp what I am saying. It was important that you understood the inner workings of Druidry before I explained what Maeve and I are doing. Besides…I did not know if we would ever see each other again."

Jessie stepped away from the fire just as a mist surrounded them in a dewy embrace. The thin veil between worlds was wispy now, and she knew their time was about up.

"I must go now, Jessie. I will call upon you after I have spoken to Lachlan and Maeve. Promise me you will not venture through the portal until you've spoken with me."

Nodding, Jessie said, "I promise."

"Good. Then off we go. Go and continue educating yourself about the world you are preparing to enter, while I try to uncover the relative safety of you doing so. I do not want you to even consider going into the past if there is an inherent danger. You have come to mean a great deal to me, Jessie. Your safety is very important to me. To all of us."

"It was really good seeing you again, Cate. Thank you so much for giving me the means to see you again. It was the best. You have been sorely missed."

"As have you. Maeve will not be pleased to know you have not found her yet."

"How did you--"

"Because you are incomplete. Your search has not yet even started, but I can feel your energy and I know you have not found that which we always seek."

"Just tell her she's worth waiting for."

"Indeed, I will do that. Take care of yourself, my friend." Walking toward the mist, Cate stopped and turned. "You know you did not have to become a Druid."

Smiling at her, Jessie nodded. "I didn't become one, Cate. I was born one."

With a silvery laugh, Cate vanished into the fog.

Jessie woke up bright and early the next morning, had a cup of coffee and a piece of toast, and headed out for class before she realized it was only six a.m. At school she studied in the student lounge, trying desperately to keep her mind on the exam. It was so hard not to allow her mind to linger on Cate and their conversation, but somehow, she managed. Then, hoisting her backpack over her shoulder, she headed for her favorite professor's office to camp out.

"Come in, Miss Ferguson," Dr. Per Lee said in her deep, booming voice when Jessie poked her head into the office.

"Do you have a second?"

"For you, I have five or six."

She sat on the chair opposite the professor. Her office was far neater than most and filled with books and texts about the Renaissance, three of which the professor had written herself.

Dr. Per Lee was the most popular professor in the history department, even if her six-foot, two-hundred-and-fifty-pound frame was somewhat daunting. She was gregarious, warm and funny, with a voice that demanded everyone's attention in a room. She was the only history professor who did not use her own textbooks for her classes.

"It might take ten or eleven, but I'll talk fast."

"What's on your mind today? Atlantis? The Bermuda Triangle? Witchcraft in the Middle Ages? What odd notion brings to you my parlor?"

"I've spent a bit of time on the Internet and in my many textbooks, but I'm not really finding what I'm looking for."

Dr. Per Lee leaned back in the chair, the leather creaking beneath her girth. "Which is?"

"The pirates of the fifteenth or sixteenth centuries—more particularly those in and around Ireland during Elizabeth's reign."

"Irish pirates? Is this for someone's class?"

Jessie knew professors did not help students if what they were asking for was something due in another class. "It's a personal quest, really."

Dr. Per Lee steepled her fingers together and leaned forward on the desk. "First off, there's a world of difference between sixteenth and fifteenth century anything, and Elizabeth reigned for forty years. Can you narrow it down a bit?"

"I keep finding the same information on a handful of pirates like Blackbeard, Grainne, Drake—"

"Drake?" Dr. Per Lee laughed in a deep baritone. "A good many scholars would take umbrage at that description of such a nautical icon."

"Western historians, maybe," Jessie replied. "The guy stole from anyone on the high seas and was supported in his thieving endeavors by his Queen. They can put Sir in front of his name, but that just makes him the pirate Sir Francis Drake."

Dr. Per Lee was still grinning. "Ah, Miss Ferguson, but you will most certainly make quite a contentious historian. I have to agree with your summation of Drake's employment. His piracy was advocated by Queen Elizabeth who put up one thousand pounds of her own money for a voyage that eventually yielded her forty-seven thousand times her initial investment. After that, she was quite taken with the whole idea of the crown getting free money and free goods from the services of Sir Francis Drake, so she gave him open reign of the seas; a reign, I must add, that made England very, very rich."

Jessie had known all this, but she waited patiently for the professor to continue.

"But Irish pirates? We don't have much about them. Oddly, Grace O'Malley is perhaps the most famous Irish pirate of the sixteenth century. She was sixty years old when she won her greatest battle. You would think there would be more information about her since she was so great, but alas, she was a woman, and as you know, there's not nearly as much written about great women in history as there is about men."

"Is this ship from the sixteenth century?" She handed over a photo and Dr. Per Lee studied it.

"That's a schooner. It was the best of all types of pirate ships. I would lean toward the sixteenth century."

"Thanks. Oh, one more thing. Is there anything in history about any of these pirates searching for…ah…some kind of box?"

"Not that I know of. There's certainly plenty of treasure booty and all that, if that's what you're looking for."

As Jessie left the office, she knew she had no other choice but to return to the past in order to find out why Spencer had beckoned her.

Ceara stood with her face to the rare Oregon sun peeking out behind ubiquitous clouds and closed her eyes. "After three years, Cate finally returned to see you. That makes her an incredibly good friend to you. Tell me all about it. How are they? Is Lachlan well?"

With her own face to the sun, eyes closed, Jessie repeated as much of the conversation as she could remember. When she finished, she looked over at Ceara just as a tear dropped off the side of her face. "Ceara?"

Ceara managed a smile. "It's all right, my dear. It is just so wonderful knowing they made it even after they buried our gifts, and that my son continues to live. He may be thousands of years away in body, but as long as I live now and he lives now, it doesn't hurt so much." She wiped her face and turned toward Jessie. "It's glorious news, really. They made it to Ireland after all and we helped them get there. We helped save my son. It's just…it's just overwhelming is all."

Jessie leveled her gaze at Ceara. "I need help again."

Ceara nodded. "I know you do, my dear. It is time, once again, for you to don your quester's shoes for yet another journey."

"I'm ready this time."

"Yes, yes you most certainly are. What did Cate tell you about this quest?"

"She had no idea what I was talking about as far as a box

goes."

"Perhaps you were mistaken. Maybe the memory you have regarding the box is actually a treasure chest. That would certainly fit into the scheme of the time period you are going to."

Jessie shook her head. "Whatever it is is really important; vital, even."

"Well, my dear, there is but one way to get the information you need about this mystery box."

Watching as the sun played peek-a-boo behind a gray cloud, Jessie answered, "I know." Looking out at the sun as it dipped in and out, she wondered if Cate were looking at a similar image. Did people from different times cast their gaze upon the moon at the same time? What was Cate doing at this very moment?

*   *   *

16th Century

Captain Spencer Morgan was hunched over his bittersweet ale in the captain's quarters, his bones tired and achy from the unsuccessful raid on the *Tia Amore*. Well, it was successful in terms of the bounty they scored, but it did not have what Spencer was seeking.

Duncan Parnell lay on a hammock across the small quarters with one arm draped over his eyes and the other stroking a Siamese cat curled on his large chest. Dancer was an excellent mouser and kept their quarters virtually rodent-free. As a reward, Dancer was part of their crew and often escorted them on land excursions. She was Duncan's favorite female, and the only one who'd won his loyalty.

"My bones are yelling at me," Spencer growled, sipping his ale. "At least the men are basking in the gold those Spaniards were saving for us."

"Aye. There was far more in her hold than I expected."

"I wish we had not had to burn her out. She was a beauty. Leave it to the Spanish to build such fine vessels."

"She was Spanish, Spencer. There was nothing else to do."

Spencer looked up at his friend and nodded. "I do not want

the Spaniards thinking there is any place to escape to, or that we are soft. We have a job to do and I'll not allow them to remain afloat once we've taken what we need."

Duncan petted the cat but said nothing.

"We have made our backers richer beyond imagination, we have more money than we know what to do with, and our men want for nothing. Still, the booty is secondary. Either the crews will tell us what we need to know or they can swim ashore."

Duncan lifted his arm from his face and stared at Spencer. "You wouldn't."

"The time is drawing near, and we have nothing but gold and jewels to show for it."

This made Duncan grin. "I wonder if Francis Drake would see the booty we've stolen out from under him in such light, my friend."

"I know of no one who has stated that the Spanish treasures are purely for his taking."

"Still, he knows of the Irishman who continues to plunder the galleons before he does. He will not be kind to you if he ever catches us."

"Then let us make sure he never does."

Spencer looked up at the sound of footsteps approaching his door. He swung the door open and stared down into the face of a frightened Spanish prisoner. "Thank you, Murddoch," Spencer said to the huge man standing behind the prisoner.

Murddoch looked like something of a giant from a fairy tale; long black beard, hands the size of baskets, and several scars running up and down the side of his face. He was more a man created from someone's nightmare. "You want I should stay outside the door?"

Spencer shook his head. "Duncan and I can manage." To the Spaniard, Spencer asked if he spoke Gaelic. He did not. Welsh? He did not. "English?" Spencer said, exasperated. He had discovered the Spanish were not interested in anyone but themselves and few learned the language, customs or cultures of the other peoples around them.

"If that glare is his only answer, Spencer, perhaps he speaks the language of the sword." Drawing his cutlass, Duncan stuck the tip up to the Spaniard's neck. "Come now, sir, I care not to have to resort to barbaric behavior to get you to talk to us. Talk is all I want and if you tell the truth, you may find that it saves your life." Duncan pressed the tip deeper. "My friend's mercy is greater than mine, but I would not press it much longer. There are others of you we can talk to after we toss your bloodless corpse from the ship. What say you?"

The Spaniard nodded. As Duncan pulled away, the Spaniard spat at Spencer, a glob of phlegm oozed down the front of Spencer's vest. In the flash of a blade, the Spaniard lost the tip of his chin, his blood dripping down onto his chest as he stood there, shocked at the speed with which Duncan had moved.

"Information, amigo. You can find your tongue for us, or we shall let the fish find it for you. Comprende?"

The sailor nodded slowly. "I…know nada," he said, his thick accent surrounding every word. "No can help you."

Spencer stood next to Duncan, whose imposing countenance made the sailor shrink down. Few men were as good with a blade as Duncan Parnell. "You do not even know what it is we want."

The sailor blinked and then nodded once. "Filthy English want gold. No work for gold, only take." The sailor spat once more, only this time it landed on Duncan's boot.

Spencer stepped closer, grabbing a fistful of shirt. "First of all, do I sound English?"

The Spaniard shook his head. "That one."

"The ship is English, but make no mistake about it, I am not." Spencer glanced over at Duncan, who kept his blade a hair's breadth from the sailor's throat.

"You no work for gold we collect. English…perezozo. Phooey!"

Duncan tightened, but Spencer shook his head. "You are making my friend angry with your less-than-flattering words. Do not think we don't know what you speak."

"I speak truth. No good Englishman."

"Then tell me this truth: I am seeking a box. A carved, wooden box."

"No lo se. I not know. Como se dice…box…in Espanol?"

"A box, you idiot!" Duncan said, hitting the sailor with t'

flat of his blade. "A square wooden box with writing and symbols carved on it. Don't act like you don't understand. You know exactly what we're talking about."

Spencer frowned at Duncan. "Easy, my friend. His ship is gone, the language is unfamiliar, and your sword is making him nervous."

Duncan lowered his sword. "You are too soft. We should dispose of him and drag out one of his compadres."

"And you, my hotheaded friend, are too impetuous." To the Spaniard, Spencer said, "The box we are looking for has odd marks all over it…like a code."

"I not know this…box, pigdog!"

The movement was so swift it caught both the sailor and Spencer off-guard. Duncan had grabbed the sailor, pushed him out the door and backward over the railing, hanging onto him with two powerful hands. "We are not playing games, little man!" As Duncan held the sputtering, spewing, frightened sailor over the railing, the sea below rushed by them as the ship sliced through the deep blue water. "The box! You know quite well what we are talking about, you bastard, and if you value your life you'll stop acting like you don't!"

"English puerco!"

With a quick shove, Duncan sent him over the side of the ship and into the cold, dark water below, where he vanished under the swells from the ship.

Spencer joined Duncan at the railing and peered over the side. "Well, we will not be learning anything else from that one, will we?"

"He knew nothing."

"Do you think we gave him enough time to tell us?" Spencer asked as he stared back at the spot where the sailor had landed. "Or are we going to toss them all into the water? Duncan, it is no use trying to get information from them. Even if they could understand what we were asking, none of them will tell us."

"Then they'll all end up at the bottom of the sea like their

be in Ireland in two days. When we arrive, I will go
h and—"

"And what? Wake up, Spencer! It does not hold the answers you seek and it is dangerous. You, dead, will not further our cause. You need to walk away from all that nonsense."

"You give up too quickly, my friend."

"And you don't give up soon enough. You are a dreamer."

Spencer swiped his hand through Duncan's hair; a movement his soul had repeated in a dozen incarnations. "We are what we always have been: questers."

"No, you are the quester, and I'll leave you to it when we reach port. But leave me with my wenches. In the end, we shall see who winds up with the good, in the light, and on the happy side of life. My wager is on me."

This made Spencer laugh. "Oh, truly?"

"Truly."

*   *   *

21st Century

Jessie could not wait to go to the Dreamworld once more. She had done everything she could to keep busy until she had the time and space to go to her room, turn on her fountain, and get herself into a state that would enable her to reach through the thin walls separating this world from that of the faeries. She and Ceara had spent hours practicing, learning, training, and doing everything in their power to give Jessie the tools to breach the barrier.

The shamans of many cultures used drugs and smoke houses, alcohol, and fire ceremonies to get to a state that would enable them to enter the Dreamworld, but Ceara had taught Jessie that it was reachable using the higher power of the mind. On this evening, she would at least discover what it was the pirate was looking for, and why it was so important to him. She wondered why he was so desperate.

It was desperation she'd felt when she was with him, wasn't it?

"He is desperate, Jessie, because the situation is."

Startled at the voice, Jessie peered through the mist and saw not only Cate, but Maeve as well. She ran through the mist toward Maeve, who scooped Jessie up in a hug that revealed how much they meant to each other in any life.

"Maeve!" Jessie cried, breathing in her scent. "I can't believe you've come! I can't believe it's you!"

Maeve released her and stepped back. Her gray eyes were warm and she smiled softly into Jessie's face. She was a tall woman for her time, towering over both the diminutive Cate and five-foot, six-inch Jessie. With long flowing auburn hair draped around porcelain skin, Maeve could have been the model for Botticelli's Venus. Still, as striking as she was, it was Maeve's regal bearing that made others stop and stare.

"Jessie. It is so very good to see you once again." Maeve took Jessie's hands in hers. "I never thought to see you once we left the island. Catie informs me you are well."

Jessie stared into those kind, intelligent eyes and nodded. "I've never been better. My life is good, Maeve. I have finally found my way and I am no longer the lost little girl I was when we first met."

"I am so happy to hear it. When last we met your life was... well—"

"Shitty."

This made Maeve laugh and the sound was like small wind chimes blowing in a gentle breeze. "An odd term, but I believe I understand." Putting one arm around Jessie's shoulders and the other across Cate's she guided them to the stone circle. "Catie tells me you have been summoned once more."

She nodded and watched carefully as Maeve raised her arms and muttered words Jessie did not recognize. As Maeve's arms rose, the mist fell like a blanket behind them, growing denser and wetter; the air, moister. Everything around them changed.

"Catie also tells me it was a man on a ship who initiated contact with you."

Jessie nodded again, somewhat disappointed that Maeve appeared more interested in the pirate tale than in her. She had envisioned this meeting a thousand times, yet it had never looked like this.

As if reading her mind, Maeve reached out and caressed Jessie's cheek. "Oh, Jessie, I, too, would like all the time in the world to sit with you and share the wisdom you have discovered and all of our experiences these past years, but your situation, our situation is quite serious. We will have time to visit and share our lives, I promise. But for now, there are things you need to know—important things, things that could impact us here and now."

Jessie's forehead furrowed. "Are you in some kind of trouble?"

Maeve shook her head, a small strand of red hair swirling around her face. Brushing it away, she answered, "No, at least, not that we've seen...yet. I cannot, nor can Catie, see that far into the future to be able to know what is happening to this... pirate man, but I can tell you what I believe he is searching for."

Jessie glanced over at Cate, who said, "As soon as I asked Maeve about the box, she knew just what it was. I should have known as well, but I never imagined...never thought..."

Jessie's heart beat faster. Now she would know what was so important that Spencer came across the seam for her.

"Important," Maeve said, in tune with Jessie's thoughts. "Very important."

Motioning for Jessie to sit down at her place around the stone circle, Maeve nodded for Cate to start a fire, which Cate did quickly.

"Now, you must listen carefully because time is of the utmost. When we all landed in Eire after the devastation on the island, we stayed on the coast for about half a year. During that time, Catie foresaw that man you called Saint Patrick destroying our scrolls and documents. When she told Lachlan, he was determined to balance the destruction by such an evil entity and find a way to preserve the scrolls. Cate tried to persuade him not to intervene, but his mind was made up. So he gathered up the chief Druids with him, and had us write down everything we could remember from our training, be it Bardic, Ovatic or Druidic—stories, poems, laws, histories, even magic. Every one of us spent the light of every day contributing our knowledge to the scrolls until at last, the box could hold no more. When the final scroll was placed into the box, which

Lachlan himself had carved, he closed it and carved the final BoibeLoth inscriptions on them. Then, Lachlan myself, and four others hid it in a cave off the coast of Eire." Cate folded her hands in her lap before continuing. "As you know ours is an oral tradition, and none of us are comfortable with the written word or with leaving our precious secrets for others to find, but we had to do something."

"So you preserved them. Who were the others beside you and Lachlan?"

Maeve sighed wearily and Jessie realized that perhaps more time had passed here than just three years. Maeve's once red tresses were now streaked here and there with strands of gray, and the slight wrinkles around her eyes had not been there before. "Dougal, Bernard, William and Quinn. Do you remember him?"

Jessie nodded vigorously. "I remember he was missing for a while and you were worried that maybe he…maybe he ended up trapped in my time like Ceara…or worse."

"He reappeared just as we were escaping the island. He was not harmed, and had helped Lachlan a great deal as we made our way to Eire. He was of great service to us as we wrote our scrolls, often working well into the night by the dimmest of candlelight."

"So you finished the scrolls and placed them all into this box. You think this is the same box Spencer is looking for?"

Cate nodded. "Indeed, it must be."

"But why? What on earth would sixteenth century pirates want with a box full of scrolls?"

Maeve shot Cate a look and it was she who responded. "Spencer is us, Jessie, and he knows who he is because that is what we do. That is what we have been doing for centuries now. We try to remember. Spencer has remembered. In his remembering, he has discovered something that could change everything about your world if he cannot stop it."

This shocked Jessie. "My world?"

Maeve moved and knelt in front of Jessie, locking her gray eyes onto Jessie's. "Tell me, what would happen in your time if an individual could turn metals into gold?"

Jessie brought her hand up to her mouth. "You don't mean… I thought turning lead into gold was just a metaphor."

"Perhaps in times after ours it came to be such, but in our time, many of us have the ability to transform one thing into another."

"And you could do it with lead and gold? I've read such things. I've even learned about it in one of my classes, but no one believes it was ever really possible."

Cate and Maeve nodded in unison. "Of course it was possible," Maeve replied. "It still is. Do they not transform one thing to another in your time?"

"In my time, alchemy on that level is a myth, a metaphor, an allegory to explain the transmutation of the soul. It has never been proven to work."

Cate shook her head. "Does everything your people misunderstand become a myth?"

Shrugging, Jessie replied, "If I've learned anything from the study of history and from you, it's that history is not a static event. It changes as information is revealed or uncovered. Even when it doesn't change, there are those who try to change it."

"How terribly sad. How awful that a thing that once happened can't stay the way it happened. Your people must be awfully confused about who they are and where they came from."

"You have no idea."

"So, the question still remains: What would happen if someone in your time could do just that?"

She shook her head. "In the wrong hands, that ability could change the entire economic structure of the world."

Maeve laid her hand on Jessie's knee. Just her touch was soothing and embracing. "Precisely. Now, that particular outcome would be the same in Spencer's time."

Jessie nodded. "To create your own wealth in any age would be…cataclysmic; economic chaos would ensue."

"Indeed."

"Then why on earth did you put that in the box if you knew—"

"We did not," Cate replied, "at least, not those of us who

knew better."

"Then who?"

Maeve shrugged. "Quinn."

Jessie rose and paced over to the fire. The sense of betrayal hung in the air with the smoke. "And how do you know this? How can you be sure?"

Maeve reached into her pouch and withdrew a purple powder that she tossed into the fire.

Looking into the fire, Jessie watched as a man took form in the flames.His head was bent down while he scratched his quill pen over a scroll. "What is this?"

"It is Quinn writing the steps down that will create the changes. We were forbidden from putting those words to parchment, but Quinn disobeyed.That was why he worked so late into the night. He needed to be alone with the scrolls in order to copy down the processes involved."

"This is amazing. How is it possible we're seeing this?"

"The faery-folk...the Sidhe. When Cate asked if, perhaps, there was something in it that would cause Spencer to seek it out, I asked them to allow me a glimpse of all the items that went into it."

"Why would they do that for you?"

"We have an...unusual arrangement, Jessie, one that not even Catie understands. Suffice it to say, I was surprised to see this image of Quinn because I believed we all did our writing together, by daylight, after rituals and calling upon the goddesses. It wasn't until much later that someone told me Quinn worked well into the night. In this image, he sits alone, writing by candlelight, with an energy about him that is not good. I was able to look closer and see that he was transcribing the alchemy forbidden to be written down."

"Hence the evil energy," Cate added.

Jessie stared over Quinn's shoulder, not able to see his face. But his face was not important. What was important was what Maeve had discovered: Quinn had added a recipe for disaster into the box that was meant to share the wisdom of a craft they didn't want to see die.

"That's why Spencer is searching for it?"

"I do not know why Spencer is looking for the box, except that maybe he has remembered what possibilities it possesses."

"Well, I've got news for him. I am not putting my life in danger just so that son-of-a-pirate can get rich off your knowledge." Jessie watched the image of Quinn fade, replaced by Spencer standing on the deck of his ship. "So, I've been running around like an idiot so he can transform lead into gold?"

Turning to Cate, Maeve asked, "Is this the man who tried to contact you?"

Cate stared into the fire and nodded. "Yes."

"What?" Jessie asked, turning from the image to Cate. "You never told me Spencer came to you. Why didn't you tell me?"

"I did not intend to omit this fact from you. I believed someone came from the future to me, but I blocked him out because the essence of the energy was not you, Jessie, nor was it good. His energy has a darkness that I did not want to take on, so I would not allow him in."

"I didn't know you could do that."

"You would be amazed at what the mind can do, Jessie."

Maeve nodded. "We were unsure who or what the dark force wanted in attempting to enter Cate, so I helped her build walls to keep him out. Perhaps it was this Spencer, perhaps not, but if it was him, we sent him on his way with nothing to show for it."

Jessie rubbed her thumb across her chin. "I see." The ship faded into the fire and the flames once again resumed their natural burning. "And if it was Spencer trying to contact you, he did not get through, but of course, I let him in. I should have known better."

"Not necessarily, Jessie. Remember, he is you and Cate. Just because his energy is dark and heavy does not mean that he is a bad being. His path may not be what either you or she would wish to have, but it is his path nonetheless."

"What are you saying?"

"His motives may not be as self-indulgent as you seem to think. He needs something from you, Jessie, from us, and until we know what that is, it is not right to assume the worst, as I did."

Maeve nodded. "We mustn't assume anything. Clearly, the man knows something of us, or else he would not have been able to use the portal in such a fashion. Do not underestimate this man."

"He's a pirate, Maeve. He kills people, steals things, burns ships and who knows what else he does? These are not good people."

"What he is doing," Cate said softly, "is remembering. Whatever it is he is remembering has led him to the box and to us. That cannot be overlooked."

"Spencer must truly be in need to have traveled both backward and forward to find one of us. He found you. It is up to you if you are going to help him."

"Why not you?"

Cate reached for Jessie's hand. "I know too much of your world from our time together. Your memories linger within me, much like how those of my time linger in you. It is a gift and a price to pay for traveling through the portal." Smiling, she continued. "I do not know what you call it in your time, but I have this craving for Turkish coffee more than I care to admit. I get this craving from you."

"Turkish co...oh...sorry about that. I do drink a lot of coffee."

Cate nodded. "That is apparent."

Maeve opened her arms and the mist lifted, and it was now lighter and drier than when they first arrived. "The box contains something Spencer desires. I cannot imagine that he wants our words of wisdom or our stories. There can be only one thing he would risk his life for."

"You want me to go?"

Maeve sighed. "That is not a decision anyone can make but you."

"But if the box is found, and someone can translate the scrolls—"

"It has the potential to change the world, yes."

Pacing across the circle, Jessie had no doubt that she would go back, even if it was just to find out why Spencer was traveling all over time. Still, the familiar shadow of fear hovered near her, reminding her of the dangers of slipping through time. "There's one thing I'd really like to know. Why did Quinn do that?"

Maeve and Cate glanced at each other. Finally, Maeve ran her hand through her hair before replacing her hood on her head. "We do not know."

"What do you mean you don't know? Why don't you just ask him?"

"Because, soon after we moved the box, Quinn disappeared."

*   *   *

21st Century

The light in Ceara's sanctuary was dim and the smell of patchouli incense lingered throughout. Celtic instrumentals played softly in the background as Ceara carefully spread her tarot deck across the aged oak table.

"And you're sure this is something you want to do?" Ceara checked her watch for the third time in as many minutes. She hated late clients.

Jessie nodded, looking out the window to see if the late client had pulled up yet. "I have to. I must at least hear him out. I don't know what he wants or needs, but I just can't shut him out like Cate did. I want to, but I…I can't."

"Perhaps she's just a tad more suspicious of him, as you ought to be. I just hope you aren't doing this because you are slightly addicted to the concept of time travel. That would not be a wise move at all." Ceara placed both hands over the deck and closed her eyes.

"Addicted? That's a bit harsh, don't you think?"

Ceara checked her watch once more. "Is it? You wait three years and the door is barely ajar and you intend to push your way through it. You're a seam junkie. Yeah, that's right. A seam-tripper." She turned over a card and showed a bull.

"Fine. I admit it. I love it. I love everything about it. It's exhilarating to be someplace so incredibly different and exotic. It's fun. It's—"

"Fun?" Ceara raised a gray eyebrow at Jessie. "You're

addicted."

"Am not."

Ceara crossed her late client off her list. "Of course you are. All questers are addicted, otherwise why would they go? There's something that connects us all, Jessie, and you are as connected to your portal as Cate is to hers." Ceara turned over a second card of the Druid Animal Oracle deck she used just with Jessie. The card was a salmon. "See here? You are strong like the bull, but you try to balance that with the wisdom of the salmon. You want the best of both worlds, satisfying neither."

"You made that last part up."

Ceara pushed her glasses back up the bridge of her nose. "There are obstacles in your path, my dear. What of your parents?"

"They have a party in Portland. They'll be gone all weekend."

"You and Daniel will run the inn?"

"And Tanner. He's working all weekend. I'm paying him cash to cover for me. I'll only be gone for part of the day anyway."

Ceara leaned forward. "Remember well, Jessie Ferguson: time travel is not a game. If you are in Spencer's time and he is run through by some buccaneer, you will die then and there, just as surely as if your own body had taken the blade itself. This is serious danger, the waters of the sixteenth century in which you are willingly about to plunge into head first; serious indeed."

Jessie stared at the salmon card. "I know. But Ceara, we're charged with remembering. Spencer remembered. So do I. I can't just turn away. You don't need to worry so much, Ceara. At least on this trip I know more about what I'm doing. I've researched the age, and I am aware that Spencer is a pirate who raids Spanish galleons, a common practice in his time. He wields a sword, steals booty, burns the ships and kills people on board. Should be a piece of cake."

Ceara whistled and shook her head. "He's no Cate McEwen, that's for sure."

"No, he's not, but then, neither am I."

Ceara turned over the Raven card and then sighed.

"Damn. Not the Raven."

"As you are aware, Raven is associated with the Triple Goddess, the Morrigan. Raven is also the totem of the pan-Celtic Sorceress/Goddess Morgan le Fay, who was also called the Queen of Faeries. In some tales, she is Queen of the Dubh Sidhe, or Dark Faeries, who were a race of tricksters who often took the form of ravens. Tha gliocas an ceann an fhitich orFice ceann na fhitich. Scots Gaelic proverbs meaning, "There is wisdom in a raven's head." Ceara studied the cards more carefully. "Any time the Dubh Sidhe are involved, it is a time for worry. If you choose to go, may the goddess be with you, my dear."

*   *   *

16th Century

"It's one of Drake's ships!" came the call from the crow's nest high above the ship's deck. The wind was whipping the masts back and forth, so the voice was battered by the snapping sounds of torn sails. "She's preparing to attack!"

"Attack?" Spencer cried, looking to Duncan for confirmation. "But we're flying an English flag! That bastard would attack his own people?"

Duncan cursed under his breath. "He cares not." He opened the telescope and looked at the ship. "It is not a ship of Drake's… at least not one that he is traveling with at the moment."

"But she's English nonetheless."

"Aye, Captain, that she is." Duncan handed the telescope to Spencer, who ignored it. His trained eyes knew what to look for in an enemy vessel.

"Bring her about broadside!" Spencer shouted to the sailor on the above deck.

"Broadside, Captain?"

"You heard what the captain said. We're goin' aboard her!"

Duncan and Spencer ran up and down the deck preparing their men for the inevitable attack from the English. The scent of gunpowder permeated the air mixing company with the sound of metal against metal and men shouting to each other.

"They must know we're carrying Spanish gold," Spencer uttered.

"We are laying low in the water, Spencer, and it's one of Drake's ships. I'd guess a patrol ship of some sort. Those cretins never can pass up the chance to steal someone's gold. It's what the Queen bade them all to do."

Spencer spat. "We'll be ready. Those buggers think they're attacking their own soft kind. Little do they know this ship has but one of the Queen's own."

"She's no Queen of mine."

Spencer drew his sword and climbed partway up the rope ladder. The wind threatened to shove him from his perch. "Fifty pieces to the bloke who finds the box first!"

At that, the men roared and yelled, and prepared to jump aboard the British ship the moment she was within reach.

Leaping back to the deck, Spencer stared into Duncan's light blue eyes as he cocked his head and looked intently at his friend. Duncan's shoulder-length blond hair whipped around in the wind as if alive. "What?"

Duncan flipped his hair over his shoulders and turned toward the approaching ship. "If Drake's on that ship, he'll kill you straightaway. The man abhors the very ground upon which you stand. He would surely find joy in watching your feet swinging a foot or two above it."

"As well he should. I have not made his life on the water an easy one."

Spencer withdrew his cutlass and the two men crossed blades. "To the old ways. May the goddess protect us and further our quest."

The Irish made the first big push onto Drake's ship, and they had the upper hand by numbers as well as by speed. Spencer's men were swordsmen first and sailors second, and he had never regretted having a ship full of killers, swordsmen and archers. They were consummate fighters.

Soon, the deck of the English ship was slippery with blood from both sides, as sailors and crew alike swung cutlasses, pikes and even pitchforks at each other. Anything that had the capability to draw blood was used against the English, who were known to fight dirty enough to win, and they won enough to please their Queen.

But the Irish advantage was short-lived. British sailors began a charge from below deck that caught the Irish unaware. Suddenly, the tide turned, as more British cutlasses found Irish flesh, leaving body parts on the deck as they made a last charge.

"Should we retreat?" a sailor asked Spencer as he fought against two British renegades.

"I'll cut your head off my own self if I so much as hear you utter that word again." Spencer managed a defensive blow against a huge, dark sailor wielding a thick Saracen sword.

"Spencer!" Duncan cried, tossing Spencer a small shield. Spencer caught it with his left hand just in time to deflect a blade of a second British sailor bearing down on him. Spencer protected himself from the Saracen and the sailor, so he did not see the ax handle coming toward his head. The flash of movement was not wasted on him, and he tried to duck out of the way, but he was too late. Spencer didn't even have time to hear Duncan's shrill warning call from behind. The only thing Spencer had time for was to block the Saracen sword that hit with so much force, he dislodged it from the hand wielding it, sending it skittering to a bloody pool on the deck of the ship.

The sword hitting the deck was the last thing Spencer saw before the ax handle cracked across the back of his head, sending him sprawling face first onto the sticky deck.

Duncan could only watch in horror as the huge man reached for the Saracen sword and turned to finish the job on Spencer. In desperate panic, Duncan tried to get to Spencer, knowing he was too far away, knowing Spencer was going to feel the slash of the big blade, knowing without a shadow of a doubt that all he could do was watch his best friend get cut in half by the enormous Saracen.

"Spencer!" Duncan cried out, not wanting to watch Spencer die, but unwilling to turn away. "Spencer, get up!"

From somewhere deep in her soul, Jessie called to him to wake up. Inside Spencer again, she found herself in yet another dangerous brawl, only this time, it didn't appear he was going to make it out alive.

If that was the case, neither would she.

She was Spencer, but she wasn't his consciousness. She was part of his Eternal Soul, part of him he would be in the far away future…and there would be no future if he did not wake up.

Panicked, Jessie was torn between saving him and herself in the process, or time slipping quickly enough to save just herself. Could she just leave him on the deck of the ship to be run through, or would she do the unthinkable and manage to let him live another day? Was she willing to take that risk?

There wasn't a choice, really. There never was. She could no more leave him to die than leave Cate.

So it was here, on the filthy deck of a British ship, where Jessie Ferguson was going to be killed by a very large man wielding an even larger sword. If she couldn't figure out how to save Spencer, his death would kill their soul, ending her life in the twenty-first century. Her parents might never find her body in the numberless room in the Inn, and when Ceara came after her, all she would find would be Jessie's dead and empty shell of a body, never really knowing why or how she died.

But she did not want to die in this century, on this ship, in this manner. If only she could figure out how to do what Ceara had done all those years ago when she took over Erma's body. Jessie knew nothing of possession, but if she didn't figure it out in the next ten seconds, this would be the last quest she'd ever experience.

"Spencer!" Duncan's terror-filled voice rose above the carnage, and to his astonishment and relief, Spencer slowly reached for his sword and twisted around just in time to block what would have been a fatal blow to his head. The shocked Saracen stepped back and into the pool of blood. Slipping and falling back to the deck, his head hit the side of the ship.

Jessie looked down at the man, at the cutlass in her hand, and then back at the man, knowing she did not have what it would take to sever his head from his body or even poke him with the sharp sword. She knew it was what needed to be done, knew it was what everyone expected her to do.

She took a deep breath, steadied the thick, muscular legs holding her up, and leapt over two dead bodies, deflecting blows along the way aimed at her…at Spencer's head. She wielded the cutlass as if she had been doing it her whole life, even though the weight of it felt heavy in her hand. This body was remarkably powerful, agile and nothing at all like the one she had in the twenty-first century. It bounded across the deck, slashing and defending, taking care of the only link she had between her and Spencer; because even though his conscious memory was not awake, his body's cellular memory moved and operated as if he were cognizant of every move she was making. His body knew what to do even if she didn't.

And she didn't.

All she could think of was getting to Duncan, who was trying feverishly to get to Spencer. But Duncan was fighting off two of the British soldiers bent on skewering him, and had his hands full. He was able to push one over the side while whacking the other one on the side of the head on his way down the steps. He fought and dispatched anyone who dared get between him and Spencer. "Behind you!"

Spencer wheeled around, lifting the cutlass in time to prevent another fatal blow. When the pirate drew his sword back once more, Murddock lumbered out of nowhere like a grizzly bear and nearly cut the head off of Spencer's attacker, spraying blood everywhere. Warm, red liquid dripped down Spencer's face, causing Jessie to momentarily gag.

"Spencer!" Duncan gasped, arriving at Spencer's side. "I thought it was…checkmate for sure, my friend," he said, gasping for air. Blood splatters dappled his attire—some of it his own, as he suffered a gash to his right eyebrow that was still bleeding. "You should have killed that bastard when you had the chance."

Jessie shrugged the heavy shoulders as she gingerly felt the blood on the back of her/Spencer's head. In her time, it would take a dozen or more stitches to repair that wound. She wondered what they would do for him in this time. "My head seems to be the main target of these scallywags." The voice had such a rich, deep timbre, she wasn't sure the words had come from Spencer.

Duncan parried a blow from a sailor, knocking him sideways, and Spencer kicked him across the deck so hard he nearly went over the railing. They fought back-to-back for several minutes, until their area of the deck was British-free and littered with both dead and wounded.

Jessie could hardly believe she had taken possession of Spencer's body. It was the strangest experience of her life being in a man's body…being in a pirate's body, but this wasn't any pirate, this was one of her past lives and as such, ignited many of Spencer's memories within her own consciousness.

When Duncan pulled his sword from the last Brit near them, he shook his head. "These bloody bastards need to learn how to fight." Turning, he looked hard into Spencer's face for the first time.

Jessie stared back at the blue eyes peering down at her and was immediately seized with the feeling of recognition. She had seen this man before. Those eyes were as familiar to her as if she had just seen them yesterday, but it wasn't the eyes she recognized as much as it was the being that possessed his soul thousands of years ago. She had no doubt who Duncan had once been.

"Lachlan?"

Duncan frowned and shook his head. "Are you all right, Spencer? It's me, you big lout. Duncan. That bump on the head must have shivered your timbers."

Spencer shook his head, and Jessie could feel him returning. "It is you."

Duncan leaned down and peered hard into Spencer's eyes. "We're fighting for our lives here, and you want to bring up our other lives? That conk on the head has made you daft. Come on. I'll take you back to the Raven and take a look at your hard skull."

Spencer looked out over a deck that now held more corpses than living beings. The British were being beaten handily by Spencer's well-trained killers, who were nearly through running the Brits into the sea. "Looks like we kicked their asses," he said.

Duncan burst out laughing. "That's quite a turn of a phrase. Come, let's return to the safety of our ship and let Murddoch clean up the mess on this one. Our men can search and secure it before stripping it down until it's nothing but a skeleton of its former self while we tend to that nasty bump." Duncan spat into a puddle of blood. "Send boys to do a man's job, will you, Drake?"

Spencer nodded. Inside, Jessie suddenly felt woozy and a strange and familiar feeling came over her. She struggled to maintain her slipping consciousness, and barely made it to Spencer's quarters before collapsing in Duncan's arms.

"Easy, my friend, I have you." Duncan turned his face toward the door and shouted, "Butcher! I have need of him in the captain's quarters! Someone get the Butcher!"

The boatswain came running to the quarters. "Sir?"

"I need the Butcher! Send him here immediately."

The boatswain nodded and headed out quickly.

As Jessie felt the thick, dark walls of unconsciousness creep in around her, she reached for Duncan's hand and stared deep into those light blue eyes she had never seen, but knew all too well. There was no doubt in her soul that this man who held the body of his friend had once been the Druid High Priest of the people known as the Silures. Long ago, he was a peaceful man, a man whose path was filled with knowledge and wisdom, not butchery and mayhem.

"Lachlan?" Spencer said softly, reaching out to touch Duncan's now blurry face. "I know you're in there."

"Shh," Duncan whispered, "you've suffered a blow to the head, not to the mouth. Hush now, so the Butcher does not have to hear your idiotic ramblings."

With the last floating light of consciousness left in her, Jessie managed to barely push out a whisper, "It's Jessie. I've…spoken with Cate and Maeve…Duncan. I know about…the box."

Ever so quietly, Jessie's world faded to black.

*   *   *

21st Century

Tanner was waiting for Jessie on the deck of Ceara's houseboat. His shoulder-length brown hair danced in the salt air swirling around the marina. His black leather biker jacket fended off the slight chill pervading the Oregon coast. With his hands jammed in his pockets, he might have been mistaken for a thug waiting to mug someone.

He was waiting, all right, but not for that reason.

When Jessie came bounding around the corner, Tanner pulled his hands from his pockets and started toward her before catching himself. "Hey," he muttered as nonchalantly as he could.

"Oh my God, Tanner! You will never guess where I've been!" Jessie said breathlessly, crossing the plank to the deck. Her cheeks were rosy from her jog down the hill from the Inn, and her long hair trailed behind her like a cape. When she reached him, she threw her arms around his neck and hugged him tightly. "It was so incredible!" Pulling away, she saw, for the first time, the look of worry in his eyes. "What?"

"You promised you'd let me know if you ever went back. You swore."

She bowed her head. That promise was made a lifetime ago, when she didn't think she'd ever really go back. "I'm sorry, Tanner. I guess I just got ex—"

"You don't get it, do you?" Turning away, Tanner moved to the side of the boat and stared down at the water gently slapping the boat.

"I do get it," she said, stepping next to him. "I should have told you. It's just...everything seemed to happen so fast and I—"

Tanner turned and put his hands on her shoulders. "This isn't about the portal, Jess. Damn it! Do you have any idea how much it kills me knowing that you're willing to toss yourself through time to land in danger you know nothing about?"

Looking up into his eyes, Jessie suddenly realized that this wasn't about the promise at all. This wasn't about danger or time travel or anything to do with it. Tanner Dodds was in love with her.

"Oh...God...Tanner. I'm...I didn't—"

He silenced her with an index finger on her lips. "Don't say it, Jess. I've heard it long enough to know that I am not your soul mate or Anam Cara, or the one you're waiting for. I know all of that, but it hasn't stopped how I feel for you." Tanner looked away. "I've tried everything I can to just stand by you and be your friend, but I can't keep quiet about it if you're going to put yourself in jeopardy again."

The pain in his voice hurt her heart. How long had he felt this way and kept it hidden? How had she missed the signs a normal girl would have seen? How could she have been so incredibly blind about her best friend?

"I've been suppressing my feelings for a long time, Jess, but I just can't any more. I know you don't feel the same way, and I really don't want to mess our friendship up, but I need to lay my cards on the table. I need you to know…I'm in love with you. I have been for a really long time."

Jessie blinked rapidly. Words escaped her.

"I know. You're shocked. Trust me, so was I when I realized what was happening."

"When? How?"

He gently stroked her cheek. "Probably from the first moment I saw you, but I knew for sure when Ceara told me you'd gone back through. I felt this…I don't know…this anxiety wash over me. That's when I knew I needed to tell you. I don't want this to ruin our friendship, Jess. I just…I couldn't…can't contain it any longer."

"Tanner, I…I really don't know what to say."

"Just say you won't let it spoil anything. It would kill me to lose our friendship." He hesitated. "And that you'll keep your promise from now on."

Jessie swallowed hard. "I should have kept it the first time. I'm sorry."

Just then, Ceara stuck her head out of the galley door. "You two get it worked out? We've got business to tend to in here." With that, Ceara went back inside.

"She knows, doesn't she?"

"I had to talk to somebody. She said you'd want to know even if there wasn't anything you could do about it. I understand that, Jess, really I do. I know that Maeve is out there somewhere looking for you, and that when she shows up, your life will be complete. I know all of that up here." Tanner pointed to his head. "But that didn't stop me from feeling things in here," laying his hand over his heart.

"I'm glad you told me, Tanner, really I am. It's just—"

"I know. You have a lot on your plate, what with school and saving the world and all." He smiled. "Do me a favor and let me save what's left of my male pride. Let's pretend it's two days from now and relieve Ceara of the burden of curiosity eating her up right about now."

"But we will talk later?"

"You betcha."

As Jessie turned to the galley she stopped and looked back over her shoulder. "Just so you know, I would never let anything get in between our friendship. I promise."

"And you'll keep that one?"

"Absolutely."

Ceara was waiting patiently at the small kitchen table when Jessie descended the stairs. "It needed to be done," Ceara said softly. "It was eating him up inside." Rising, she poured three cups of tea and set them on the table. "We cannot move forward dragging that kind of baggage with us. We needed to clear the air."

"Consider it cleared," Tanner muttered, sitting across from Jessie at the small table. When he slid in, their knees touched as they always did, but this time, there was something more to it.

"Now, my dear, tell us all about your visit to the sixteenth century."

It took a pot of tea and three biscotti for Jessie to tell Ceara and Tanner the entire story of what happened on the deck of the ship. When she finished, Tanner was white, and Ceara was shaking her head. "You are very fortunate that nothing terrible happened to you."

"Yeah," Tanner added. "Good thing Duncan was there. I can't see you stabbing some guy."

"I should have killed that guy with the Saracen sword, but you're right. I just couldn't. Spencer might be a killer, but that's just not a hat I'll ever wear."

Ceara waved at both of them to be quiet. "And then what?" Her cheeks were rosy red, and her eyes sparkled. "Finish the story."

"That's where it got really weird, and I totally wasn't expecting it." Jessie inhaled slowly. "I figured I was just slipping back to my present body, but that isn't what happened."

Ceara shook her head. "You went back to the Land of the Sidhe, didn't you?"

Jessie nodded. "Yes, ma'am, I sure did."

"Wait a sec," Tanner interjected. "How come? What did they want with you?"

Ceara turned to him. "Remember those strange pictures if you looked at them long enough and the right way, you'd be able to see another picture all together?"

Tanner nodded. "I hate those. I could only do it when I was high."

Ceara nodded. "The second picture is always there whether or not you actually see it, correct?"

"Yeah."

"And according to the directions, if you relax your eyes, if you just sort of let them go, the second picture will reveal itself to you. Well, that's how the Otherworld operates. It is always there. Sometimes we can see it without trying, other times we need assistance. Jessie has learned how to reach that state without really trying. This time, however, she received assistance in the form of an ax handle." Turning back to Jessie, Ceara folded her hands on the table. "My guess is that your Captain Morgan pulled you into it."

Jessie nodded. "That's what I think. He was out of it, he knew I was there, and he pulled me with him thinking it might save me."

Tanner held his hand up. "Wait. Spencer pulled you into it?"

Ceara and Jessie both nodded, but it was Ceara who answered. "I'm sure Spencer and Duncan have done more than merely remember. They are, in their deepest hearts, still Druids from long ago. They have obviously remembered a great deal more than just who they were and what they're looking for. They understand the import of the box."

Jessie nodded. "They do."

"What else do they know?" Tanner asked.

Turning to him, Jessie could barely make eye contact with him. "More than I could ever have imagined..."

* * *

Jessie was surprised to find herself standing in a large clearing with a huge monolith towering in the middle. Spencer leaned against it, a crooked grin on his blood-smeared face. He was wearing the same clothes she'd seen him in earlier, a white swordsman shirt, brown doublet, those short black pants and knee-high hip boots, all spotted with the blood of dead men. His black curly hair hung in ringlets to his shoulders, and he bore a scar that cut his left eyebrow in half.

"You came back," he said, grinning like a fool. "You've a courage I'd not expected from just a lass."

"Of course I came back. You came through the portal to get me, and I answered, as I did for Cate before you." Jessie took a step closer to him. "And it's a damn good thing I did, too, otherwise, you'd be in two pieces right now."

"And for that, I thank you," he said, performing an elaborate bow. "And not a moment too soon, I might add. Please, Jessie, won't you sit down?" Spencer waved toward the smaller stones encircling another fire pit.

"Sure. But we don't have long, Spencer. Men are fighting and dying on your boat."

Sitting on a stone next to Jessie, Spencer stuck a twig between his teeth. "It's a ship, lass. The Raven is a ship."

Looking around, Jessie wondered where, exactly, they were.

"We're in the Land of the Sidhe, lass. It was the only place I could think of taking you that might save your life."

"What will save my life is if you get up and fight."

"And I will, but I need to make sure you're safe. She would have me hide if I let anything happen to you."

"She?"

"Maeve, of course." Ever so softly, so quietly, his lips barely moved, he whispered, "Have you found her yet?'"

Jessie's hand went to her mouth. "You know."

"Aye. I know more than you might think a salty dog like me ought to know. I've paid attention to signs and portents, lass. I've known for quite some time that you'd come help us if only I could find the way to reach you."

"Tell me about that, Spencer. Tell me how you knew to reach me, of all people."

Spencer rose and paced a few feet away before turning to her. The sun behind him illuminated him like a halo. "I did not know where else to turn for help."

"You tried Cate, though, didn't you?"

"Aye, but she snapped closed faster than a clamshell on a fish, that girl. She would have nothing to do with the likes of me, I'm afraid."

"Do you know why?"

"Of course I know why. Look at me. I kill men for profit, for posterity, for just about anything you might imagine, and a few you would never think of. If Cate allowed me in, she would be forced to take my memories…to relive those bloody moments of slashing and bloodlust. Can you blame her for shutting me out? I certainly don't."

"But you did manage to get to her once."

"Aye. Just the once, and that was just for a fleeting moment. In that flash of time, I was able to see a few scattered memories of hers before she shut me out altogether. One of those memories rang like a bell, lass, and that bell was a young girl from the future named Jessie."

"You came through to me shortly after Cate closed down on you, huh? Only you discovered I have very few of Cate's memories and I may not have the memories you need."

"Perhaps not, but you have the next best thing, don't you?"

"Cate?"

Spencer nodded. "Cate." Sitting back down, he waved his hand over the fire pit and it turned into a perfectly still pond.

"You have the power!"

"Not much, but some, yes. There is very little I can do save remembering and even then, I am not as sharp as Cate once was." Picking up a stone, Spencer tossed it into the pond. "Tell me, Jessie Ferguson, what caused the ripples in the water?"

"Is this a trick question? The stone."

"What stone? I see no stone."

"Because it's at the bottom of the pool."

Spencer put his hand up to his mouth to hide a grin. "Would you wager your very life on it?"

Jessie stared at the water before looking into Spencer's eyes; and though the eyes were his, the wisdom she saw was not. "I would not."

"Good. You see, the stone causing the ripples is gone, but its effects are still lingering, aye?"

Jessie nodded, wondering where he was headed with this. "Yes they are. I follow you, but have no clue where you're going with this."

"Think of that stone as the British Queen Elizabeth. Ripples are made by her, but no one can really say whether or not she is the stone at the bottom of the water. There, but invisible, as it were."

"Okay."

"Elizabeth wants the box, Jessie. That is why Francis Drake is such a busy little man poking about here and there and everywhere in between. She is the reason why Duncan and I are doing everything in our power to get to it before anyone else can."

"Wait a minute. You're telling me the Queen of England wants the box?"

"Aye. Drake was paid a great deal of money to get the box to her in one piece. The box is the reason we've turned our attention to and are raiding the Spanish galleons. If that is where Drake is going to be searching, then so are we. We must reach it before he does."

"Wait." Jessie held up her hands. "How does the Queen of England in the sixteenth century even know about the existence of the box carved in the first century?"

"Do you know who Elizabeth's mother was?"

Jessie nodded. "Of course I do. Anne Boleyn, wife of Henry the Eighth. She was beheaded for apparently bewitching Henry. Many accused her of being a witch."

Waving his hand across the water, Spencer waited for it to reveal a young woman sitting at the knee of an old crone. "The accusations about Anne being a witch were true. She did possess the sixth digit on her hand, and did, in fact, enchant Henry. The woman had always dabbled in the dark arts, and apparently, during one of her more successful dabblings, she discovered something about her past lives that led to her knowledge about the box. Anne Boleyn, Queen Elizabeth's mother, knew about the existence and the contents of the box. Had she lived long enough, she might have been able to benefit from her knowledge." Spencer flicked his wrist and the vision disappeared. "Henry never realized that he killed the goose who could have laid him many golden eggs."

"So you think it's possible that Anne Boleyn found a seam, and that's how she knew about the box?"

Spencer nodded. "What I have discovered most since heeding the call long ago is that anything is possible. Just look at yourself in this very moment. You are sitting by a lovely pond in a world your world no longer bothers even denying, talking to a pirate who's killed more men than you've danced with, and yet, here we are...on the same side, after the same prize."

"It is an amazing notion, Spencer, but I'm not so sure that I can be of any help to you in this quest. There is no historical information about a mysterious box."

"Do your history books mention anything about Drake's interaction with the Spanish galleons?"

"Yes. It's what he is most known for."

"And is it on record that Elizabeth and her cousin, Mary, have quite the contentious relationship?"

"Yes, again. Are you suggesting this is all Elizabeth's doing?"

Spencer was up and pacing now. "Most excellent. Yes. You see, Anne told her daughter about a mysterious box the Spanish picked up from the Portuguese explorers. The box, maybe forgotten in the hold of some ship, contains the one thing that would secure Elizabeth's reign and give England the power she needs to be the strongest monarchy in the world for all time. The key to England's power would be the ability to turn lead into gold, which would give her unlimited riches with which to expand her kingdom. With unlimited wealth, Queen Elizabeth could remain unmarried, deal however she pleased with the French, reign in the Spanish, and perhaps rid her of her cousin Mary without touching the coffers or marrying a prince."

"Wait," Jessie said. "What about Mary? How does finding the box affect the Queen of Scotland?"

Spencer rubbed the knot in the back of his head. "That is Elizabeth's other most important use for the contents of the box. If she can prove to the Protestant Scots that their Catholic Queen is harboring the Druids and using Druidic wisdom, Elizabeth will be able to pluck the contentious Scottish throne away from Mary without having to go through an expensive and costly war. It would give her every right to dispose of Mary without fear of reprisal from the Catholic nations."

Jessie's mouth dropped open. "You don't mean..."

Spencer nodded. "Elizabeth intends to use the box to blackmail Mary. If Mary doesn't step down from the throne of her own accord, Elizabeth will create a situation where Mary's followers do it for her." Spencer moved his head from side to side and rubbed the knot from his neck.

Now, Jessie was up and pacing. "Okay, wait a second. The box was hidden fifteen hundred years earlier in Ireland. You think that Anne somehow found out about it, told her daughter, who has since developed a superior navy, to look for a box that will give her the recipe to turn lead into gold. Then, she is going to use the information inside the box to destroy her cousin's reign so that she can rule Scotland as well? Does that about sum it up?"

Spencer ran his hand through his hair and sighed. "If Elizabeth gets her hands on the box, she'll destroy Mary, the French, the Spanish, and anyone else who gets in her way. She'll unite Britain by ruling both England and Scotland, and she'll send her navy to bring the Irish to its knees."

"And that's not the worst of it, is it?"

Spencer stepped closer to Jessie so their faces were about a foot apart. "I wish it were. Someone else has come through in search of the box. Someone who cares naught about politics, my people, or the Queens. If he manages to secure the box before Duncan and I can, he will do more than upset the balance of power in my time."

"He could upset the economic balance in every century."

"Exactly. So you see now why I need your help? Without some guidance, without a head start of some kind, everything that has come before could be altered, including your own time period."

Taking Spencer's callused hands in hers, Jessie shook her head. "Then I say we make sure that doesn't happen."

*   *   *

21st Century

Tanner rose and stretched. Two more pots of tea and several biscotti later, Jessie had finished her story of her visit with Spencer in the Otherworld. "Sorry to bum you, Jess, but it sounds like you're getting mixed up in a historical catfight that ended over five hundred years ago. Elizabeth lopped off Mary's head for conspiracy charges, and as far as we know, no one has ever really turned lead into gold. Is it really worth risking your life for?"

Jessie motioned to Tanner to sit back down. The tension she felt was not so much about her possible death in Spencer's world as it was about her life here in this time. "That's just it, Tanner. That's why Spencer came through. He doesn't just need my help…he needs mine and Cate's assistance because whoever is coming through the portal has been time-slipping for quite a while. It's someone who knows the old ways…someone who wants to use the box for his own design. I can't allow that to happen."

"So is this the sum total of your life, then? To go here and there saving people from the past from things they should handle on their own?"

Ceara cleared her throat as she rose and collected the teacups. "You two have unfinished business that has nothing to do with boxes or Queens. Whatever may come of this, remember one thing: 'There is nothing we like to see so much as the gleam of pleasure in a person's eye when he feels that we have sympathized with him, understood him. At these moments something fine and spiritual passes between two friends. These are the moments worth living.'"

When she went upstairs, Jessie and Tanner sat in silence for a few moments before she licked her lips and quietly said, "You're my very best friend, Tanner."

"Don't, Jess."

"Let me finish. Please. I heard you out."

Tanner looked resigned. "Fine, go for it."

Leaning over, she laid her hand over his. "You mean more to me than you could know. I can't imagine my life without you, but I am only now beginning to see who I am. I've been lost for so long; it's taken me three years to get back on the right path."

"From where I stand, that's a pretty lonely path, Jess. You think I don't see how you look when you think of Maeve? I know how lonely you are. I see it in your eyes—hell, I feel it whenever you are anywhere near me. You're lonely."

"I don't deny that, but just because I'm lonely doesn't mean I'm okay with turning to you to fill that void. I'd never do that to you."

"I know I can't fill that void, Jess, but I'm not asking to be Mr. Right. I'll settle for Mr. Right Now."

Jessie stared at him and stared and stared until she burst out laughing, and Tanner's laughter followed. "Oh my God, where did you get that line?"

Still laughing, Tanner rose and sat next to Jessie. "From a stupid movie. Was it a bad line?"

"Not bad…just…how long did you work on it?"

"Coupla days."

Jessie threw her arms around Tanner's neck. "It was very sweet. So are you."

"Sweet enough for you to consider maybe loving me back?"

Pulling away, Jessie locked eyes with him. "I have so much I have to do."

"Is that a no?"

Jessie shrugged. "Consider it a definite maybe, Mr. Right

Now."

*　　*　　*

16th Century

Spencer always enjoyed a return to land, and this time was no exception. Being at sea was a bit like existing out of time; life ashore continued without you. Babies were born, wives went astray, siblings died, and when you finally rejoined those you'd left behind, you were so weary all you wanted to do was nurse an ale and sit back listening to all the silly tales people wanted to share.

It was this listening Spencer was known for. Whenever he and Duncan visited taverns together, Spencer would listen for hours at a time to Duncan's embellished stories and prefabricated tales. The man could weave a story so thoroughly, Spencer had no doubt that his skill at oral storytelling was a result of many lives spent as a Druid. Only a bard with years of traveling the world could beat him in storytelling, and Spencer had yet to meet that man.

It was, after all, one of Duncan's stories that had caught Spencer's attention ten years ago, when he was just a boy of fourteen and had already been at sea for years with his father.

Young Duncan had been standing in the middle of a town square in a small village on the coast of England, relating an old Druid myth. Spencer inched nearer and nearer until Duncan caught his eye and held his gaze. As the tale came to a close, Duncan walked toward Spencer, and finished the story as if he were telling it only to Spencer. Then, Duncan held his hand out to Spencer and said, "Do you know me?"

Spencer looked hard into those light blue eyes. A kid at sea learned to trust no one on land, but this blond-haired young lad was somehow different from the others. A deep-set knowing transpired between them, and it did not take Spencer long before he understood what all of the dreams, visions and other memories he'd had meant. The instances he could not account for nor explain that had captured his mind were all clear to him at this very moment.

"I believe we've met before," Spencer said, releasing Duncan's powerful grip and stepping back. Duncan was as familiar to him as his own father, and it was frightening. He had heard of such occurrences back in Ireland, but not in this part of the world.

Duncan cocked his head. "How about we sneak us an ale and you remind me of when that was."

Spencer didn't know if it was the stolen ale that had loosened Duncan's tongue, but two hours into their visit they were sharing memories they had never themselves actually experienced or shared with anyone before. The truth became clearer and clearer, and they arrived at the same conclusion simultaneously.

Two boys from different places, one raised on land, the other at sea, and yet they had still managed to find each other in their sixteenth century lives. From that day on, they met each day on the dock, sitting for hours reliving events from ancient Egypt to the Middle Ages; events sometimes only one of them remembered.

Spencer had always known he was different. He had thoughts that felt like dreams, dreams that felt like reality, and real-life experiences which he successfully handled because of wisdom and knowledge he should never have possessed in the first place.

There were others out there in the world looking for him. He thought he knew their names, but it wasn't until Duncan mentioned those very names that he was sure they had existed. When it became evident that they had known many of the same stories and incidences from times long ago, Spencer did what all good questers do: he sought a Shaman from one of the forest tribes to help him understand what was happening to him...to them. It wasn't easy finding a Druid in England during this time, so many of them had gone underground during the Dark Years. But Spencer had an unerring ability to find like-minded people.

The Shaman, a wizened old woman known only as Sheridan, became the single most influential person in Spencer's young life apart from his father. Sheridan explained who the woman was in Spencer's dreams, and her connection to the gray-eyed one Spencer was searching for in this life. She also explained that the triad in their many incarnations had always sought each other out as well, and one of those was sitting right next to Spencer.

"You must go out and find the other," Sheridan had said. "She will be searching for you as well, and it is your destiny to unite. That is the way it has been, so shall it always be. Always."

"But how will I know them? It was a coincidence that I—"

"You will know," the crone replied, "as easily as you know your own name. And know this: there are no coincidences in either life or death. When souls are connected across time, they know when they discover each metamorphosis, each changeling, each being who carries within them the memories of another life. Those memories are residual memories. Sometimes we remember them as if they happened yesterday, sometimes we remember them not at all."

"We'll know by just looking?"

Sheridan shook her head. "You'll know by feeling. You will know because night will become day, the moon will shine next to the sun, and everything within you will remember things you did not know you have done or can do. There are two things on this earth you cannot escape: your past, and your destiny, and for you, my fine young man, both are so deeply entwined, they may never be separated. It is how you have always intended it to be."

Spencer started to ask another question, but she sent him away, telling him that his past and his present had started coming together, and that the rest was up to him. "She will be searching for you as well. Do not hesitate to fulfill your destiny, my son. Your quest...your journey has only now begun."

And so it had. Spencer had reached the shores of France and Spain, Sicily and Sardinia, Greece and Crete. He had traveled all over the world trading wools and wines with his father, but it was on that rare summer day when Spencer found Duncan, that his world had opened up and his destiny took shape.

"Many find each other, but few remember," Spencer told Duncan that night as they lay in a field looking up at the stars.

Duncan was sixteen, had seen little of the world, but had amused himself with women and the sword. Countless numbers of young girls could not fill the void he'd felt for as long as he could remember. So, he worked hard to perfect his blade skills, hoping that someday he would be the best armsman in Britain, and that being so might give him that which he sought. When nothing came close to filling that empty chasm, he jumped at the chance to learn how to be a seaman, hoping the sea held more answers for him than the land.

"Do you see the woman with the gray eyes?" Duncan had asked that night as he contemplated his future on the high seas. "The one they call Maeve?"

"Who were we in Maeve's time?"

"We were Druids, like Sheridan; powerful, powerful priests and priestesses who…" Spencer hesitated, shaking his head when Duncan belched out a laugh.

"You might have been a…a…woman, but I…oh, that I'll not believe. Not ever."

Spencer sighed and shook his head. "When one comes to you in your visions and dreams, who is it?"

"The priest, Lachlan, and that boy-o never kicks up his heels, if you know my meaning."

"Chief Druid of the Silures." Spencer shook his head, and frowned. "I did not know I knew that."

"Yes? So? You should not be surprised I was a great leader. It is what I do best. What else do you know that you did not know you knew?"

The two boys laughed until they cried, and for the next few days, months and years, they continued to share visions, memories and dreams, until eventually they knew a great deal more about who they once were and what adventures they'd been on together. Soon, they had compiled a great many pieces of their lives as Druids, and they understood why they needed to remember and why they were so important to each other.

And so, when the elder Captain Morgan's merchant ship pulled out, Spencer and Duncan began a journey of two boys growing into men, and now, they were two grown men of twenty-four and twenty-six transforming into questers.

It had been quite a journey.

Five years into their path, when Duncan and Spencer were nineteen and twenty-one, they were in a tavern off the coast of

France. Duncan was preparing to bed yet another tavern wench when he leaned across the table to Spencer and said, "You cannot wait for a ghost that might never arrive. Besides, what if she shows up and she's a man? You'll have wasted all this time brooding over a memory…and an ancient one at that."

The look Spencer shot Duncan contained daggers, and they never spoke of it again. Duncan had always had a lust for women that was never quenched, and Spencer was always finding women who never suited him. He always pictured that gray-eyed beauty, always came away disappointed by the brief, physical connection with the women beneath him. He had stopped looking for Maeve long ago, resigned to the knowledge that he would find her when he least expected it.

Duncan wanted nothing to do with those Druids who kept calling him back, begging him to remember. He remembered the love Lachlan had for Maeve and how she had gently kept his feelings for her at bay. He remembered the longing, the ache, the yearning to hold her in his arms just once. That had never come to pass for Lachlan, even though he had remained true to her on a spiritual level, never breaking her trust, never crossing the line she so clearly had drawn for him and any other man trying to get too close to her. Duncan marveled at the kind of man Lachlan had been. Who among them today had such a respect for a woman to honor her with the title of friend? How could Lachlan have spent his entire life wanting her and yet never so much as kissed her? In Duncan's mind, Lachlan was either a saint or a eunuch, and he wasn't sure which was worse.

He truly enjoyed the pleasures of the flesh, and there certainly was much of that to be had. As Lachlan had been true to himself on the spiritual plane, Duncan was to himself on the physical one. Maybe he was the balance for their eternal soul, because together, he felt they would have made one damn good man.

But Duncan seldom shared this opinion with Spencer because Spencer was bent on finding his Maeve in this life of theirs; waiting for the day when the Goddess brought them together again for another quest or adventure. Spencer was sure she was out there, and Duncan just let him go on believing it.

"You think the box will lead us to her, don't you?"

Spencer glanced up into Duncan's eyes and shrugged. "I do not know which path will take me to her, Duncan, so the more paths I try, the better my chances are of finding her."

"And are we getting close?"

"To the box? Yes. I can feel it. I don't know how, exactly, but I know we're on the right path."

"And you are sure it needs to be destroyed? It will be lost for all time. The works that Lachlan and the rest took so much time creating will no longer be here for future generations. Are you so sure that is the right thing to do?"

Spencer raised an eyebrow. Duncan was usually so aloof and noncommittal when it came to the Druids' dilemmas. "When they wrote the BoibeLoth, they left them in Ireland anticipating that the box would be found by people of like mind, not those who would use the writings to benefit their own end. They had no idea that Quinn had slipped so lethal a document within."

"Lachlan was both wise and foolish."

Spencer sipped the ale. "Aren't all men?"

This made Duncan laugh. "Indeed. And I should stop acting like a fool by standing here talking to you, when I could be consorting with that lovely lady."

"Be off with you then. Enjoy your trollop. I'll be up before you and we shall meet back here for supper."

Watching Duncan swagger up the stairs to greet his young lady, Spencer wondered if there was ever anything on their path that would fill Duncan's empty soul.

*   *   *

1st Century AD

Lachlan was still cursing when Maeve rode off on his gray horse, leaving him and Cate standing in a cloud of equally gray dust. "How could I have been such a fool?" Pacing back and forth, Lachlan spat on the ground, which he seldom did. "There were reasons why those before us did not write down our deeds, rituals or most sacred traditions! It is my arrogance that has struck a blow to our kind."

Cate reached up to caress his back and then thought better of it. "How could you have known?"

"I should have known! People count on me to know!"

"How? Can you see fourteen hundred years into the future?" Cate lowered her voice slightly. "Could you have predicted the evil that lay in the breast of Quinn?"

"It is my job to see the evil in men's hearts, Cate."

Cate reached out hesitantly toward him, her hand brushing up against his. "Oh Lachlan, you have taught me that man is an ever-changing creature to approach with caution and an open heart. Who could have known how unimportant integrity would become to men? Who could have predicted that the value of one of the earth's metals would become god and goddess to cultures all over the world? Not even Maeve could see how ugly greed would make man."

Cate looked down the slope at the Donnaugh Valley and at a field which had just been sown. As healer of the village, Maeve had been given land on which to grow many of the herbs she employed in the relief of pains and other illnesses. As Cate studied the land, a sudden chill swept over her and she wrapped her arms tightly around herself.

"What is it, Cate?" Lachlan asked, sensing her unease.

Cate studied the small center of the village below. It was only a few huts of woadspackled buildings, but it was a special village she had grown to love. She could see three men standing together smoking pipes. Gray mist curled up from each pipe, mingled together slightly above their heads before dissipating. A fourth man hobbled lamely up to the three others and spoke with them briefly before starting up the path toward them.

"Cate?" Lachlan walked over to where Cate stood and followed her gaze. "What is it?"

Cate inhaled slowly and shook her head. "I…I am not sure."

"Is it those men?"

"Maybe." Turning to Lachlan, Cate stared into his eyes. "In all the years I have known her, I have never heard her express a violent intention. Not once." Cate watched the man on the path. "It worries me to hear her sound so cold."

Lachlan stared openly, taking a protective step in front of Cate. "Who is that man?"

Cate swallowed the trepidation rising within her. She knew...yet...she did not for sure. "I believe he is the reason Maeve left us."

Lachlan was squinting now. "There appears to be something not right with him. His gait is all wrong and awkward."

Cate shuddered, stepping another half foot behind Lachlan. "Be wary, Lachlan," she whispered. "Be very careful."

She studied the man as he neared. Although dressed in typical ill-fitting peasant garb, there was definitely something about him...something off...something unnatural. The air around them crackled as the man slowly approached, his gait unbalanced, and his legs out of synch with each other. She had only felt this once before, and it felt just as menacing then as it did now.

The filthy, wrinkled old man strode up to them, looked from one to another, and then ever so slowly grinned, showing blackened teeth that were chipped and rotting. The stench of ale wafted through the air, assaulting Cate's nose. The hackles on her neck rose, and Cate took another step back.

"I do not suppose you recognize this smile, Cate, but I imagine if you peered deeply through the windows of my soul, you would know who I am."

Lachlan held his hand up. "We are not in the habit, sir, of being approached in such a manner, nor do we play guessing games. Is there something you need help with?"

Again, the man smiled broadly. "Actually, dear Lachlan, there is something I can help you with."

Cate held up both her hands with her palms extended as if feeling the vibrations in the air. She immediately recoiled as if burned. "Oh my—"

Lachlan turned toward her. "Cate?"

Cate shook her head as if trying to rid something from it. She put her palms up one more time. This time, she took the energy as if taking a physical blow.

"Cate?"

Slowly lowering her hands, she stared at the still grinning

old man. "Quinn."

Lachlan shot a look over to the man who was, most assuredly, not Quinn.

"Do not be fooled by this appearance, Lachlan. This man… or, should I say, this body houses me. And yes, it is I. Quinn." The man laughed. It was an ugly, unnatural sound, like rocks being dropped on metal. "Very good, sorceress. You are perhaps stronger now than when you left Eire. Your mentor ought to be proud." He looked around. "Where is she? Where is the woman you'd both throw yourselves off a cliff for?"

Cate shook her head sadly and pulled her robe tighter around her. "You have lost your way, Quinn. You sought to save the Druids on the isle, and yet—"

"I found everlasting life in an age too wonderful, too incredible to be believed. Do not pity me, Cate, for I do not need it nor do I want it. I have found paradise in a time when man can fly, wear fine clothes, get money from a machine and talk to someone far away as if they stood right next to you. It is nothing short of heaven, little priestess. Far better than any gift the Sidhe have to offer."

At last, Lachlan found his voice. "Why have you come, and in disguise no less? What trickery is this?"

Quinn absent mindedly scratched himself. "Because I ran into a bit of a…problem, you might say. I had to possess this body in this time so I can complete my final quest." He wagged a filthy finger at them. "And you ought not to try and stop me."

"Final quest? Are riches in the future all the wisdom you've learned from your travels? Is that how you are choosing to use the skills you were born with?"

The man belched, and Cate waved the stench away from her face. "You have taken over a drunken man's body, for what use?"

Nodding, Quinn laughed. "It is so easy, Cate. I have never had so much fun in all my lives. With the portal, our souls can go anywhere we will them to. If the being within cannot fend us off, we can live forever. Imagine the wisdom you both can have if only you would—"

"No." Cate stated, holding a hand up. "That is not our way.

It is unnatural and—"

"And nature, Cate, is on its way out. You think the cutting of the oak groves by the Romans was terrible?" He chuckled. "You ought to see the people of the future and their destruction of the planet. Forget about nature or what is natural, Cate. Your precious nature is doomed."

"Just what is it you want, Quinn?" Lachlan demanded.

"Ah, ever the pragmatist, eh, Lachlan? Or has that word not yet been developed?" He waved the question off. "Nevertheless, as you know, I've put a little plan into action that will enable me to create my own wealth in a time where cash is king." Chuckling, Quinn shook his head as if he'd told a joke. "I just love that line. Anyway, I have chosen a life to live but to acquire it, I need the contents of that box."

"You must be addled, Quinn, to think we would help you. We would never help you. You have already put something into motion that we cannot reverse."

"I have done nothing more than travel to the sixteenth century to retrieve the box for the Queen of England. Only that bitch will never see it. Once I get my hands on it, it will never be seen again."

"Why the Queen of England?" Cate asked. "Why then?"

Quinn tottered unsteadily a bit before answering. "She has more resources than anyone. More ships, more men, more power. She has what it takes. Believe me, I've been to other times, but I have a better shot at it in that time. I've become quite the quester, Lachlan. I come and go through the portal as I—"

"Enough of your boring boasts, Quinn. We tire of you and whatever game you're at. Cate was wrong. You are not lost. You are beyond lost. Now, be off with you." Lachlan stepped up to the drunk. "And leave us alone."

Quinn glowered at Lachlan through bloodshot eyes. "Do not presume to dismiss me, Lachlan. I am not to be trifled with. I hold all the cards in this game. All of them. Every one and every thing you hold dear is at my mercy…including your dearly departed mother, who has somehow managed to land herself in the twenty-first century."

Lachlan clamped his jaws together, every muscle tightening.

Cate laid her hand on his shoulder. "That is surely your greatest boast of all, Quinn, and perhaps the most fantastical. To assume you have some sort of power to wield in other times is not only arrogant, but foolish as well."

"What is foolish, Cate, is your constant meddling. You criticize me for choosing to live in a time where medicine comes from a bottle, yet you are truly no different than I. You just want to visit, not to live. You want to befriend your future being, not co-exist with her. It is a minor discrepancy. We both use the portal to grant our desires. We are not as unalike as you presume."

Cate felt his energy changing to something more ominous; darker. She stepped in front of Lachlan much as he had done to her earlier. "Leave us." Cate's voice was cold and commanding.

"Oh no...Not until you've heard why I am here. You are curious, are you not, as to my...occupation of this dreadful being?"

"We care not, Quinn, and if it were in our power to destroy you here and now, we would."

Quinn's grin broadened, his blackened teeth looked like rotten walnuts. "Ah yes, ever the pacifists, we Druids. I counted on that when I first made my plans." Quinn glowered up at Lachlan. "If you persist in interfering with me in any way, those you employ to stop me will perish. I have no illusions of peace and serenity other than what money will buy."

When Cate and Lachlan looked at each other, Quinn spat on the ground. "It is Spencer I speak of. He and everyone else you send to do your bidding."

"Spencer is not as easy a target as you might believe."

"Ha! His weak attempts to prevent me from retrieving what is rightfully mine are pathetic. He has not the mind, nor the means. If he persists—"

"Which he will."

Quinn waved this off. "If any interfere, I shall be forced to exact punishment on the one thing you hold above all else."

Cate felt her blood run cold. "You have no idea what we—"

"But of course I do. Everyone here knows...it's Maeve you all cherish like some goddess. It is Maeve who sets the wheels in motion. It is Maeve—"

"Maeve has nothing to do with this."

Quinn laughed and his laugh turned into a coughing spasm. "Maeve," he said, spitting a glob of phlegm at Lachlan's feet, "has everything to do with this, you silly girl. She is the only one powerful enough to get in my way."

"And she will."

"Perhaps she will try, Cate McEwen. I do not doubt that she is trying as we speak." Turning slowly, Quinn started back down the hill. "Funny thing though," he said over his shoulder, "it was not Maeve I meant—though it is anyone's guess why you all risk so much for her. No, the one I refer to is that woman-child you and Spencer called upon for help who need stay away from me. She will rue the day if she tries to stand in my way."

Cate and Lachlan exchanged glances. "Jessie? Why hurt her? She has done nothing—"

"I saw what she was able to do for you on the island. If you value her, you will leash that dog so she can live out the remainder of her life where she is."

Cate stepped toward Quinn, disregarding both the stench and her own fear. "You will not harm that girl."

The odor coming from Quinn's stolen body was palpable. "Of course I can. Can and will, but you can save her, Cate. Tell her to stay in her own time and disregard the beckoning of that madman, Spencer Morgan. Impress upon her how sorry you are to have involved her. It isn't too late to save her."

"Do you honestly believe I have some sort of power over her? She is a headstrong girl from a time I know little about."

"Then she will be a dead strong girl. You brought her into this. You can uninvolve her just as well. Get her out of my way, Cate, or I guarantee I will dispose of her." Quinn started back down the path. "Remember what I said, Cate. I will kill them all. Do not disbelieve me or my intentions."

Cate and Lachlan stood quiet and still, those final words reverberating in their heads.

"Come," Lachlan ordered, pulling Cate up the hill toward

the craggy bluff. They made their way through a crashing waterfall into a passage leading to an underground cavern and toward the newest portal Maeve had found.

"Cate—"

Cate turned to Lachlan and covered his mouth with one finger. "I must go. You know it as well as me." With a wave of her hand, Cate opened the portal. It looked like a slight crevice in the wall of the cavern where a bright light shone from, but Cate knew what was on the other side; a world she did not know, but needed to protect anyway.

It was their way, the way of the Druid.

"Perhaps Maeve has the right idea. Maybe we should have destroyed him. It may not be too late." Lachlan's voice was low and barely audible.

Cate stared up at him. "I cannot believe that you, of all people, would suggest such a thing."

"He is evil, Cate, and there is no end to the evil he can do. He has threatened the very fabric of time."

"But destroy him?"

Lachlan sighed. "Why do you think she returned to Eire?"

"To talk him out of this."

Lachlan gazed deeply into her eyes. "No, Cate, not to talk to him. Maeve knew what she was doing when she left so abruptly."

Cate felt as if a hood had been lifted from her eyes. "She knew?"

Lachlan nodded. "She left because Quinn is after her. He said as much when he told us she was the only one powerful enough to stop him. He isn't as afraid of Jessie as he is of what she will do. She left to do exactly what she said she was going to do: to destroy him."

*   *   *

21st Century

With her parents out of town, Jessie had to work overtime during the weekend, which, from all appearances, was going to be a busy one. The Inn's two floors of guests were busy from the end of April until the beginning of November, and this week was no exception. Every room had been booked for nearly two weeks, and that meant she, Daniel and Tanner should be hopping all weekend long. Already, Daniel had been up helping the maid with the first five rooms. Then he announced he was meeting his friend, Harold, at the pier to watch the sailboats come in.

"You get all your work done?" Jessie asked, checking the refrigerator to make sure the ice was in the ice bucket for the Newmans' third anniversary. They had come here on their wedding night because they got caught in a downpour on their way from Seattle to San Francisco. They never made it to the city by the bay, choosing to stay on the Oregon coast in New Haven at the newly refurbished inn. They had returned the next year to celebrate their first anniversary, and Jessie did not doubt they would continue to do so until they were too old to remember who they were married to. She hadn't seen very many people as in love as the Newmans were, but she was sure if anyone could go the distance, it would be them.

"Daniel?"

"I heard you. I got as much done as I could, considering this place is a never-ending job. It's got to be harder than working for someone else."

A part of her agreed. She had seen her parents sink their every dime and invest every ounce of energy to make this place work, but it truly was a never-ending job. She didn't know if inheriting the Inn from them would be a gift or a curse. "Then knock your socks off. Don't do drugs, have sex or rob any banks."

"Sheesh. You take all the fun out of fun."

Watching him run down the street, she sighed. A minute ago, it seemed, he was just a five-year-old boy. Now, he had the beginning of facial hair and was no longer her little brother. His doctor had said he would be a little over six feet, like their father. Jessie wanted some of that height, but it didn't look like any was coming her way. At five-feet-six, she was done growing.

The front doorbell chimed.

"You're late," she said, scowling playfully at Tanner. It had taken her father over a year, but he'd finally accepted the fact that even though Tanner might resemble a druggie, he most definitely was not one. The Fergusons had hired him to work the front desk on the condition that he would cut his hair a bit shorter and come to work without the trademark leather jacket that was his second skin. Soon, Tanner was taking guests on beach treks, driving groups to Eugene or Portland, and arranging for bike, canoe and kayak rentals. He'd become a fixture around the Inn, and everyone loved him.

"You're a ball-buster; you know that, don't you?" Tanner brushed hair off his forehead. "I had to stop by the store for the Newmans' strawberries, remember?"

"Oh, right. The strawberries."

"You forgot, didn't you?" Tanner crossed his arms over his chest.

She hated that he was right but knew better than to lie to him, even in fun. As an empath, Tanner immediately sensed dishonesty anywhere near him.

"I didn't forget," Jessie said. "I just knew you'd remember."

Tanner stepped closer and lowered his head to look into her face. "You tired?"

"No. Why?"

"Carrying around all that denial must be exhausting." Tanner just managed to get out of the way of the towel that Jessie snapped at him. She grabbed the strawberries and started washing them in the sink. "We've got another full house."

Tanner stood so close to her, she could feel the heat from his body. "Is it later yet?"

She swallowed and kept washing the strawberries. "I haven't had much time to catch my breath."

"Jess, I understand my role in your life. I've known that since the day Madame told me who you were and what you were doing. While you're traveling around to the past, we're still living today…in the present. Do we have to worry so much about the future? Can't we just be intimate in the here and now?"

Wiping her hands off on the towel, she turned to him. His eyes were more intense than she'd ever seen them, and there was a rough masculinity emanating from him she'd never felt before. "Intimate. That's a big word, Tanner. Being intimate means—"

"Do you love me?"

She backed half a step away. "What?"

"Do. You. Love. Me?"

"You know I do."

"Right. And I love you. We're two people who love each other. Why can't we find a way to express that until she—"

"Because you don't do that to your friends, Tanner. I can't be with you and then drop you like a hot rock when she shows up. I couldn't live with myself. You mean too much to me."

"So you're determined to keep me at arm's length to save our friendship?"

Jessie nodded.

"She said you'd say that."

"You've been talking to Ceara about this?"

"Jess, I'm in love with you! Who else would I talk to about that?"

"What else did she say?"

"That I was a fool." Tanner bowed his head. "I am, aren't I?"

She wrapped her arms around him and pulled him into a hug. "Yes, you are, but that's what makes you irresistible."

Hugging her tightly, he buried his face in her hair. "I'm not going to give up."

"I didn't think you would."

Pulling away, he tucked a piece of hair behind her ear. "I know where your heart is, Jess, but she could come in five days or fifty years. Are you just going to wait around forever?"

"You know, I have no idea. Just the use of the female pronoun kinda freaks me out. I mean—"

"I know. You're not gay. I'm aware of that."

"It has nothing to do with some archaic labeling system of how to be with each other. When the time comes, her gender won't matter. I know that in my heart of hearts." Jessie slowly pulled away. "Just as I know that you're my very best friend, and I won't do anything to jeopardize that."

"For now. Just know that my charms are wily. They can

sneak up on you on a moment's notice."

Laughing, she replied, "I'll keep that in mind."

Grabbing the strawberries, Tanner opened the refrigerator. "Think we'll need the kid for breakfast tomorrow?"

Jessie nodded. "I cut him loose for lunch. He worked really hard this morning, but I think we'll be okay."

The front doorbell chimed again. "It's been like this all week."

"The beaches are really busy this morning. People are gonna be looking for a place to crash."

"I'll take the desk. Will you check the pantry for tomorrow morning's breakfast goodies? Reena has a habit of forgetting Sunday's breakfasts."

"Sure."

She took her apron off and tossed it back at Tanner before stepping out of the kitchen and behind the front desk.

The desk was like that of the European Inn tradition. It was a long, dark wood, about five feet tall, that allowed the guests to sign in much as they would at a fancier hotel. Her folks had paid a fortune for the antique, and it was one of her favorite pieces in the Inn. Stepping behind it, she welcomed the well-dressed gentleman who had just walked in.

"Good morning," Jessie said, looking up into his Ray-Bans. Graying sideburns framed a George Hamilton-style tan. He appeared familiar, but she couldn't place where she had seen him before. When he flashed his twenty-thousand dollar veneers, hackles on the back of her neck jumped to life. "Welcome to the Seaside Inn. How can I help you today?"

The man did not remove his glasses as he leaned casually on the front desk. "Do you have any rooms available in your lovely facility?"

"We're completely booked for the weekend, I'm afraid."

"Busy, eh?"

Jessie felt a tingle on the back of her neck. "Very."

"Too busy to go meddling?"

She stepped back, as the tingle now itched. "Excuse me?"

The man leaned closer. "You're a busy girl, Jessie Ferguson, running an inn in one world while questing and saving yourself in another. How ever do you manage?" He whipped off his sunglasses and glared at her.

Jessie cut her eyes to the kitchen door, but she could not see Tanner. When she looked back into the man's eyes, she knew who he was—not because she recognized him, but by the way he felt. Although she had never met him, Cate had, and the memory was strong and frightening. Theirs was not a good relationship.

"Oh my God...Quinn?"

The man's smile was cold and distant, vicious beneath the salt-and-pepper goatee. "Well done. I appreciate you not wasting time with foolishness. Perhaps you have gained some wisdom in this life."

The fear in Jessie's neck ran down her arms to the tips of her fingers. "I may know who you are, but I have no idea why you're here."

Quinn was still smiling. "I'm afraid I may have frightened your little brother."

At the mention of Daniel's name, her fear dissolved into something closer to anger, and she took a step forward. "What do you want?"

"You know what I want."

"I'm afraid I don't."

"So, now you're going to play games."

"This is no game, Quinn. Get out. I don't have it...and if I did—"

"I'd kill you and your family without a second thought, so be glad you don't."

The anger diffused, leaving her feeling more panicky than brave. Her fear regrouped itself and now lodged in the pit of her stomach, its tentacles reaching into all parts of her body. She looked once again toward the kitchen and this time Quinn followed her gaze.

"I suggest you find a way of keeping your friend in the kitchen unless you want him sent to the hospital before lunch."

"Take your threats and get out, Quinn. I'm not afraid of you."

The smile dropped from Quinn's face as he leaned even

further over the desk. "Don't you dare presume to tell me where to go or what to do, Jessie Ferguson. You ought to know one thing very clearly before you use that tone with me again, and that's that I hold all the cards. All of them. Everything and everyone you hold dear is in the palm of my hands and I can crush them at a moment's notice, so you take care how you speak to me."

When Tanner walked out of the kitchen the thought crossed her mind to act like Quinn was one of her professors, or a customer. Tanner would know the second he got close enough that neither was true.

"Tanner, would you mind checking the basement for those blackberry preserves Reena bought the other day?"

Tanner cocked his head as he looked at her, then quickly joined her protectively at the desk. "Who the hell are you?"

"Please, Tanner, just do as I—"

"Who the hell are you?" Tanner repeated, shoving his face into Quinn's.

Quinn tilted his head at Tanner like a dog trying to hear a sound. "Ah, an empath. Well, Jessie Ferguson, it appears you have surrounded yourself with quite a variety of sages and wizards even in this time. You are so much like Cate, even here."

Standing shoulder to shoulder with Tanner, Jessie felt her courage beat back her initial fear. "Get out, Quinn."

Quinn stared hard at her. "There are conditions that need to be met in this life that will assure me of my safety in other lives."

"Conditions about what?"

"There are...things I need to do, and I cannot have you or Cate meddling in my affairs or the affairs of the portal. If you agree never to return through the portal again, I will allow those you love in both realms to continue living. Do whatever you wish in this time, but if you go through the portal again, I will kill every member of your family, Cate McEwen, Maeve, Lachlan, Spencer and this young man who loves you enough to risk his foolish life. Is that clear enough?"

She put her hand out to stop Tanner from making a move. "Don't—"

"Come on, Jess! Haven't you heard enough?"

"I have." This voice came from the side door. Ceara entered the room and closed the door, her gaze never leaving Quinn's. "I should have known you would show up sooner than later; although later would have been preferable." She strode into the room, her scarves swirling about her. She made a beeline toward Quinn, her multi colored, multi layered scarves still moving even after she landed in front of him.

Quinn squinted at her. "My word. Ceara?"

"I felt your evil the moment you came through the seam," she replied. Turning to Jessie, she stood more erect. "I am terribly sorry it took me so long to get here, my dear, but this old body has a heck of a time getting up the hill." She approached Quinn and looked up into his eyes. The body he was using now was almost an entire foot taller than she. Chuckling, she shook her head. "Just as I thought."

"Your meddling, Ceara, has become hazardous to their health. I believe—"

"Oh, hush, you intolerable lout. I heard why you are here and what you want from the poor girl and you're not going to get it. So be off with you."

"You do not fully understand the situation, old woman."

Ceara winked at Jessie and Tanner before stepping even closer to Quinn. "I understand enough to know you are the same spoiled brat you always were, and when you don't get your way, you become a bothersome bully. Well, go bully someone else and leave these kids alone."

Red anger crept up Quinn's neck and turned his cheeks pink. "You are making a fatal mistake."

Ceara waved this away, bracelets clanging. "No, Quinn, it is you who are making the mistake, and if you are stupid enough to bring this battle to my home, you had better be prepared to face a wrath the likes of anything you've ever seen. You will rue the day you came into this age. Now be off with you before I allow this young man to tear your arms out and beat you with their bloody ends."

Quinn glared at her, but made no move.

"Quinn, I can tell by the sweat on your brow and the color

of your fingertips that you've overstayed your welcome in that body. You are getting weaker, aren't you? Perhaps you aren't as savvy a quester as you gave yourself credit for."

Quinn pointed at them. "The old woman may have saved your life this time, but if I see you again on the other side, I will kill you where you stand." With that, he exited.

Ceara said anxiously, "Jessie, my dear, are you all right? Tanner, would you be a dear, and get her some water?"

"Sure. Man, that was something."

As Tanner left for the kitchen, Jessie fought back tears. "That was…something, all right. What was he doing here? How did you know who he was? What did you mean when you said—"

"One question at a time, my dear. Please, let an old lady get off her feet first. That hill liked to have killed me."

Jessie took Ceara's elbow and helped her over to the sofa in the parlor. Tanner joined them with three bottles of water. Jessie opened and drank half of one while Tanner settled in next to her. "That was some weird shit, man. Twilight Zone. I've felt a hell of a lot of weird things, Ceara, but I've never felt anyone who had absolutely no emotions. It was like he was dead or something." He opened another bottle and handed it to Ceara.

"In a way, he was." Ceara drank from the bottle before taking a few cleansing breaths and beginning her explanation. "First off, my dear, as a creature who has come and gone and is tied to the portal, I feel the otherworldly disturbances whenever it's been entered or disrupted."

"That's how you know when I go through."

Ceara nodded. "I knew that day three years ago when we first met that the plane had changed. This gift is also the reason I became stuck in this time. When I was a little girl, I often felt these odd sensations right here." Ceara pointed to the space behind her earlobes. "My parents knew there was something special about me and sent me to Mandrake, the Chief Druid of the Silures, to learn how to control my powers as well as my destiny."

Jessie leaned forward as she listened. "So you became a priestess."

"That, and a few other things. I entered the portal for the

first and, as it turns out, last time."

Jessie nodded. She knew the rest of the tale. "You knew evil had come through when Quinn slipped in."

Ceara drank more water before answering. "I'm certain that man felt like a corpse, Tanner, because in a way that's what he was. That man was merely a body Quinn possessed so he could come and talk to you."

Jessie and Tanner both leaned back as if Ceara had pushed them.

"Yes. Quinn is no longer a Druid, for what he is doing is against all Druidic practices."

"But you—"

"I have the permission of my host to take over her being. You can bet that Quinn did not. Wherever Quinn's real body is in this time, is probably ensconced in a safe place. He has obviously managed to learn how to take over another being."

"Why not come himself?" Tanner asked.

"Too risky. If we did decide to kill him, he risks losing his link to this life. He's not going to take the chance with his own life, so he borrowed one."

Jessie leaned forward again and took one of Ceara's hands. "You say he is powerful, yet you scared him away."

Ceara gripped Jessie's hand. "Not so. Do not make the mistake of viewing retreat as fear. He came to deliver a message. He had no intention of harming you—otherwise, he would have borrowed a body that was more up to the task."

Ceara gazed out the window at dark clouds threatening more Oregon rain. "The important part of all of this is to recognize that you frighten him, my dear."

"I do?"

"Of course. His coming here was an act of a desperate man. Something you are doing makes him nervous, and my guess is it's your visit to Spencer."

Jessie rose and paced across the room. "I don't know, Ceara. I just don't see how Spencer is going to be able to find that box among all those ships in all those seas." She stared out the window trying to put all the pieces together. "Anne Boleyn tried to ally herself with the Spanish just before Henry had her killed.

By giving them the whereabouts of the box, she hoped they could save her. It's just conjecture at this point. As far as we know, the box could be at the bottom of the sea."

"No, we have to assume it's on a galleon." Tanner finished his water in one large gulp. "There can't have been more than, what, a hundred on the seas at that time?"

"Try thousands." Jessie turned to Ceara. "The question I have is why Quinn isn't camped out on Drake's ship?"

Ceara's eyes narrowed. "Maybe he is. I think it is safe to assume that Quinn has positioned himself somewhere close enough to react swiftly once the box is produced. The better question, my dear, is whether or not you are going to push on with your quest. It would be understandable for you to be afraid of—"

"I am not afraid...well, maybe not for my own safety, but for Daniel's and my folks, and the two of you, of course. Do you think he can hurt Cate or Spencer?"

"Cate can take care of herself. As for Spencer—"

"He's a pirate."

"Enough said then." Ceara studied Jessie for a moment. "Right now, Quinn can ill-afford to be slipping around time threatening everyone. If he is going to be successful, he is going to have to concentrate on his sixteenth century life in order to insure that Spencer does not get to the box first. That doesn't mean—"

"I refuse to be intimidated, Ceara. What would Cate or Spencer say if I picked up my jacks and went home because the creep paid me a visit? I owe them both more than a yellow stripe down my back. They deserve better. So do I. Screw him."

"That means you'll need to continue moving forward."

"It means I'm going to have to spend time outside this life if I'm to help Spencer reclaim the box. I won't be around to protect Daniel. How can we keep Quinn away from my family if I'm not here?"

"You don't worry about your little brother, Jess," Tanner declared. "I'll make sure he's okay. You just do what you have to do."

"He's right, Jessie. I'll be able to detect it if Quinn returns.

Tanner will come and get your brother to make sure everything is all right. You know, maybe it's time to tell Daniel the truth about you."

Jessie paced to another window. The clouds seemed to darken with her mood. "The kid's already dealing with ghosts and poltergeists. No way."

Turning back to them, she said, "Sorry. I didn't mean to snap. It's just…one second, I'm excited about slipping through time again, and the next minute, my family is in danger. It's just not how I pictured it." Remnants of fear clung to her like new tar on a tire, and there was a chill in the marrow of her bones. Quinn was evil, and she had felt his darkness as if he'd reached his hand through her chest. "I hope whoever else I have inside knows some kung fu or karate, because the next time I see that creep, I'm gonna kick his ass."

Ceara smiled. "Atta girl. Now, before we send you back, everyone must be warned."

"Right."

"Because if he cannot get the box, the man will take it out on everyone you hold dear."

Nodding solemnly, Jessie replied, "He won't."

"You sound awfully sure."

"You've never met Spencer Morgan."

*   *   *

Jessie and Tanner finished out the day saying nothing further about their strange and somewhat intimidating visitor. Perhaps, she thought, that happens when such darkness enters your life. This felt like a muddy imprint on her soul. She felt dirty, as if he had somehow molested her and her life. It was, she supposed, what happened when you tested the bridges of reality. Sometimes they swayed, and left you with a sense that you needed to hold on tighter to the railing.

She was holding on now, but she wasn't sure to what. She knew she possessed a brand of courage beyond that of most young women her age, and she knew where it came from: Cate and Spencer and everyone else she had ever been. She could not, would not turn her back on them. If she did, she would never get her self-respect back again. Ever. And she had fought too hard to retrieve that self-respect three years ago when she was mired in a world of drugs and meaningless sex; she wasn't about to kick it to the curb now.

Tanner returned from lighting the fire in the large brick fireplace to ward off the cool winds brought by the darkening weather. "You've been really quiet today."

Standing at the door, she crossed her arms tightly and nodded. "Lots to think about."

Tanner looked up from the hearth. "You really stood your ground today."

She walked over and knelt down next to him, studying his profile as he fed newspapers to the fire. "So did you. Heroic, really."

Tanner blushed and kept stuffing the fire. "It was nothin'."

"It was something to me. I mean, suddenly, you're thrust into this bizarre world of past people who seem to be dictating our present. Is that too weird for you?"

"Too weird happened in my life a long time ago. I'm not normal. I'm weird. I say in for a penny, in for the whole fucking enchilada." Tanner crumpled newspapers into a ball and tossed it into the heart of the flames. "I wasn't getting jack from that creep. For a minute there, I thought I'd lost it. The power, I mean. And you know what's really weird?"

"What?"

"It scared me. I mean, I never thought about what my life would be like if I wasn't an empath, and for a split second, I thought I didn't have it anymore." Tanner ran his hand through his blond hair; his normally sharp eyes held a melancholic haze.

"I would have thought you'd be glad."

"Me, too. Isn't that strange? To take something like that for granted until you think you might not have it anymore?"

"Well, it's kind of cool that you get to see how much it means to you."

He nodded and rose, his back to the fire. "For better or worse, it's a part of me...like being a time slipper or quester is part of you."

Jessie shook her head. Slipping through time was altogether different from being a quester. A quester had a job to do, a role to fulfill, a destiny in her hands. It was important and vital to the balance of things. She saw that now. She realized that her little girl fantasies of being friends with her selves from the past were merely that—fantasies. Cate and her other selves hadn't worked so hard to remember so Jessie could use the portal as a playground; they had done so because they knew she would be needed. And she was needed now.

"It's a bit overwhelming."

Tanner lightly rubbed her back. "You're up to the task, Jess. And besides...you're not alone."

She watched the flames greedily take his newspapers. "Ceara's pretty amazing, don't you think?"

"Now there's your hero. She was incredible."

She stared at him until her looked up at her. "That body is old, Tanner. Every day, she gets up and down the stairs slower and slower. It worries me."

He pulled her to him. "The cycles of life, Jess. You've been studying them from a Druid point of view for three years. When it's Ceara's time to go, you're going to have to let her."

She held onto him tightly. "I don't know that I can do that."

He lightly kissed the top of her head. "Let's worry about that when it gets here, okay?" He looked into her face. "What are you going to do about this mess?"

"That's just it. It's here." She thought about a life without Ceara. "I can't even imagine—"

"Don't do outcome, Jess. She's here now. Stay in the here and now with us."

Nodding, Jessie nevertheless felt the fear hook onto her heart and dig in. "You're right. If I'm going to go for an extended stay, I have to be ready physically, and I just don't think I am."

"Of course you are."

"You know, three years ago, Cate made me promise not to go back through. For the longest time I never really understood why...until today. Today, when I was ready to go up against

Quinn, I realized, finally what I really am. I understand both my legacy and my destiny. I am what Cate and Spencer and all the others have always been. I am the keeper of the gate. It's not a coincidence that we moved to where the portal is. It's how it's supposed to be. Protecting the portal is my job. I see that now, and I am not going to let them down. I refuse to fail."

"You're up to it. Come on. You look beat. I'll watch the front desk for the next couple of hours." He lightly ran his finger across her forehead. "You know, you and me...we're not like everybody else. We live in a world where the boundary between reality and all else is blurred. Before today, I didn't know if that was a curse or a gift. Now I know."

Two minutes later, when she laid her head on her pillow, those were the last words she remembered as she gripped the ankh and waited to step over that very blurry line.

"Hear me, Cate," Jessie whispered as she began her deep breathing. "I need you."

Cate was murmuring almost the same words from another plane, another time.

Jessie found herself standing on the bow of a Spanish galleon. A thick fog surrounded the ship, and the only sounds were the creaking of old wood and the sea slapping the sides of the ship. It was eerily quiet as the fog parted for the wooden female figure clinging to the bow of the ship like some preternatural gymnast. She wondered if the sea was always so quiet.

"Only when there are no other ships around."

Turning around, Jessie smiled at Spencer. Maybe it was his lopsided grin or his laughing blue eyes, or maybe it was just how much he reminded her of Tanner. But whatever it was, she found herself instantly liking this cutthroat.

"It just feels so—"

"Lonely?"

She nodded. "That's it exactly. Is it always so...eerie?"

He stepped next to her and stared out at the green sea. He was clean-shaven, which surprised her, and he smelled of allspice and something else she couldn't put a finger on. How very different this sea world was and how anyone could possibly ever get used to the loneliness of standing on the deck of a ship was beyond her. The fog alone seemed like some living creature that came and went at will, without warning, without care.

"Sometimes, when you stand here, the fog is so cold it bites the marrow of your bones and leaves teeth marks."

She glanced sideways at him. This was a surprise. "I never expected poetry from you."

He stared down into her eyes. "Life is poetry, Jessie Ferguson. Some of us live it in rhythm, some of us need to be freer, less confined, but we all need the visions poems give us."

She studied him for a moment. "Wow."

This singular response made him laugh. "You should not be so surprised, Jessie. I do have the spirit of a Druid, after all."

"Not just any Druid."

"And I'm not just any privateer."

"I think I'm beginning to see that."

"I am lucky enough to have the soul of a Druid priestess who could memorize thousands of verses, laws, stories and poetry. Cate did not work so hard in one life only to have those words forgotten in the next."

She was astounded. "You mean…"

"That I remember them? Not all, but many. So could you if you worked at it. I am somewhat surprised at how little you seem to remember. Something must have happened to us between my time and yours to have made you know so little."

It wasn't an affront, and she didn't take it as such. He was right. She didn't remember nearly as much as she wanted, and no matter how hard she tried she could not gain access to those memories. It was frustrating.

"Do not be too hard on yourself," he said, scratching his armpit. "When I first realized what was happening to me, I wanted to know everything I could, but there was so much to know, so much to remember. I felt…inadequate."

"That's the perfect word for it."

"You will remember more and more as you get older and wiser. That's what happened to me. You are all of what, twenty?"

She nodded.

"Even Cate did not have all of her memories at such a young

age."

With a frown, she said, "Only today did I figure out why you and Cate summoned me."

Spencer did not reply, but returned his gaze to the sea. Together, they stood side-by-side watching the green water roll and curl ahead of the ship.

He spoke above the waves. "You are afraid."

"I have reason to be."

Spencer nodded. "He came to your time and threatened you, too, did he not?"

She started. "Too? What do you mean, too?"

He did not answer. He turned toward the mist that had suddenly enveloped the ship. At first she thought it was the fog, but then she realized it was the same mist that separated the stone circle in her Dreamworld from Cate's reality. Spencer offered his hand to Cate who appeared from the fog like a specter.

"Cate!" Jessie threw her arms around the small priestess and hugged her tightly. "You're here!"

"Indeed." Cate leaned back in Jessie's arms and studied her. "You are well?"

Jessie nodded. "As well as can be expected."

Cate released her and nodded. "Quinn has been very busy spreading his darkness, but I am so glad you are here nonetheless. You are very brave, indeed."

Jessie pulled away, a look of confusion on her face. "But I thought—"

"That I would not harbor Spencer's violent memories with my own? This is the Dreamworld, Jessie. I do not absorb his memories here, nor shall you."

"But I was calling you, Cate," Jessie said, glancing over at Spencer. "No offense, Spencer."

He bowed his head slightly. "None taken."

"I sought Spencer in his Dreamworld last night and asked him to join us. If we are to protect ourselves, we need each other. We cannot go blindly into the unknown, and we cannot face Quinn without each other."

Jessie cocked her head toward Spencer, but he said nothing. "Is that why we're on a ship?"

Cate and Spencer both chuckled. "The ship is your doing, Jessie. We are in your Dreamworld now."

"Oh."

Spencer ran his hand along the railing of the stairs. "Not a bad replica, either, except for the woman on the bow." His smile broadened and two deep dimples appeared. "You have a knack for detail."

Cate released Jessie's hands and gently brushed a stray hair from her forehead. "It is only natural for you to be frightened, dear, but you are not alone. We are here, and together we'll deal with Quinn."

"The only one he hasn't come after is me." Spencer, standing next to them, towered over the diminutive Cate by well over a foot. "And that means he's a coward who will threaten women, but when it comes to taking on a man who might not care if his head remained attached to his shoulders, he remains in the shadows."

Cate said, "Quinn could never understand the bond that traverses space and time. He was always too self-aware to connect with anyone in his time or any other. That might very well be his downfall."

"We must find that damned box before he does," Spencer growled.

Jessie glanced from Cate to Spencer. Looking into his eyes, she gazed into a man who was heroic, sensitive, courageous and tenacious. A man carrying around the wisdom of her little Druid priestess. She realized how badly she had prejudged him…how wrong she had been about the man he was; for who he was contained remnants of who they had been, and Jessie found herself loving Cate McEwen fiercely. Perhaps, in time, she could love this grumbling pirate as well.

"What you see is true, young one," he said. "Look beyond the scars and my handsomely set jaw. See me. See me, and remember, for my memories are within you as surely as Cate's are. I am in there. You just need to remember."

She felt the chill in her bones suddenly disappear, and everything she ever thought about pirates, about treasure, about men like Spencer, evaporated into the fog. He was in her, and she remembered being a little girl of five and begging her mother to let her go to a Halloween party dressed as a pirate. Her mother insisted she go as something more feminine, but she didn't want to be a ballerina or a princess. She had wanted to be a pirate.

"That's why this boat has such vivid details," she murmured.

"Then you do remember something."

She nodded. "More than I realized."

"Good," Cate said. "For we must trust each other and work together to find not only the box, but Quinn as well."

Jessie tore her gaze from Spencer and looked at Cate. "You sound worried."

"We should be. Quinn can move in and out of time in any form he chooses to possess, and he has a definite goal that would disrupt the balance of every time he is a part of."

Spencer linked hands with them. "It seems most likely the box is in the hold of one of Drake's ships already. He may or may not be returning it to the Queen. The man continues to elude me and appears to be eluding Quinn as well. What you can do for us, Jessie, is discover where Drake is in my time, and maybe even the name of the next galleon he plunders. I fear I am always a step behind."

She nodded and answered, "That should be no problem. What date is it in your time now?"

Spencer flashed Cate a brief smile. "May second, 1567."

"I'm all over it."

Cate and Spencer exchanged curious glances.

"Uh, it means I'll get it done."

"Good. We knew you would."

She turned to Cate and smiled into eyes she now saw in her sleep. "What's with all this we stuff?"

Blushing, Cate replied, "Spencer remembered me, and within me you are. You are with me always, Jessie. Not a day goes by that I don't think of you and wonder what you are doing. When I look at the moon, I wonder if you are looking at it also. When I see my reflection in the water, I wish it were your face staring back at me. You are in every part of me, and this has changed me…changed my life. I am a better person because of you."

Jessie swallowed her emotions and asked the question she had asked every single time she met up with Cate. "Where's Maeve?"

"She has gone to find Quinn."

"What? No! How could you let her go?"

"No one lets Maeve do anything, my friend. She returned to Eire to take care of Quinn."

"She's not safe."

"She's luring him away from us," Cate said. "From me and Lachlan. We did not realize what she was doing until it was too late. She must have known that he would be coming and wanted us away from any danger."

Taking Jessie's hand, Spencer placed it on his chest and laid his large, calloused hand over hers. "Cate and I are the same. You and I are the same. It is my hope that you look beyond your judgments of me and my kind and remember who I am."

Jessie did not pull away nor did she look away from his probing eyes, eyes much keener and probing than Cate's. "I'm trying."

"That is all I ask." Releasing her hand, he stepped back. "Perhaps you fail to realize just how odd you appear to me; a young, rebellious lass, full of hopes and dreams that would choke the life right out of me. You appear so soft and frail compared to me, yet, your tongue is indeed sharp and quick to strike." He smiled almost sadly. "But I do not prejudge you, Jessie, because I know one thing about you that matters most; you are willing to risk your life for the one soul all three of us hold dearest to our hearts. If you know nothing else about me, remember that, I, too, risk my life for her, now and forever." He strode over to the mist, allowing Cate a chance to say her farewells.

"He's right," Jessie said. "I never looked at it that way. I guess I should cut him some slack."

"I know not about slack, Jessie, but I do know that what he says is true, and anyone who stands to protect my Maeve is someone I trust. You need to trust him as you do me." Hugging her one last time, Cate whispered, "You know where to find me. I will always answer you, Jessie. Always."

*   *   *

16th Century

Duncan was ruffled up like an unmade bed as he sat at the table with Spencer. He reeked of cheap alcohol, sweaty sex and early morning.

"You look bad, my friend, but you smell even worse." Spencer waved the air in front of him.

"And a good morning to you. I daresay I stink, but I would bet my last coin I am a happier man than you this morning."

Spencer shrugged. "You might very well be. I take it your evening went...well."

"She was a fiery beastie, she was. Barely held my own. Spencer, why don't you let me find you a dainty thing tonight? It is not good for your only female companionship to be the past and present forms of yourself. There's something almost... incestuous about it."

"I have seen the wenches you dally with and will be amazed if your pecker does not decay from some disgusting disease before you are forty."

"Bite your tongue."

The two men shared a relatively quiet breakfast and conversation, with Spencer relaying his meeting with Cate and Jessie. He did not acknowledge an immediate connection to Jessie, perhaps because he was still surprised himself at the pull she had on him. He liked her...no, he more than liked her, he had a respect for her, and that was not a gift he gave out lightly. She displayed a courage and a willingness to go to battle against a being who could conceivably destroy her in the blink of an eye.

As they ate, a young man swept through the tavern door like a leaf blown by a strong wind. He was dressed as the Queen's man and everyone in the tavern stopped to stare.

"I have been informed that Captain Spencer Morgan has come ashore," the young man said breathlessly.

Before Spencer could say anything, Duncan rose and drew his sword. "I am he."

The Queen's man was not the least bit impressed and did not even reach for his sword. "I have been told of a certain thing which you seek and I know a man in south Wales who says he knows where it is and is willing to show it to you for a price."

"And it is he who sent you? You are the Queen's man, are you not?"

"I am. The man I speak of is my cousin and he needs money I do not have. He knew you would soon be land-bound and bid me to seek you out with this information. It is all I know."

"And how did you find me?"

"Your friend, the swarthy one the women are drawn to, has quite a reputation. I merely inquired about him among the ladies."

Duncan glanced over at Spencer, who nodded, so Duncan continued the ruse. "So your cousin wants money for this information? How reliable a man is he to make such a boast as to know what it is we seek?"

"He is very reliable. He would not reveal to me what he knew, or where it is. He simply said you would want to hear what he knows and that it would be worth something to both your interests. Are you interested?"

"I am," Duncan said, tossing a coin to the man, who caught it neatly with one hand. "Your cousin lives where?"

The man gave all the pertinent information to Duncan before catching a second coin crisply in the air and leaving as quickly as he'd come. Duncan put his sword away and sat back down at the table. "It is an obvious trap, Spencer. We cannot be deceived, nor can we go."

"You are right. We cannot. But I must."

Duncan's eyes grew wide. "What?"

"I must go. If it is truly a trap, and we cannot be so sure that it is, then it could be a trap that might lead me to Quinn. It is a risk I must take for all our sakes."

"Are you mad? This Quinn will slit your throat and use your body to hide coins if you are entrapped by him. Don't be a fool, Spencer."

"Not if I get him first."

Duncan rubbed the back of his neck. "Then we go after him

together."

Spencer shook his head. "Not this time, my friend. I need you to stay and ferret out the truth about Drake, his whereabouts, and the Queen's cause in all of this. Mark my words—Drake is more involved in this than ever we realized. We find him…we're close to the box and to Quinn."

Duncan spat onto the hay-strewn floor. "I do not like this one bit."

"Think about it, Duncan. If someone is making such a desperate attempt to ensnare us, then we must be closer to our goal than we imagined. We've become a threat."

"I cannot merely sit back while you walk right into his hands." Duncan shook his head. "I like it not one bit."

"You do not have to like it, Duncan, you just have to help me with it."

Duncan shook his head. "I'll not help you to your death. You do what you feel you must for Jessie and the rest of you, but if you start playing this too loosely, if you worry too much about a woman who will not be born for another five hundred years, I will walk away from you and leave you to your insanity. I'll take no part in such foolish behavior."

"I know what I am doing, Duncan."

"I truly hope so, because if you are not careful, you will take a journey from which you may never return."

*   *   *

When the third day came and went and Spencer had not yet returned, Duncan recalled the crew to the ship and headed to sea and to the only port he knew where to find help.

After docking his small British vessel, Duncan left the crew and started for the hills of Tewkesbury. It did not take him long to find the person he sought.

"Ennia!" Duncan called out, seeing the door to the small thatch-roofed house ajar.

"I am over here," Ennia replied, waving from the garden.

For as long as he'd known her, which was most of his life, Ennia McFadden had loved her gardening. Her garden was filled with herbs few knew how to find and even fewer knew how to grow. As a healer, she was second to none, with the exception of her grandmother, who was still practicing somewhere in The Hollows.

He had first met her when another young man challenged him in front of the girl Duncan had been unsuccessfully trying to impress. Not long after the boast, Duncan was carried to a young Ennia's house to staunch the blood from a nasty hip wound received during the fight. Duncan had lost his pride, some blood and the girl. Humility, it seemed, came at a heavy price, but it was a price worth paying in exchange for a long-standing friendship with a woman five years his junior; a woman who was a Druid priestess in a world that had all but turned its back on them.

She and her family had remained hidden in the forests of Tewkesbury for as long as anyone could remember. They had trained her to be a healer from the moment she could walk, and when she did walk, she spent hours collecting roots and plants with which to make her great-grandmother's special unguent.

"You are forever tending this garden, Ennia," he said, kneeling next to her and kissing her cheek. Ennia had been the one woman immune to his charms and good looks, and she had made it clear to him that she offered him the love of friendship, but nothing more, further scarring him when she had rejected his pitiful attempt at more.

"Your destiny is not tied to the land or to any woman tied to the land," she'd said on the day he was finally healed. "There are great things in store for you, but not here, and not now."

She had never taken a husband, and as far as Duncan knew, she had never had a relationship with any male in the village. Magic and healing were the passions in her life.

Ennia's green eyes sparkled. "Working with the soil breathes life into me as the sea air does you. It is, as always, good to see you again, Duncan." She bowed her head low. "I see the salt air has done you well."

Duncan studied the way the sunlight played upon her red hair as he took her hands in his. "You look well, Ennia. Time is a friend of yours."

Pulling a hand free, she gently pushed his chest. "I appreciate your flattery, but time is not your ally, Duncan. It nips at your heels like a hungry wolf. Come." She took his outstretched hand and led him to a small fire burning behind the woad house in which she had grown up.

"As always, your ability to read my energy astounds me. You have not lost your edge."

She chuckled. "And your inability to acknowledge that power within you astounds me. You have a heritage of greatness that could help you defeat this evil seeking to destroy you and Spencer Morgan. Instead of harnessing your own powers, you keep coming to me for answers you could very easily find for yourself."

Duncan gazed into her wizened face and stepped closer to her. "I come to you because I care for you. It does my heart good every time I see you."

"You have never changed, Duncan. You care for that which you cannot have." She smiled to blunt the sharpness of her words. "But you do have my friendship, and most certainly my attention for whatever it is that brought you up here. So please keep me waiting no longer and tell me what answers you seek this time."

"It is Spencer."

Ennia looked away from him and into the fire. "This evil pursues Spencer as well, I take it?"

He blew out a breath and nodded, his hair falling into his eyes. "Aye," he said, brushing his bangs aside, "through time as well as space. The dunderhead has allowed himself to walk willingly into a trap. There is nothing he would not do for a woman who died fifteen hundred years ago. And now..." He shook his head one more time. "Now, he is going to risk all for a woman from the future."

Ennia laid her hand on his. "She is not any woman, though, is she?"

He shook his head, his gaze lingering on their hands. "I need to know what I can do to get him out of trouble. It's been three days and I have not heard from him. I fear the worst."

Ennia gazed into the fire a bit longer and then turned to

study Duncan. "What does your heart tell you? You've never learned to listen to it, have you? After all these years, you still do not understand the power of your heart."

He shrugged helplessly. "Apparently not."

"Why do you continue to struggle with what you are? Your life could be so much easier if you accepted the truth of your pasts."

"This is a discussion better left for another time. Is Spencer still alive or not? Have I allowed my best friend to walk into danger he could have avoided?"

She reached into her pouch and tossed a purple-colored powder into the flames and they sprayed and sputtered. "You allowed nothing of the sort. It appears Spencer left in order to keep you out of danger. He fears this thing that chases him. He fears for you."

Duncan cursed and kicked a rock. "Damn him!"

"This danger…is it capable of hurting the one he calls Maeve?"

His anger vanished, and he ceased his cursing. "Bloody hell! How could I have been such a fool?"

"Is that a yes?"

Bowing his head, he nodded. "I should have known it had to do with her! It always comes back to her."

"Perhaps because he listens to his heart. You could learn a thing or two from that man. If he felt there was a danger to her, he would do what was necessary to protect her. Apparently, he feels almost as strongly about you."

"So he tricked me?"

She shrugged. "I do not know. I was not there."

He thought about it and shook his head. "There is this item…"

"The box. I know."

He stared at her. He had never fully comprehended her powers until this moment. "A man named Quinn has made threats to Cate and Jessie both. They're—"

She waved his explanation off. "I know who they are. This Quinn knows how important Maeve is to Cate and Spencer. He will exploit that. He will do what is necessary to split his attention in two."

"Spencer told me Maeve is trying to draw Quinn out and away from the safety of the portal."

"And Spencer knew this. He cares about you so he has distanced himself from you."

"Like she did them." Duncan shook his head sadly. "Damn her. How is it possible for a woman long since dead to have such an effect on people?"

This made her smile. "She understands that she is all of their Achilles' heels. My friend, if you could only realize how much we have to learn from the past, you would know why Spencer Morgan is on this current path. The question is will Spencer sacrifice himself in this life in order to save someone in his past life?"

They looked at each other. The answer needn't have been spoken.

"Can you at least tell me where he went then? He mentioned a farmer by the name of—"

She shook her head. "That ruse was for your benefit. That was not the path he's chosen to take."

"Then, where is he?" Duncan's voice boomed into the forest, echoing loudly.

Ennia studied the flames, threw various colored powders into it and watched as the flames leapt and jumped. "He has gone to the only woman powerful enough in this time that can help him."

Duncan's face drained of all color. "He didn't. Oh please tell me he did not go there."

Nodding, she took his shaking hand. "He has. He has gone to see the Queen."

* * *

When Cate slipped through the fabric of time and into Spencer's presence, she was not prepared for his reality. The room was dank and dark, and reeked of human fluids. There was but one window high above the tower wall, placed there, it would seem, to torture the beings held within the walls. She did not need to have been imprisoned to know where they were.

His cell was cold, dirty and drafty. Wet and filthy straw and debris littered the stone floor and there was a rusty pail next to a small door cut from a larger door. The tiny window cast an eerie shadow on the floor, and what little breeze there was smelled of sweat and fear, human waste and decay.

As Cate began to meld into Spencer's conscious being, he glanced around the tiny cell and grinned painfully. His mouth hurt, his ribs ached and he thought he might have a few broken fingers, but at least now he wasn't alone. He had barely felt Jessie's presence when she entered him, but this feeling was far more powerful. Her energy coursed through his body like a drug. It could only mean one thing.

Cate.

"Well, for now, my little Druid, I must concentrate on the task of staying alive. Until tonight then." Spencer rose and felt a sharp pain in the side of his ribs, a simple reminder of his first attempt to see the Queen and the beating he'd taken for it.

It had been a long shot, but he had to do something to separate himself from Duncan, who was too good a friend to lead into the mess Spencer was headed toward. To be an Irishman—a pirate, no less—who had stolen plenty from the Queen's own buccaneers, and yet to still ask for an audience with her was inconceivable to the entire court. But Spencer had to try. He bowed his head now, thinking about the amazed looks on the guard's face when he said, "Tell her Majesty that Spencer Morgan, Irish pirate and buccaneer, requests an audience with her."

He had heard that Queen Elizabeth admired audacious men—men who were bold and who walked their own paths. He had hoped his audacity would be enough to at least spark an interest. She was an astute businesswoman, after all, and her foreign policy was perhaps the most brilliant in all the world. Surely, she would hear from the man who might be able to tell her where her precious box could be found.

To explain his request, Spencer had told Sir Walsingham that he wanted to see the Queen; that he knew "where her mother's jewels were." The guards promptly beat him, tossed him in the cell, and returned a few hours later to kick him a time or two more for good measure. Perhaps using his own name had not been such a brilliant move, but he needed to get the Queen's attention. The use of her "mother" was a means of letting her know just how much he knew about the box. Spencer was certain the Queen would eventually call for him, even in secret. She desperately wanted what was in that box, and she would brook no delay in getting it. It was only a matter of time—time and the ability to survive any further beatings from her overzealous thugs.

He had hated deceiving Duncan, but he knew Duncan all too well to know that he would never have agreed with the plan to see the Queen. For one thing, Duncan had some sort of sickness where close spaces made him weak and ill. He could handle the smaller spaces of the ship perhaps because it would not take much for him to get out of them. He would have preferred floating alone in the sea to a smallish cabin on board, which was why he was more often on the deck than within. He could fight his way out of a bar, out of a bed, out of trouble, but to be enclosed in stone and rock would have sent him into madness, and Spencer could not ask that of him...even to stop Quinn.

Quinn.

Spencer so wanted to know who Quinn was in this world. Around every corner on his way to London, every shadow Spencer saw was Quinn. It was so disconcerting knowing that his enemy was here, but that he would not be able to recognize him.

Lying on the cold stone, Spencer winced as he closed his eyes. His whole body ached to the core of his being. He knew who he was. He had remembered Cate so long ago, she seemed a part of his own memory. She was that part of him that was good. She was the white light in a sea of darkness. She was his wisdom, his knowledge, his insight. She was the best parts of who he was. She was a powerful priestess who had lived her life in a peace he would never know. Cate was wise beyond her years, compassionate and giving. He remembered that she laughed easily, communicated with nature, and loved very, very hard. He knew...he remembered her ties with Maeve, the depth of their bond, the intensity of their relationship, and it was these memories that had stayed with him most of his life...ever since he began remembering.

To know there was someone out there, not just any someone, but someone who had loved you before they even knew you were out there looking for them; before they knew you were longing for them...before they knew you, was almost inconceivable.

Almost.

He hadn't become a sailor because his father had passed it along to him. He was a sailor because he knew she was out there somewhere. He had been needing to find her since his dream of a gray-eyed woman who came to him and bade him remember, the first in a long string of dreams featuring the beautiful woman who called herself Maeve, his Anam Cara. Anam Cara, a Gaelic phrase literally translated to "soul friend." There was a deeper meaning to the Celtic term. Anam Cara happened when kindred spirits found each other, and Spencer knew who his was by the age of twelve. He just needed to find her, and a ship seemed the best way to search the world over for her. He needed to find her soon, or him.

It didn't really matter to him, either way, and that was how he knew the incredibly deep bond they must have shared, and how it must have deepened over the centuries; grown stronger than any other relationship. It hadn't mattered to the Celts the gender of the one you loved because they understood that the body was a house for one's spirit, and that spirit had no gender.

And so he had sailed into many ports—Turkish, British, French, Scottish—and anywhere else he felt like sailing just to see if she might be there. He would sit outside the busiest taverns for hours with a pint of ale, watching people walk by. Watching, waiting, hoping she would come to him in this century, as she had for centuries before and would centuries after.

He had been doing this for over ten years; in one sea and out another, searching coastlines, taverns and holds of ships. He had even been to Egypt once because some of Cate's memories had some sort of Egyptian symbolism to them. It had been a long and somewhat arduous trip, and in the end, he left Egypt having had a few nice encounters with women who were simply too exotic for his tastes, and...well...not her.

When privateering became too lucrative to ignore and allowed him to go everywhere he ever dreamt of going, Spencer let Duncan play the swashbuckling hero as long as they had enough funds to stay afloat. So, they attacked Spanish galleons searching for gold and treasures.

Until the box. The box had changed everything.

Now, Spencer had a two-fold goal—find the box and keep Quinn from hurting people he had never met, but loved all the same. If only he could get his hands on that damnable item Lachlan had foolishly buried. He would, of course, give the Queen the box, knowing full well that there was only one man in the kingdom who could translate what lay therein. No one at court would know the language the scrolls were written in. None save Quinn.

It had been the only thing he could think to do in order to flush Quinn out of hiding. If Cate's memory served him correctly, the scrolls were written in BoibeLoth, a long lost language used by the Druids. If Quinn knew the Queen had the box, he would come forward to translate the scrolls for her. Of course, the risk to Quinn would be whether or not the Queen would kill him afterward. Maybe it didn't matter. It didn't appear he had any intentions of staying in this time, anyway.

Closing his eyes, Spencer tried to ignore his throbbing ribs and the cold fear creeping into his soul. If Quinn hurt Maeve, it wouldn't matter what time he planned on living in. Spencer would spend the rest of his life hunting him down until he destroyed him in every age his soul existed.

And that was a promise.

"And a promise I am quite sure you'll keep," Cate said, coming through the mist. "How are you?"

He rubbed his ribs, which were not sore in this Dreamworld. "Been better. Is Maeve well?"

"Yes. She has gone in search of Quinn. I have come to let you know that her plan has been set in motion. There may not be time here, Spencer Morgan, but there is help. I have information that can help you find your way out of here as well as a way to get what you need from this Queen."

Spencer stepped closer. "And what made you change your mind and help me out of this bind, Cate?"

"Jessie."

"Jessie?"

"Aye. If she trusts you, then I can do no less. Your heart is in the right place. Now all we have to do is make sure that your body follows."

*   *   *

21st Century

Jessie looked up from the laptop she'd been staring at for the last few hours, and pinched the bridge of her nose. Her eyes were burning and the caffeine she'd consumed in the form of coffee and chocolate was giving her the jitters. She said to Ceara, "I would love to hear what the Welsh think of good old Sir Frankie Drake. I've got nothing here but either accolades or innuendos."

"Hah! The Welsh are still suppressed by the British, and anything we get from them has been edited, re-edited and transformed as if through the hands of a magician."

"Then what do you have?"

Ceara's eyes danced. "According to my source, there's a log of Drake's early activities sitting in some obscure maritime museum awaiting authenticity reports or some such blather. So far, it has yet to be authenticated because scholars and historians already have a number of logs, and there's some doubt as to its origins. Apparently, this log casts a dark shadow across the entire forty-year reign of Elizabeth, and so no one wants to see that in the light of day. You know those Brits and their history. They still refuse to acknowledge why the pilgrims left their silly little island in the first place. Where history is concerned, the British people and their scholars have selective and very creative memories. My friend is going to do everything he can to get his hands on that log to see what he can see."

"Thank heavens. There's a ton of info online, and snippets of logs here and there, but none near the date we're looking for." Jessie leaned back and stretched. Time bunched itself on her shoulders like a gargoyle.

"So maybe relying on history isn't such a great idea."

"I just read a few pages here that said when Drake was searching for the Northwest Passage, historians assumed the bay he wrote about was the San Francisco Bay, but plenty of other evidence suggests otherwise." She hit the back button of her browser and kept reading. "A guy named Bob Ward believes Whale Cove here in Oregon was the harbor Drake spoke of, and not the San Francisco Bay. I guess when Drake got back to England, the Queen confiscated all of his logs and charts, and they were never to be seen again. There was a great deal of secrecy around his voyage, and nothing was written about that voyage for ten years."

"Ten years? Now there's a woman who can keep a secret."

"And it's no wonder. According to this, the Spanish King wanted Drake hanged, yet Elizabeth knighted him instead. That woman hated the Spanish."

"Ah yes, and that would be one of the reasons why the Spanish King sent his Armada."

"Yes, but that's too far after Spencer's time. We need 1567." Jessie continued to scroll around the many Drake sites online before standing and stretching. "This book from Dr. Per Lee has some good details in it." She glanced at the lecture notes Dr. Per Lee had lent her. "There is a ton of information from 1570 on, and we practically have a play-by-play of Mary's whereabouts, but as for the elusive Drake, there's hardly a thing."

"Perhaps your professor can help when she gets out of her meeting."

An hour later, the phone rang and Jessie crossed her fingers as she answered it.

Dr. Per Lee said, "What would you like to know about Francis Drake?"

"I need his whereabouts in May of 1567. There's tons of stuff for 1570, but I am only interested in that month of that year."

"Well, that's quite specific, isn't it? Jessie Ferguson, what are you up to?"

"Well, I could be honest with you and tell you I travel

through time using historical data to save my old selves who are now friends of mine, but then you'd never help me, would you?"

Ceara's eyes bulged and she covered her mouth to stifle an enormous, bemused laugh.

"Oh, I'd help you, dear—right to the psych department. Okay, here's what we know about the 1567 time period. Seems he and his ships ran into the Spanish somewhere along the coast and he barely escaped with his life. It was an embarrassment of sorts that historians have never really sorted out from the bits and pieces we've uncovered thus far. Drake doesn't write much about it."

"Are you sure it was the Spanish?"

"Now Jessie, you know that no one is sure of anything in history."

"Right. What happened to his ships?"

Dr. Per Lee chuckled under her breath. "You are going to make a fine historian some day. The sketchy details of the entire affair come from Drake, himself, corroborated, of course, by his few literate crew that survived. Apparently, all ships were lost, as were most of the crewmen. Like I said, it was an embarrassment to the crown."

"Was it common Spanish practice to destroy the vessels of their enemies?"

"You are coming along quite nicely, Ms. Ferguson. Sometimes they did, sometimes they didn't. In this case, however, it appears to have been overkill, though few historians have speculated as to why. The Spaniards' moves were calculated and well-thought out. If that act was an act of the Spanish crown, it was certainly out of character."

"And yet, Drake still managed to…to what? Swim away?"

"Highly unlikely unless the battle was just offshore. What are you getting at?"

"His whereabouts, that's all. I'm interested because the man was knighted for being a pirate and—"

"Privateer."

"Whatever. The man was a thief, plain and simple."

"Well, that's not entirely true. He was called a privateer

during his time. Pirate came later."

"Okay, so our little enterprising Drake has some sort of run-in with someone who might have been Spanish, and then his logs disappear for over ten years after he returns from the Oregon Coast, yet—"

"Oregon? So, you're going to take the angle that he actually landed in Whale Cove and not the San Francisco Bay?"

"I'm not sure what I believe. I do know the evidence bears hearing. I also think Queen Elizabeth would have, and did, lie to protect an area of our coast that would have been an incredible investment for the crown. The woman was a greedy, enterprising monarch."

"There are certainly many historians who share your opinion, but that does not dilute her greatness."

Jessie doodled thunderbolts on the top of her paper. "She was, by all accounts, a master of manipulation, an astute business woman, and a single-minded ruler. I'll give her that much."

"Therefore? Connect the dots, Ms. Ferguson."

"It stands to reason that with the Spanish already coming up the Central American coast, she sure as hell wouldn't have wanted them or anyone to know of her find in the New World. This would be one of the times when boasting of Drake's finds would not be beneficial. But that's not really the time period I'm worried about, as much as I'd love to discuss this with you."

"I see. Your point is simply that anything we get as authenticated material from Drake must be dubiously questioned and scrutinized."

"Yes." She heard Dr. Per Lee clapping.

"Bravo, Ms. Ferguson, you have just exited the novice stages of history 101. Yes, everything from Elizabeth's time regarding Drake and his exploits should be questioned. Unfortunately, they aren't, and the English are intensely self-righteous when it comes to anyone casting aspersions against her. She was, after all, responsible for returning England to greatness. One doesn't rule for forty years unless they're accomplishing wonders. She did that, and more."

"Okay. The Queen was a great leader. She was great because she used men like Drake to line the coffers."

"I imagine that relationship was quite symbiotic."

"Then is it safe to say that she allowed the notion that Drake may have lost his ships at that time, but not necessarily to the Spaniards?"

"To what end?"

"Propaganda. The Spanish were to England in the sixteenth century as Russia was to the United States in the twentieth century."

"I applaud you once again, Ms. Ferguson, for making connections beyond your age."

"Can I ask you what you think happened in 1567?"

"Let's see. He would have been about twenty-two years old and hadn't risen to the kind of prominence he would experience in his life. As you said, it wouldn't be until three years later when he really starts to get the Queen's attention. At twenty-two, full of himself and trying to gain access to his Queen, he would not have gone too far from home. I'd say it's possible he was in or around France, maybe a bit more south, but surely not so far away. Drake loved action and France and Spain would have provided him with plenty. I would guess he sailed the English Channel dipping down as far as Portugal in order to keep the Spaniards at bay and looking for easy pockets to pick. Remember, this was a young man who would become famous the world over. He had ambitions."

Jessie had stopped doodling and was taking notes. "So you think he'd be cruising around on the Golden Hind looking to make a name for himself."

"And, of course, he sailed the Seagull with his cousin John Hawkins, whose name you'll find on many a pirate manifest online. They were quite a pair of hooligans and...well, they made the Queen of England and England herself very, very wealthy." Dr. Per Lee spoke in a muffled tone to someone in her office, and then said to Jessie, "I have another student waiting. Give me a call later if something else urgent comes your way."

Jessie ripped a page out of her notebook and held it up to Ceara. "Victory is ours! The name of his ship was Seagull, and the professor thinks he might be near France."

*   *   *

As Spencer looked around him, he was surprised to find himself standing in a stone circle not unlike Stonehenge. A cool mist swirled like a curtain on the edge of the forest about a hundred paces away. Treetops poked their heads from the mist in the distance, making him wonder how far this place extended.

"Where are we now, Cate?"

Coming through the mist, Cate smiled warmly as a single shaft of sunlight landed at her feet. Her robe did not move as the mist blew around her. "This is my Dreamworld, Spencer, and I am here to help you."

He looked around, awed by the beauty yet somewhat ill at ease by how he got here. "Is this—"

"Where souls meet, yes." She stepped closer and looked over at the quiet fire pit. "It is where Jessie and I come when we wish to talk face-to-face."

He nodded, his eyes following her. "You enjoy her company often?"

"Not often enough, I'm afraid. She is in training and there is much for her to do yet in her own time."

He backed a step away when Cate neared him. "I don't blame you, you know."

She turned and cocked her head. "Blame me? For what?"

"For not wanting anything to do with me. I am a far cry from the peaceful warrior you are."

Cate smiled slightly. "Peaceful warrior. I do so like that."

"It's true."

She sat on a large rock opposite him. "I do not know what happened between my time and the fifteen hundred years before your time to create the soul I am looking at, but obviously, there were lessons still to be learned. Do not ever apologize for what you aren't, Spencer."

He sat down and nodded. "If I did that, I'd be apologizing for the rest of my life. I'm a privateer, Cate. I make money by taking it from those who earned or stole it. Not a very glorious place for our soul, don't you think?"

Folding her hands in her lap, she answered, "I think you

are young, still. Perhaps this is not your destiny but merely the path you must be on now in order to help right this injustice we face."

He heaved a heavy sigh. "It does seem odd that we need a crusty being such as me to ward off one who can travel through time. I feel ill-equipped or I'd not have called you."

"I am sorry I did not answer sooner, Spencer, but your memories are somewhat haunting. There is so much bloodshed and misery in your world. Now, tell me what it is your corporal form is doing in the vile, fetid place in which it currently rests."

"I believe I know where to go now, Cate. I know what I am doing. I have a great plan."

"Oh do you now?" Cate moved so smoothly back to the fire, it was as if she were gliding on the very mist itself. "You think allowing the Queen's men to beat you unconscious is a plan?"

Spencer stared down at his bruised hands. "That wasn't really part of the plan, but if it gets me in to see the Queen, then it's worth it."

"You must listen to me. While the box and its contents are precious, my interests are purely selfish. I mean to protect Maeve even as she believes leaving me has kept me safe." Cate raised her hands and the fire rose with them and then separated, revealing Maeve as she rode on the bow of a ship. Her long dark hair blew like a curtain in the wind as she closed her eyes and smelled the salt air. "She nears Eire and will attempt to handle Quinn from there."

Spencer walked over to the fire and stared at it, mesmerized. It was the first time he had ever seen Maeve outside of his mind's eye. There she was, gray-eyed, long flowing hair, a hooded cape billowing behind her, and a regal bearing. "She's beautiful, aye?"

Cate grinned. "Oh, aye, but beauty or not, she has put herself between danger and me, and I fear what she will do to protect me from Quinn."

He sighed. How deep must a love go that one would give their life for another without thought, without hesitation? There was but one he would do so for and he'd left him back with the ship. "Can she protect herself then?"

"Yes, she can, but she needs you alive, not playing the hero. This is what you do not understand: If Quinn is to be stopped, he must be stopped in all ages. We must get to him in your time as well as in mine."

Spencer could not take his eyes off the woman he had been searching for his whole life. His heart stepped up a beat as he stared at her hair blowing behind her. "That is what I am trying to do, Cate. How can we attack someone when we do not even know who they are?"

Cate started to close the flames over the image of Maeve, but Spencer reached out to stop her. "She's so majestic. I...I can't—"

Cate slowly pulled away and motioned for the flames to become one. "You would risk your life, everything you have ever accomplished, for a woman long dead?"

Spencer's eyes narrowed as he turned to her intensive gaze. "You did."

She turned away.

"And so did Jessie. It's what we do, isn't it? Our whole lives are devoted to her, past, present, even future. Her life was in danger and you called on Jessie. Now, Jessie is in as much danger as Maeve. We cannot afford to lose Jessie, either. My plan is a sound one. I will get to the Queen one way or the other. Once I fully inform her of what is about to happen with the box, Quinn will have to show himself in order to read the scrolls. That is when I'll know who he is. That's when I'll have the bastard in my grasp."

"Not if you are rotting in the Queen's dungeon."

"I won't be. I'll use the box to bargain for my freedom."

She reached out and held the end of his sleeve, their eyes locking for the first time as she gauged the integrity of his character. "You are a good man, Spencer Morgan. The path you have chosen may not be a good one, but the soul of the man is."

He shrugged. "I am glad one of us thinks so."

She put her hand on his cheek and forced him to look at her. "I do not wish for you to die trying."

"You would not even allow me entrance, Cate, because of

who I am and what I do."

"That was before."

"Before what?"

"Before I learned what kind of heart beats beneath that chest of yours. You need to live. And I am going to make sure that you do."

*   *   *

16th Century

Duncan and his six-man crew made it through London without much trouble or notice. Maybe it was divine providence, or maybe it was the fact that he'd made sure he only took Englishmen with him when he sailed an English boat bearing the Cross of St. George. Whatever the case, they had gotten further into the city than he had imagined, and without incident. A good omen, to be sure.

Acting like drunken sailors on shore leave, they moved from tavern to tavern tossing money on the table and ale down their parched throats like it was the last day before retribution.

It was working very well until a British sailor who had once lost an ear to Duncan's sword turned from the table he was sitting at and spotted the man responsible for his disfigurement.

"You!" the young sailor roared, grabbing his sword and coming at him. Duncan's men all started for their weapons, but he bade them to be still with a flick of the wrist.

"We cannot afford to give ourselves away yet," he said in a low tone, especially to the hotheaded Murddoch. Raising his hands in a nonconfrontive gesture, Duncan appeared to be surrendering.

"Do I know you, sir?" Duncan asked, a crowd gathering now, mostly in support of the one-eared pup standing over him.

"Damned right, you do! Or do you not recognize the mate of the ear you removed from my head over the right to bed some whore?"

Duncan frowned as he looked at the tip of the sword only inches from his chest. He could feel Murddoch's breathing quicken as he prepared to go for his own sword. Long ago,

Duncan had saved Murddoch's mother from a band of drunken gypsies out to entertain themselves with the women near a tavern. Duncan took on six men, and by the time a young Murddoch arrived at the scene, Duncan and Murddoch's mum were the only two left standing. Ever since then, Murddoch had not allowed anyone to trifle with Duncan, and this young nobody was going to be no exception. A slow, ominous growl rumbled from deep within the giant as he cracked his neck left and then right.

"No, Murddoch," Duncan said softly. "Do not bear arms against this lad. He has confused me for someone else."

"The hell I have! Stand, man, so that you may look eye-to-eye to the man who will deliver you to death."

Duncan slowly rose, sensing his tenuous control over the quick-to-strike giant who had pledged his loyalty to him. Duncan had seen Murddoch crush the skull of a man like a nut underfoot, and all because the man accused Duncan of stealing his woman and came at him in a threatening manner.

He had, of course, done the transgression, just as he had relieved this lad of his ear.

"I am not your enemy."

"But you are. A man does not forget the face of the man who cut off his ear because of a whore." The crowd murmured acknowledgment of this fact.

"Perhaps, but only a boy would exact his revenge on an unarmed opponent, and as you can plainly see—"

The crowd nodded and seemed to agree with this point as well.

Duncan pressed the crowd advantage. "And if you do not remove your sword from my person, I will be forced take it from you and remove your other ear so quickly, not only will you not see it coming, but the pain will be secondary to the humiliation you will feel."

This, the crowd wanted to see. And they grew ever restless as they pressed in closer. The boy turned to scowl at them, so Duncan kicked the hilt of the sword from the young man's grip sending it high into the air. In one swift motion, Duncan caught the sword and brought it down perilously close to the boy's face, shearing his remaining ear off like a piece of ham off the brisket. The appreciative crowd roared at their good fortune, and the now earless boy grabbed the side of his head, felt for an ear that was now being gobbled up by a dog on the floor, and promptly passed out.

Tossing the sword on the young man's chest, Duncan glanced over at the crowd. He'd been around long enough to know when an enthusiastic crowd was transforming into a mob, and this crowd was just about there. Having seen the drama played out, they would soon want revenge against the outsiders who dared attack one of their own. It happened all the time.

"Murddoch, get the men out of here. Callaghan, pay the barkeep and meet us out back. Snap to it man before we have to fight our way out of here!" Duncan turned back to the crowd to offer a smile before heading for the door. When all of his men were out, they quickly moved down the darkened streets only to hear the door of the tavern crash open behind them and the mob spill into the streets.

"Run!" Duncan yelled, leading his men through the filthy streets of London's back alleys. He could have stopped and fought, but he had precious few men as it was and he didn't want to lose any in a bar brawl.

Zigging and zagging, Duncan could hear the crowd behind them gaining momentum. This was their city and they had the advantage of knowing every inch of it. It was only a matter of time before he led his men into a dead end. And then what would he do? Fight his way out and wind up in a cell or worse?

No, that would never do.

Scanning for any way out of this maze, he had just started taking a right turn when a blond boy of about sixteen came running toward him, waving his arms.

"Follow me if you want to save yourselves!"

Murddoch swung his blade toward the boy and shook his head. "Naw, we ain't a gawn indoors lad. Bea' it."

The boy ignored Murddoch and turned to Duncan. "Lachlan, you fool! You can escape the crowd if you'll follow me!"

Duncan reeled. "Did you—"

The boy jammed his face into Duncan's. "Remember." His

eyes glowed like a wolf's at night. "Remember quickly, or you and your men will die right here."

Duncan peered into those eyes and saw something he never imagined he'd see. "Mother?"

The boy grinned. "That's my boy. Come now. Follow me lest that crowd get a hold of ye."

Duncan turned to the men. "We're following the boy."

"Duncan—"

"If you wish to live, follow me. Otherwise, it has been good knowing you all." To the boy, Duncan nodded once. "Lead the way."

A few minutes later, Duncan and his men were safely behind the doors of a small cottage tucked away among the maze of shops and homes.

Once the footsteps from the crowd retreated into the night, the boy lit a lamp and motioned for Duncan to follow him into another room. "Your men can stay here, but what I have to say is for your ears only."

As Duncan followed the boy into the other room, he heard one of his men ask Murddoch, "Did I hear him call that boy mother?"

Murddoch cuffed the man on the ear. "Ye jackass! He said, mother, like inna Mother of God or sumptin' like it. Donna be an idjit."

When Duncan entered a dark bedroom thick with the odor of sickness, he saw a man and his wife huddled in the corner. The air was stuffy and dense, as if the windows hadn't been opened in weeks. The bed was unmade and there were herbs and water next to the bedside table. The two people looked at him, frozen fear on their wan faces.

"We won't hurt you, folks." Duncan said softly. "It was just…a tavern brawl got out of hand. We're not here to disturb anything or steal from you. You have my word on that. There is nothing to fear from us."

The husband shook his head and pointed to the boy. "It is not…you…who frightens us."

Duncan looked at the boy, and for the first time, saw how white and piqued he appeared, his very skin translucent. "Are you ill, boy?"

Ceara whispered, "I am not, but the boy is." He turned to his parents and told them to go be hospitable to their guests and to get the men something to eat and drink. When they scooted out of the room, the boy turned back to Duncan. "This was the best I could do on such short notice."

Duncan stepped closer to the boy and raised the light to his face. "You called me Lachlan."

"And you called me mother." The boy smiled. "Which I was in another life." Ceara sighed sadly. "It is I, Ceara, Lachlan's mother who addresses you. My lovely son's spirit has turned into you, and now you need me. This is quite a mess you've gotten yourself into."

Duncan lowered the light and Ceara gazed into his eyes and whispered, "Remember."

He stared into her face, slowly shaking his head in disbelief. Memories from the farthest, darkest reaches of his soul inched their way from deep within him until they surfaced and broke through his denial. "It is you, Mother. You are in there, aren't you?" Duncan reached out and hugged the boy. "What on earth are you doing here?"

"Helping you, what else?"

Duncan lowered his voice and looked around. "What did you mean, short notice? Are you not the boy? Are you not of this time?"

Ceara shook her head. "I am not. I am only borrowing him while he is in a state of fever. I needed a body somewhere close to the palace, since that was where you were sure to be heading. And look! Here you are."

Duncan stepped back. "You have enchanted him?"

"I prefer the more modern term of possessed, and yes, I have. I had to get to you before you wound up in the tower, or worse. You know not what you are heading into, nor why Spencer left you behind."

"And you do?"

She nodded again. "Lachlan had a fear of enclosed places and—"

"As do I!"

Ceara replied patiently. "Yes. Many of our phobias come with our souls. A little like mud on our shoes."

"PhoBeeUhs?" Duncan shook his head as if the word were distasteful. Shaking his head to make the many unimportant questions go away, he asked the only one that mattered. "Has something happened? Is Maeve—"

"Everyone is all right. Listen to me. You must, for the first time in your life, truly believe in the powers within you. Duncan, you can get Spencer out of harm's way, but you can only do it with Jessie's help. You must believe in who Lachlan was, in his spiritual energy, his talent and skills. You must embrace who he was within you."

Duncan stared at her. He felt out of balance, talking to a young boy who held his mother's spirit from fourteen hundred years ago, who spoke as if they knew each other. How was this possible? How had he fallen into this mysterious place? "This Jessie…the one Spencer seeks…is she as powerful as—"

"Cate? Almost. She is young yet, and just starting her training, but she is fearless and cares almost too much about what happens to you all. She can help you. I know this is difficult, but it would be easier if you could acknowledge within you what you truly are. You have fought remembering for so long. You must not do so now."

"How can you know this? You do not know me."

"I know my son. He may have been a little boy when I left, but Jessie met him, and I know enough to know what kind of man he was and how powerful a priest he was. If you had remembered, you would have found a better way than coming to London. You would never have allowed Spencer to trick you. There were a hundred things you would have done differently."

"Then I am a failure to you."

She shook her head. "Not at all. Not everyone who remembers wants to remember, and there is nothing wrong with that. But just because you have chosen not to remember does not mean you are a failure. You have a chance to change that and to succeed here." She patted his hand. "I know this is strange for you, Duncan, but look within and you shall know that I speak the truth."

He stared at her. "You sound so much like Spencer. He has been bothering me about that for nigh on ten years."

"Well, it's time for you to listen. He is your friend, he is in danger. Tell me how you intended on getting Spencer out of the Tower."

Duncan furrowed his brow. Truth to tell, he had not thought about it, so intent he was on just getting his men through London in one piece. "I...I do not know."

She stepped up to Duncan and took his face in her hands. He tried to pull away, but her grip was strong. "Remember. That's how you can help Spencer."

He wanted to look away, but he was caught by those eyes that bore into him, demanding that he finally allow Lachlan's memories to surface; a choice he had refused his entire life.

Lachlan was the antithesis of himself. A priest versus a sinner. A peaceful man, not a killer. Lachlan did not pander with women; Duncan could not get his fill. The fact that he carried many of Lachlan's memories and had allowed, ever so briefly, for Lachlan to come through to him, didn't mean he was ready to remember entirely. He did not have the connection with his past that Spencer had, nor did he have much interest. His only connection was with Spencer in this life. This life was all that mattered to him.

But he could remember, and though he did not share these memories with Spencer, he did dream often of Maeve and their lives in Ireland.

"You do remember," Ceara whispered, not taking her eyes off his, nor her hands from his face.

Duncan sighed. "I do."

"And it pains you."

"I remember you leaving and never coming back. It is a wound he carried deep within him until the day he died."

She sighed sorrowfully. "I went through the portal years before Cate, and my body was destroyed by the Romans before I could return. I was trapped in the twenty-first century in the body of a joyless woman who cared not about life. I managed to make something out of her horrid existence all the while waiting for someone else to come through the portal. I waited years for that to happen, and when it did, I went right to her."

"Cate."

Ceara nodded. "She changed my life. She gave me Jessie, and by extension, the chance to participate in her journey. She gave Lachlan the chance to say goodbye."

"He thought of you often, to the very end."

"Shh." Ceara placed a hand over Duncan's lips. "I do not wish to know his end. I prefer to think of him as a robust young priest helping his people."

"That, he did."

Ceara released Duncan and stepped back. "And so, I lived. Waiting. Wondering. Learning all I could even though there are too few Druids in my current time. I lived, and now it's time to help Spencer live. There is a way to break into the Tower. I will need to return to my time in order to get that information. I wanted to get here before you ran blindly to your own death, but I must return to gather the information you need."

"We're to stay here?"

"Yes. Spencer must do his part first. We need to see if he can bring Quinn out into the open."

"And if he can't?"

"Then it's up to you."

Duncan raised an eyebrow. "Me? What would you have me do?"

"Can you still write BoibeLoth?"

Duncan had to search deep in his memories for the meaning of the word. He was not good at tapping into Lachlan's memories, but the word was so odd, he surprised himself by being able to get to it pretty quickly. When it came to him, a slight grin played on his lips. "I believe I can."

*   *   *

21st Century

"You did what?" Jessie was pacing back and forth across the deck of Ceara's houseboat.

Ceara continued watering her plants on her boat as Jessie

paced behind her. "Keep your voice down, my dear. I do know what I am doing."

"But I thought you couldn't—"

"I can't. I cannot go back to Cate's time...to my time, because I'm dead. I know I should have been more forthcoming with you about what I am capable of doing and the extent I am willing to go, but there just wasn't time."

Jessie turned and stared at her. "What else don't I know?"

Ceara turned. "Probably quite a bit."

"We're talking about possessing people, here, Ceara. You possessed that boy."

"I thought you'd be pleased to know that Duncan was not clobbered by a mob."

Jessie shook her head. "I am, I guess. I just...it's so...I don't know."

Putting her watering can down, Ceara said, "It had to be done."

Jessie nodded. "I tried to get to Spencer through the Sidhe, but he was unreachable, and very unclear in the dream realm. I think his injuries are adversely affecting him. I had to go through the portal. I did the only thing I could think of to do. I concentrated everything I had. It was all I had to give him."

Ceara paused her watering and turned around. "So, I'm not the only one who's been busy. Go on. Tell me more."

"I left my memories in him."

Ceara's eyes grew big and she wrapped her arms around Jessie and hugged her closely. "Oh, my dear, you have come so far! I am so proud of you!"

"What can I say? I like the pirate bastard. He may not be Cate, but he cares about her like I do, and that has certainly endeared him to me."

Putting her watering can on the ledge, Ceara motioned to Jessie to follow her into the kitchen. "My friend, Liam, from Wales called this morning. He confirmed what we already suspected." Dropping two tea bags into cups, she opened the refrigerator and took out the half and half. "In Drake's log, he simply calls the box it." Setting the carton on the counter, she touched the touchpad on her laptop.

Jessie leaned over the laptop and read aloud. "I finally have it. After several near disasters and quite a bit of booty, I finally have it deep within the hold, carelessly tossing it aside as if unworthy of even being opened." Jessie's heart raced as she continued. "New day. I know not what she wants with it. There is nothing but old paper scrolls not worth a farthing and unintelligible. But as long as she seeks it, I shall have the necessary backing to do whatever it is I would wish to do in this life. So for now, it will remain in my possession." Swallowing hard, Jessie glanced over at Ceara, who was smiling.

"He has it." Jessie jumped to her feet and hugged Ceara too tightly, forcing the wind completely out of the old woman. "Finally, something to go on." Releasing her, Jessie poured the water onto the tea bags. "We're actually closing in on him. Now, all we have to do is get Spencer out of the Tower and—" Jessie's grin dropped from her face as she met Ceara's eyes. "We can get him out, can't we?"

*   *   *

16th Century

Spencer felt the boot before he saw it coming. The one eye already swollen from his first beating took too long to focus. When it hit him, it forced all of the air from his body.

"Get up ya lazy Irishman. Her Majesty has granted your filthy hide the audience you seek, though God only knows why she does not want us to just hang you."

Spencer looked up at the guards. When it appeared they were truly not going to hit or kick him again, he rose unsteadily to his feet, his ribs aching with his every breath.

The guard grunted to the other two men standing at the door. One of them said, "If he is who he says he is, her face is the last thing he will see."

The men laughed as they dragged Spencer down the fetid hall of the Tower. The walls dripped with some sort of slime, and the air was stale, but he was glad to be free of his close quarters. He could understand why the English feared this tower, this jail. One might go mad just from having to inhale the stench of slowly rotting human flesh, excrement and diseased spirits.

"The Queen expects you to be on yer best behavior, Irishman…if ye have one, that is."

His companion laughed, and the sound was like breaking glass under the heel of one's boot. "Do you have any idea how many people, real people, true Englishmen, request to see Her Majesty? Too many to count. This here is a privilege you had better respect, or it will be the last conversation you ever have. That, my friend, is my own personal guarantee."

Spencer drew himself up, straightened out his clothes and ran his hands through his greasy hair. It had been a very long time since he had been this filthy.

"Remember…" whispered the guard who had kicked him. "One ill thought or move and one of us will run you through so fast you'll be dead before you can blink. Are you understanding me, boy-o?"

Spencer nodded. "Quite clearly. There is no need for any more of your threats. I am a gentleman and shall behave as such in front of your queen."

The massive door to the Queen's audience chamber was befitting someone of monumental stature. Carved from some great tree, it had a regal bearing befitting the entrance to the chambers of the most powerful monarchs in the world. Everything about this place conveyed riches and royalty unlike anything he had ever seen.

Before the great door stood a beanpole of a man with a gray goatee and the same color beady eyes rocking back and forth from heel to toe. The air about him was electric as his eyes locked onto Spencer's like a leech onto human flesh. His demeanor might have been more intimidating had he not worn a purple velvet suit with ruffles and all the accoutrements of a dandy.

"Walsingham, I presume," Spencer said, ignoring the shooting pain from his ribs and bowing before the man. "Spencer Morgan."

Lord Walsingham stepped up to Spencer. The scent of lavender wafted beneath Spencer's nose. "I do not know what you could have possibly said to Her Majesty that would cause her to waste her time with the likes of you, but you had better watch yourself."

Spencer forced a grin. "Do all Englishmen feel the need to bare their teeth and utter threats to unarmed and restrained prisoners?"

Walsingham stepped closer to Spencer, their noses nearly touching. "A threat, Mr. Morgan, is an unclaimed promise. I guarantee you a painful and protracted death if you so much as look wrong at the queen."

Spencer nodded. "I came to talk, Lord Walsingham, and since she has graciously granted my request, I am quite sure that is all I shall have time for."

Lord Walsingham whirled around, effortlessly opened the large door and, several long strides later, entered the queen's chamber ahead of Spencer, who remained between the two armed knights, each holding onto one of his arms.

The chamber was much warmer than his prison cell and the great stone fireplace nearly took up one entire wall. A long, oak table sat in front of the smooth stone fireplace and colorful tapestries hung from the ceiling in front of every wall. Only the one large window afforded the room any fresh air or light, but it was sufficient for Spencer to see the gray clouds looming above the castle.

The room was lit by dozens of candles, but even with the fire in the fireplace and the tallow burning, Spencer could smell the flowery and clean scent of a woman.

Four women, to be exact, three of whom were huddled as if afraid he might reach out and touch them. When they parted, there stood Queen Elizabeth wearing a peach-colored gown with cream lace and intricate beading throughout. Even with his one good eye, Spencer could see that this dress cost more than a dozen of her subjects would make in a year. It was both exquisite as well as unnecessary; her beauty needed no elaborate wrapping.

When Lord Walsingham introduced Spencer to the queen, he stepped aside so she could see Spencer's face. She cocked her head, as if studying a variant of a bug, her blue-grey eyes searching for things unspoken. Spencer was amazed by both her height as well as her stature. Her bearing was so regal, he wondered why her men had felt the need to carry on so. She was nothing if not intimidating.

With her beautiful red hair and fair complexion, she seemed to belong more in Ireland than in England. Her carriage, the fire in her eyes, and her entire manner reminded him of another queen in another time who also possessed flaming red hair and a fiery personality to match.

Queen Boudicca of the Iceni.

Although Spencer had never met the first great queen, he did remember her. Jessie had seen to that. It made him wonder where Jessie was now.

"I understand you have something you wish to share with me, Mr. Morgan. Please, come forward three paces so that I can hear you better." She sat on a large wooden chair and held her hand up to still her ladies from hovering.

Lord Walsingham stepped in front of Spencer. "Your Majesty, this man, this privateer, is an Irishman of some questionable integrity and I feel—"

"Thank you, Lord Walsingham, but I am the Queen of England and as such, it would be in your best interest to do as I've commanded. Now, step aside, and allow Mr. Morgan to make his request."

Spencer could not stop his grin. This woman most assuredly had to be of his former heritage, for no other British woman he had known had ever spoken to a man in such a manner.

"Now, please bring him closer."

Spencer walked the requested three steps and stopped. The guards' grips tightened, but Walsingham was not to be quieted. "I apologize, Your Majesty, but this man claims to be that privateer who has been raiding Your Majesty's best vessels. He says he is Spencer Morgan, and—"

"Lord Walsingham, you are trying my patience. We are well aware of who he is. What I would like to know is what he is doing here."

"Well, Your Majesty, our men caught him and—"

"Oh, pshaw," the Queen said, waving his words away as if

they were a bad smell. "From my understanding, Mr. Morgan here has yet to ever be captured on the seas where he continues apparently unabated to steal from my ships, plunder my goods and destroy my crews, and yet, you want me to believe some fantasy that he allowed himself to be captured on land? And here in England?"

"Well, we were—"

"And where are his men, Lord Walsingham?" Queen Elizabeth shook her head and again waved away any reply. "Oh, never mind. The man is here because he chose to come here." Turning to Spencer, she asked, "You did come here on your own accord, did you not?"

Spencer answered, "I believe I have information about an item that is of some concern to you, Your Majesty." Spencer saw his words register on her face. It was clear by the change in her countenance that she knew exactly what he spoke of.

"I see. And why would you wish to share this information with me?"

Spencer frowned. Was she testing him? Surely, she did not wish for him to discuss the box openly? She was a master manipulator capable of getting her way with some of the most powerful men in the world. She did not manage this feat by mere beauty alone. Everything about her, including the rumors he had heard all the way out to sea was that she was an astute adversary on many levels. If this were a game of chess, she would be trolling her pawn in an effort to see if he would bite.

He would not.

"Because we both have something to gain by having this discussion."

If there were any sign of a grin or a lip twitch, it disappeared as quickly as the thought preceding it. "Leave us," she commanded Lord Walsingham and his men. Walsingham looked as if she had just slapped him.

"But Your Majesty—"

"It would not be in your best interest to question me twice in one day, Lord Walsingham. If you are concerned for my safety, then you may remain outside my doors. My ladies shall stay with me. I doubt Mr. Morgan poses a threat."

Lord Walsingham glared at Spencer as he and his men removed themselves from her presence. After all of the men were gone and the great door closed with an ominous click, Spencer braced himself for his next interrogation. The Queen and her attendants remained. A fourth appeared in the chamber carrying a tray with two goblets and a carafe of wine.

Watching the newest lady enter, Spencer could not take his eyes off her. She possessed wickedly blue eyes that returned his gaze with the same intensity as his own. Those eyes and the power behind them nearly brought him to his knees, and for a moment he thought he might end up on them.

She set the tray down before bowing and backing away from the queen.

"That will be all, Louise."

Louise nodded once, and then cast a glance at Spencer that rendered him helpless. She was the most beautiful creature he had ever seen, with porcelain skin, dark black hair, and eyes that seared his soul; a soul that recognized instantly that he knew her. He'd known her. All he wanted to do was walk over to her, take her in his arms, and…and…

"Mr. Morgan, are you all right?"

Spencer tore his gaze away from Louise and looked up at the Queen. "Perhaps a bit of water for my throat, Your Majesty?"

The Queen barely made a motion, and in an instant, Louise was in front of Spencer holding a goblet in her delicate hand. Her eyes slowly traveled from the goblet to his hand, to his strong forearm, until their eyes met.

Spencer blinked his one good eye rapidly, as if she might disappear. As the blue-eyed lady-in-waiting handed him the goblet with both hands, she made it impossible for him to take the goblet without touching her.

Time stopped for him at that moment, and all he could hear was the blood rushing through his head. He felt dizzy, he felt elated, he felt emotions he could not name.

It wasn't her manner, or the way she moved that caught his heart as she stood waiting for him to take the goblet from her. What riveted him lay behind those brilliant and inquisitive eyes.

"Sir," she whispered softly, as if trying to wake him. "Your wine."

Spencer blinked rapidly and shook his head. "Forgive me. I do not intend to be rude." Taking the goblet, his hand barely grazing hers, he smiled slightly and bowed his head to her. "Thank you, my lady."

She smiled with just the barest corners of her mouth, as if they had just shared a secret between them.

"Your manners are impressive for a seaman, Mr. Morgan," the Queen said, bringing him back to his senses.

He swallowed hard and bowed his head. "Thank you, Your Majesty. My mother would be proud to know that not all her lessons were wasted."

Queen Elizabeth raised one eyebrow. "Your reputation as a brute among men appears to be incorrect."

"As are most reputations and rumors. I am merely Spencer Morgan, Your Majesty. Only my dearly departed father was Captain Morgan, and far more deserving of the title than I." He took another sip of the wine. It was far better than any he had ever had in Ireland.

The Queen tilted her head back as she looked at him. "Humble as well as polite, and apparently you believe you have information about something I wish to have."

"I can help locate that item you seek." Spencer glanced around the chamber at the ladies surrounding the queen. The energy coming from Louise pulsed through him, and he had to shake his head to clear it.

"We can speak freely here, Spencer."

He nodded and drank more wine. He wanted to bridge the gap between them so he could lower his voice, but he did not want to alarm her or her ladies. Then, as if reading his mind or perhaps this was just a taste of the diplomacy she was known for, Elizabeth motioned for one of her women to bring a chair, which she did, and Spencer instantly sat down, glad to be off his feet. He handed the goblet back to the lady and thanked her, wishing he were giving the goblet to Louise.

"I am quite intrigued at what it could possibly be that would drag you from the relative safety of your ship and crew. To come here alone—"

"If I said the love of a great woman, you would not believe me."

His answer surprised her and she did not bother concealing it. "Love? Oh, Spencer Morgan, I do believe there are any number of things in this life that a man would do for love."

"This life as well as others, Your Majesty."

The Queen's right eyebrow imperceptibly lifted. "Indeed. Now what is it, exactly, that you risked your life to tell me?"

Spencer would not have wanted to play real chess or engage in foreign affairs against this woman. She had a keen wit, a sharp tongue and an ability to size up her opponent within seconds. He could not afford to make a mistake. It was time to let her take all of his pawns. "I know of the box you seek."

"Oh, really?" The Queen motioned for all but Louise to leave them, and off they scurried. "What is this box that would bring a wanted man into shark-infested waters?"

"You know why, Your Majesty. The box is the Druid chest you have sought since your mother died." She'd gotten his pawns, but he had just taken her rook. He pushed on, taking advantage of her surprise. "I also know why it is so important to you."

Recovering quickly, she nodded once and sipped her wine. "Do tell me more."

Spencer leaned forward, elbows on his knees. He could sense her eager anticipation. "The box that Drake is actively seeking, I can give it to you."

The Queen was unable to hide the sparks of interest leaping from her blue eyes. "Is it in your possession?"

"It is not." Spencer could see the disappointment in her posture, but her face did not change. "But I do know where it is…and I know what it contains."

The Queen leaned back and studied Spencer for a moment, with only the crackling of the fire speaking. After several moments, she said softly, "No one knows for sure what lies within the chest, just that it contains power beyond mortal comprehension."

Spencer saw the gauntlet before him. This was the moment

he had been waiting for. "You know, Your Majesty, and you are well aware of the potential riches if it contains the…recipe you seek."

Queen Elizabeth leaned forward once more, her eyes now wide with excitement she chose not to conceal. "You do know. How? No, never mind." She waved her own question away. "That is not important. What is important is that you speak the truth, because your very life hangs in the balance if you cannot do what you say you can."

"Let's assume you and I both know the secrets within the box. I understand why you want it. I understand why you have ships and sailors searching for it."

"Then help me understand what it is you want for delivering this to me in a timely fashion. I'll not be blackmailed by any man for any reason. So if you believe there are endless gains to made—"

"I do not want gold."

Again, she raised an eyebrow. She had bought and paid for entire countries, knowing that greed greased the wheels of foreign relations. "All men have a price, Mr. Morgan. What is your price if you can, in fact, retrieve the box?"

"Your Majesty, I may not be a man of the court with an elegant tongue, but I am a man who makes his own way in this world, so my request may appear somewhat strange."

"No stranger, I must admit, than your presence here. Though my men claim to have subdued you, you are here of your own free will. Therefore, nothing you say will surprise me, Spencer Morgan. Just be wary of not wasting our time."

"Then might I be so bold as to be frank?"

"I wish you would."

"There is another who seeks this box, besides your man Drake. This other seeker is a very dangerous man who will stop at nothing to get it. It is he I want delivered to my hands. This man, nothing more."

The Queen did not move. She stared at him for a long time before quietly asking, "And why do you need my help to do this? After all, you are one of the most feared men on the sea. Why can you not take care of this man yourself?"

"Because...as strange as this sounds, I do not know who he is, only that he exists, and that...well...that his existence threatens the ones I love."

"Ahh...so now I see." Queen Elizabeth leaned back. "This really is about love. How peculiar. What an intriguing man you're turning out to be."

Spencer cut his gaze over to Louise, who did not return his gaze. "You asked for the truth. As hard a man as I seem, there is a heart within that beats for one for whom I would do anything."

The Queen studied him again, and at some length. "You are a very courageous man, Mr. Morgan; to come to a Queen you do not support in order to offer a service in an effort to protect the ones you love. If I were my cousin, Mary, I would see you hanged."

"Then it is my good fortune that you are not she."

She actually smiled, and it illuminated the chamber. "Indeed. In that, we can both count our blessings. Tell me more of this man who so threatens you that you would risk everything to come to me." She narrowed her eyes as she studied him. "And make no mistake, Spencer Morgan, you have risked much in coming to me."

He inhaled slowly. "The man who threatens those I love is ruthlessly ambitious and seeks that which you desire. He believes he may know where it is, and he uses witchcraft to aid his search." This was a tenuous reach, but he could not hold back.

"You don't say." The Queen's voice was cold and flat.

"It is the Druid secrets he seeks, Your Majesty, and he is contacting witches to help him retrieve it." He waited. It was a known fact throughout the kingdom that Queen Elizabeth sought guidance from seers and other sorcerer-types even though her own mother had once been accused of being a witch.

"The Druids' secrets," Elizabeth murmured more to herself than to him. "Yes, you seem to know a great deal about the contents of the chest. How is this so?"

"My grandmother was a Druid, and so were many others in my family before her," Spencer lied. "Their histories, as you may know, were mostly oral. Except for the box and a few pieces of obscure, undecipherable writing here and there, we do not know much about their past."

"It was your grandmother who told you of the chest?"

Spencer shook his head, digging deeper into the lie he was now committed to. "I overheard her one day when I was but a boy. She believed the chest could restore the faith and the old ways if they could only find it."

The Queen was riveted. "Restore it. How?"

"By proving that the priests of old did perform the transformations they claimed to have made. It is this transformation recipe you seek, and would prove that the old ways were valid and true."

"And this man you seek...how is it you believe I can be of help to you?"

"The writings in the box, Your Majesty, are written in a language called BoibeLoth. BoibeLoth is an ancient Celtic tree alphabet used by the Druids. It was the first of two forms of such an alphabet."

The Queen leaned on the edge of her chair as if she were afraid she might miss a word.

"The Druids used what they called Ogham, which is a writing system using notches on sticks or stones. BoibeLoth is a bit like it. The scrolls within the box are written in this language, and so if one wishes to utilize the information within the box, he will need one who can actually translate the ancient symbols."

"And?"

"And he is the only person I know who can."

The Queen cocked her head slightly. "I thought you said you did not know him. How is it you know so much about him?"

"I know of him and of his threats to my family. I have my means, Your Majesty, when it comes to protecting those I love."

"Threats? Mr. Morgan, are you not threatened daily on the seas? Do you not carry the scars of numerous battles on your body? It would seem to me that words would be useless against you."

"Against me, yes. Against my loved ones, well, Your Majesty, that frightens me."

These last words seemed to startle her and endear him to her all at once. "My, my, a man who can admit fear and love in the same breath. The woman who has your heart is a very lucky woman, indeed."

Spencer glanced once more over at Louise, who ducked her head. She had been looking at him. "It is never lucky to love a seaman, Your Majesty, as our lady is the sea and our ship our mistress."

"Are all Irishmen so poetic, Spencer? If so, I must go there someday." Rising, the Queen nodded slightly when Spencer scrambled painfully to his feet. "Before I can continue this conversation, I must check out this BoibeLoth first. If it is as you say, what would you suggest we do then?"

He chose his words. "Send out word, Your Majesty, that you seek someone to translate this BoibeLoth. Appear secretive and clandestine in your offering to pay someone to translate an ancient language. If he believes you have the box, he will come offering his services."

Queen Elizabeth appeared to be pondering this. "A strategic move bringing him out into the open. And what then? How do I get the chest?"

"I will bring the chest to you. You allow him to first translate the scrolls in private, telling you all you wish to know. When he has finished, you hand him over to me and allow me to take care of him in my way. You get the recipe, I get the man."

This seemed to greatly amuse her. "You make quite an assumption about your freedom, Spencer Morgan. You believe that I can afford to allow a man who has stolen from me over and over to escape my clutches to begin anew?"

"If you would do this, you would have my word as a captain and as a gentleman that my privateering days are over. I would retire to the land if it would save my...family."

The eyebrow twitch he had come to read made its move, but she gave nothing else away. "Give up privateering?"

Spencer nodded. "I would give up my very life to save those I love, Your Majesty. Perhaps this is the first and singular moment of altruism for me, but I am a man of my word, and I will rob from you or your men no longer. Just let me have the man who threatens my world."

The Queen rose and walked over to the window, her gown shushing as it moved stiffly around her. A shaft of sunlight made its way through the opening in the arched window. Dust and smoke wafted through the ray of light that seemed to bend and refract when she walked through it.

She stared out the window for a moment, her brow furrowed, and Spencer wondered at her discomfort.

"You are an intriguing young man, Spencer Morgan. If you were not an Irishman, I would be half tempted to offer you a position within this court." Turning, she tilted her head as she studied him. "As it stands, however, you are, and I cannot. You do strike me as a man of your word...among many other qualities, not the least of which is your devotion to your loved ones. You see, I may be Queen, and there may be many unkind things said about me, but what few know about is my own capacity for love. I am moved by your inclination to protect those you care for. I will let you know shortly what becomes of my inquiry."

Spencer bowed. The Queen motioned for one of her ladies to open the door, and no sooner was it scarcely ajar, Lord Walsingham and his men barged in, as if the Queen had summoned them to her aid. "Your Majesty—"

"Is well, as you can plainly see, though your concern for my welfare warms me, Lord Walsingham. Please take our...guest back to the Tower, and do so without incident."

Walsingham bowed. "Yes, Your Majesty." As he spoke the two guards hurried up to Spencer and grabbed his arms.

"Oh, and Lord Walsingham, I do not want him harmed. Bullying a man who is outnumbered is...distasteful. Please see to it that it does not happen again."

Lord Walsingham looked at Spencer as if trying to discern the nature of his conversation with the Queen before bowing his head. "Yes, Your Majesty. I will be sure to talk to the men."

"Be sure that you do."

Just as Spencer reached the door, Queen Elizabeth asked her final question. "Oh, Mr. Morgan?"

Spencer looked back over his shoulder at her. "Yes?"

"Is she really worth it, this woman you love?"

Smiling, Spencer nodded. "Absolutely."

* * *

16th Century

Duncan had wanted to flee. This whole affair was enough to drive him mad. Here he was, waiting for this sickly young man to suddenly spring to life with the soul of a woman who had once been his mother. It was more than he could take.

He was, after all, a fighter; a man who preferred swords over words. Waiting wasn't for a man of action, and he could feel the tension mounting in his shoulders. Already, his men thought him a bit off, having seen him call a young boy his mother, and being willing to stay in an enclosed space that smelled of rot and death. It was only a matter of time before they, too, became restless and left the safety of this small, dark cottage.

Murddoch lumbered over and sat down across from Duncan. "The men are wonderin' if you have a fever, sir."

"I do not. Perhaps I should take the sword to anyone who suggests so again."

Murddoch shrugged. "We came to help Spencer, sir, but none of us sees how sittin' cooped up here is goin' to make that happen."

Before Duncan could answer, the boy opened his eyes, blinked twice and then sat up in his bed. Duncan held his breath and motioned for Murddoch to leave. Then Duncan leaned over to the sweaty boy and whispered, "Ceara?"

"Ah, Duncan, good lad. I knew you would not let us down."

Duncan sighed and pinched the bridge of his nose. He'd seen many an odd spectacle in his years with Spencer, but nothing, nothing compared to this.

The boy rose slowly and patted Duncan's shoulder. "I understand how difficult this must be for you. This is not an easy place, I'm sure, but—"

"I came to help Spencer. If you don't know how to do that—"

"Easy, lad. I came to help you." Ceara moved over to a small table. She picked up some pebbles, a feather and a few other items and set them on the table. "Now, pay close attention. What we have here is the Tower of London." Ceara pushed the pebbles and other props around the table. "We're going to make our way to the tower and get him out of there."

Duncan looked at the table and shook his head. "We may get him out of the tower, but getting him out of London is another story altogether."

"Are you on a British ship?"

Duncan nodded. "It was the only way to get close to the English ports."

"Excellent. Can one of your men bring a boat up the Thames?"

He shook his head again and laughed. "Are you crazed? You want us to bring a boat up the river?"

"It is the only way."

"We cannot..."

"I can."

Duncan and Ceara both turned and stared at Murddoch, who had quietly slipped into the room.

"I can get a small boat up the river. When I was a boy, I stowed away on one and traveled up and down for weeks."

They both looked at the giant of a man, neither knowing what to say.

"Trust me, Duncan. I can do it." Murddoch cut his eyes over at the boy. "Done it before, and can do it again, with me eyes closed." He added, "I know this lad isn't who he appears to be. Heaven-sent, maybe. Beyond my ken—but I'm with you."

Sighing, Duncan walked over to his friend and shipmate and looked into his eyes. Their connection ran deep, and Duncan knew he'd carry the men out on his broad back if he had to. "Are you sure, man?"

Murddoch nodded. "I came to help Spencer, and if this will do it, then what choice have we? I want to do it."

Duncan looked at Ceara, who nodded. "Do it."

Grinning, Murddoch put a meaty arm around Duncan's shoulders while Ceara began pushing the stones around the table. "Good. Now that that's settled, here's what we have in mind."

*   *   *

21st Century

Jessie felt the energy of Ceara's spirit in the seam the second she stepped into it. It was the first time she had ever felt spiritual energy inside the portal, and it was an odd sensation. Sitting in a chair in the numberless room on the third floor of the Inn was Ceara's body, an empty shell without her soul. Her breathing was barely noticeable, her chest hardly moving at all. Her eyes were closed and a look of serenity floated across her face.

Jessie never sat in the chair when she went through the portal. She would always just walk in, and the next thing she knew, she would be somewhere else, someone else. By the time she returned, she was always on her feet, with no memory of how she got there. For all she knew, she just stood there the entire time.

As she moved forward through the room, Jessie sensed the vibrations from Ceara's energy. It was weird not feeling alone in a place she had always come to alone—strange, yet oddly comfortable, for though they were heading to different places in the same time, their souls would still be there together.

And she liked that idea, was her final thought.

As she slowly absorbed her new surroundings, she realized where she was, and winced at the hard rock against her back. She was cold and hungry and felt the intensity of Spencer's thoughts as he replayed his conversation with the Queen in his head.

Opening his one good eye, Spencer felt her presence. He wasn't sure if it originated from within or if there were actually someone in his cell with him. He had been asleep when he felt it, and had no way of knowing how long he had been lying there, but he was definitely not alone.

When his eye finally adjusted to the dim light, he realized that he was not alone. Someone was in the cell with him, and that did not bode well for him.

Scrambling too quickly to his feet, he had to lean on his knees to catch his breath. The pain shooting through his side was much like being run through with a blade. As he crumpled to the ground, he could hear and feel another's movements across the stone floor and braced himself for another beating.

"Your Queen won't be happy to hear you have disregarded her orders," he growled, trying, but failing to stand up. His ribs were too sore and he could not straighten up; another beating was likely to kill him.

"I've not come to harm you," came a woman's soft voice from above him.

Spencer turned so he could see her with his good eye. It was Louise.

"I have brought you some food."

Spencer recognized the voice of his angel, and he sat up, gritting his teeth at the pain. When he saw her gentle smile and kind blue eyes, he knew. There was no doubt, no question in his mind or his heart. He knew. It was her.

"You," he uttered under his breath.

She helped him to the stone bench before picking up a small basket she'd left in the shadows. Spencer watched her in silence as she withdrew some bread, fruit and a piece of cheese.

"I know you," he said softly, watching her arrange the food on a platter.

"Of course you do." She cut an apple and pear, plucked grapes off the vine, and set pieces of cheese in between the bread and fruit. "You need your strength if you are going to live through this. And you are going to live, Spencer Morgan."

He started to reply, but she gently put her fingers to his lips. Her hands were soft and slightly cold, but they burned his lips nonetheless. He could smell the essence of the fruits she had just cut, and was barely able to keep himself from reaching his tongue out to taste her fingertips.

She was much younger than he, probably by a good six years or so, but there was an aged wisdom in her eyes and carriage that told him more than any words could. He needed no words to remember this one. She was unforgettable to him.

Louise carefully lifted a goblet out of the basket. It was half filled with wine and the sides were wet from sloshing during the journey. She pulled what looked like herbs from her apron and sprinkled them in the wine. Handing the goblet to him, she smiled. "It will ease some of the pain." She studied his sealed eye, turning his face gently with her hand. "They beat you pretty severely."

"I have had worse."

"I am sure you have." Pulling a twined pack of some plant from her basket, Louise dipped it into the wine and pressed the sopping mess to his eye. "Hold that there for awhile."

He held the concoction to his closed eye and felt immediate relief. "Thank you. I do not wish to appear ungrateful, but I do not believe your Queen would be too happy if she knew—"

"Hush. She knows. She sent me. Sometimes, Lord Walsingham's men get a bit overzealous. She wants to make sure you are kept well. You made quite an impression on Her Majesty."

He lowered the compress and tried to focus on her face, but she gently pushed it back to his eye. "I would surely be well if the Queen could see to it that I kept quarters elsewhere. This cell is not fit for even the rats that plague me nightly."

She smiled and shook her head. "You have much to learn about the ways of the court. The Queen cannot afford the appearance of having dealt kindly with you, Spencer, and it is her appearance and people's perceptions of her that make her who she is."

Spencer lowered the medicine once more and this time, when she tried to push it back, he resisted. For a full minute, he scanned her face, feeling the very same emotions that had nearly knocked him off his feet earlier in the day.

She bowed her head slightly, the smile disappearing from her face. "In all our lives, you have never forgotten. I do not expect this incarnation to be any different." Suddenly, Louise reached out and grabbed his head, pulling his face a mere inch from hers. The last time a woman's face was that close to his was when Duncan had paid for her services in celebration of a huge plunder.

Louise stared hard into his face, her gaze never wavering. Finally, she whispered in a voice he had been hearing his entire life:

"Remember."

It felt as if hot liquid had been poured into his veins from the top of his head, melting him from within. The world blazed before him as his head caught on fire and his fingertips tingled from an invisible warmth. His good eye focused on her eyes, and ever so slowly, Spencer knew.

He remembered.

"I remember," he said, as the heat transformed into something deeper, something eternal. "I've been looking all over the world for you. Where have you been?"

She smiled and released his head. "You know how it is with time. It has to be right, and there's no way of knowing when that is or what our destiny holds for either of us."

"Destiny brought me here."

"No, fate brought you here. Being together is our destiny. You are here now, and that is all that matters. That is all that has ever mattered." Louise lightly ran her hand through Spencer's hair, her eyes softening. "You must drive the ladies mad in this form."

Spencer took her hand and turned it over to kiss her palm—an act he had performed thousands of times in dozens of different bodies. "There is but one lady in my heart, Maeve, and you well know it."

Louise smiled and leaned over to kiss Spencer's forehead—an act she had been doing for just as long. "Your soul, yes, but your heart? I doubt that. You are quite a handsome prince this time around. I am sure there is a woman waiting breathlessly for your return somewhere."

He chuckled. "You are goading me. I wait nigh on a quarter of a century for you and the first thing you do is tease me?"

"That is not the first thing I did, Spencer Morgan. If you recall, the first thing I did was wait on you...as I have been doing for the entire eighteen years of my life." Louise shook her head. "I never suspected...a privateer? We have been many things on our journey together, my love, but it never occurred to me to look for you in such a role."

"Then why did you not recognize me in the Queen's chamber?"

"Oh, she has a keen eye, that one. Nothing gets by the

Queen. I swear I could hear your heart pounding beneath your chest when you first saw me." Louise ran her hand over his chest and smiled. "You have always reacted the same way each time we've met. Your heart always gives you away."

"It has been a lonely heart, filled with searching and journeys, quests and long, lonely oceans. I am quite certain those are things your Queen would have seen with her eyes closed."

She nodded. "I do know that, and I am terribly sorry I have not been here, but you know how that can be. It is not always easy for us to find each other."

He nodded, flashes of another time long since gone running through his head like a dream. "I recall one life where we were both over forty when we met again."

"Do you? I remember it not." Louise lowered her voice to a whisper. "But this body is young yet and has so much to learn. It is…difficult being a lady to the most powerful woman in the world. I must be careful not to show a wisdom that ought not to exist yet."

"Then you remember much? You are practiced in the old ways even here?"

She smiled and kissed his forehead again. "I always remember much about you; maybe not the particulars of a certain time or age, but you…are unforgettable."

He licked his lips and lowered the herbs from his eye. "I've managed to find you under the worst of circumstances. I—"

She hushed him with her fingertips once more. "Time is not our ally. I am here for a reason, and right now we must mend you and keep you safe until we can get you out of here."

"We?"

"Shh." She took the herb mixture from him and dipped it once more into his wine. "You did the right thing by going to Jessie. We will need her if all of us are to get through this alive."

He cocked his head. "All of us?"

Louise shook her head sadly. "Spencer—"

"All is well. I think my plan has succeeded. Once she summons Quinn and he arrives to read the Boi—"

"She will have you killed." Louise looked him in the eyes

as she said this. "Do you honestly think she is where she is by showing mercy to those who have acted against the throne? Are you so unaware of how the world operates here under the guidance of Queen Elizabeth that you believe her to be soft and weak? Spencer, she may like you, she may even respect you, but she must have you executed. It is the way of the kings and queens of this world. Don't you know that?"

He stared at her. "She would truly have me killed?"

"Not would. Will. She will hang you. You have overplayed your hand in coming here, my love. You know not the kind of monarch this Queen is. Once she has the box and a translator for its contents, she will see you dead as an enemy to the throne, she will have the scrolls translated, and then she will hang Quinn as well. The Queen is the most powerful monarch alive, and she did not get there by niceties or gentility. She is ruthless, and you are but a pawn in her own greedy game. I have come here to protect you, my little pawn, from winding up on the Queen's side of the board."

He bowed his head. "As long as Quinn is destroyed, then that's all I—"

"In this life, it matters not if he lives or dies. Do you not understand that? Is that why you have so foolishly risked your life?"

He looked up, puzzled.

"Oh, Spencer, if only you had spent less time on the seas and more time remembering our craft, you would have remembered. Once Quinn reads the scrolls, he comes ever nearer to utilizing them, whether that is in the past or the present. He cannot even be allowed to see them, Spencer. Not ever. They cannot become part of any memory."

He felt the air leave his body. He was so tired and there was just so much that he didn't understand.

"Do not worry so, my love, for you will not die at the hands of the Queen. There is still much for you to discover in this time, and much for us to do yet."

"Together?"

She smiled broadly and brought his scraped up hand to her lips. "Perhaps. But first, before we can dream the dreams of our future, we must find a way to survive the present. We must get you out of here."

He sighed. "We?"

Laughing, she replied, "Who else do we know can work miracles for us?"

Spencer sighed once more. "Jessie."

"Aye. Jessie."

*   *   *

Jessie hadn't expected to go from Spencer into the Dreamworld, but suddenly, there she was, standing in the familiar stone circle she had come to love with its brightly burning fire and cloud-like mist. On either side of the fire stood Spencer and Louise.

Spencer and Louise? Who the hell was Louise?

"Maeve?"

Louise ran over to hug Jessie. "Oh, Jessie, thank you so much for everything you have done for us thus far. I cannot begin to express my gratitude. I have waited so long...to lose him before I even began to know him—"

"I wouldn't want to be anywhere else." Jessie stepped back and looked at Louise. She was about Jessie's age, tall and slender, with piercing blue eyes and a haunting smile. "But it's odd seeing you as...well...as someone else."

Louise's smile revealed a single dimple on her right cheek. "It is as Louise that I came here, so it is she you see. I've brought us here so we might be apprised of the situation and move forward with releasing Spencer from his bonds."

Jessie stated, "Make no mistake, Spencer, you are her enemy, and she will dispose of you the same way she does everyone else."

He nodded. "Louise has warned me as such. I was a fool."

"You were trying to do what you thought best. That is never a foolish thing." Louise reached out and gently touched his cheek.

"But Quinn—"

Finishing his sentence, Louise said, "Will walk right into

Her Majesty's presence as well as my own. With Maeve to guide me, I shall know who he is and he will find out what it means to betray the priest and priestess of the Druids. Your plan was a sound one, Spencer, but you cannot simply kill Quinn without first getting the box, and you can't retrieve the box and not kill Quinn. To be successful, we have to achieve both goals."

Spencer removed her hand from his cheek and held it between his hands. "I am beginning to understand now. You intended to handle Quinn all along, didn't you?"

Her blue eyes softened, and she turned to Jessie. "You think it is a coincidence that I am lady to the Queen?"

"Coincidence is not in our vocabulary, Maeve." Jessie's mouth may have answered, but it was Cate doing the talking.

Louise nodded. "When Cate and I were Druids, we became very, very powerful. Together, we worked for years learning how to find each other in the next life. It takes work in every life, Jessie…work to remember, work to pass those memories on. Because she and I are so connected, we did something we ought not to have done."

Jessie was mesmerized.

"Think, Jessie. Remember. Remember the stone circle, the moon, the smell of fall. Close your eyes and remember. Remember."

Jessie closed her eyes and listened to the fire crackle and snap.

"That's right. Listen to the fire…remember the fire you looked into all those lives ago. Remember how you felt, how we felt when we stood there, side-by-side. Remember."

Jessie could see the stone circle in her mind's eye, and as if she was zooming in with a camera. The moon was full, a slight breeze carried a clean smell in the air, and even the oak leaves whispered as they rubbed together high above. Next to the fire, she saw two familiar figures. Cate and Maeve, and they were praying…no, they were chanting. The full moon watched also as Jessie felt herself drawn closer to the scene. Then she was no longer watching Cate, she was Cate, and the words she had heard were now coming out of her mouth. "Annal nathrack uthvas bethud dochial dienvay."

The Spell of Making...the most potent of all Druidic spells, and she was casting it right then and there. It was said that Merlin had employed the spell to transform Uther into the Duke of Cornwall so he could sleep one night with Igraine. It was powerful, indeed, and once uttered, Cate watched as a barbarian attacked a Roman. The man beside him protected him from the Roman soldier, but before she could see the outcome, the scene changed as quickly as it had materialized. A young man and woman sat by the hearth while several children slept in front of the fire. Again, the scene transformed, showing two lovers entwined near a brook, then again, as two children playing together. Sometimes the scenes showed a man and a woman, and sometimes they were the same gender, but it always centered on the two of them. Still, the scenes were fleeting, and she caught barely a glimpse each time.

And then she saw it.

Spencer in the tower and Louise administering to his wounds.

Jessie stared at Louise. "You used the Charm of Making to see glimpses of your lives in the future."

Louise nodded. "It was wrong, and we both felt terrible afterward, but Catie would not be talked out of it. Her exposure to you when you were both quite young convinced her that we could keep our olds ways alive even in the face of a changing world. She felt that the very spirit of the planet was at risk if we did not do everything in our power in our time to try to reverse the damage done by your time."

"But my time is just a continuation of the damage."

"Indeed. But you must remember, Catie has been within you, and she knew. She saw how very little consideration even you gave to those things that are a gift from nature. Of course, that has changed for you now, but years ago, you were no different than anyone else who takes nature's treasures for granted. Catie wanted a chance to change things, to further the Druidic cause and spirituality, and nothing I could say would dissuade her. In the end, she won out, and together we wove a Charm of Making so strong it actually frightened us."

"Is that how she spent the rest of her life with you, then?

Worried about the fate of Druidry?"

"Not just Druidry, Jessie. Catie would never be so short-sighted. No, she worried about the fate of our home, and she spent the better part of her later years training her spirit, training our spirits to be able to remember so that maybe, one day, when we were needed to once again bring nature into the hearts of mankind, we would know how to do so."

"And can you? Have you been able to remember?"

Louise nodded. "More than most. There are certain memories I carry with me from one life to the next, but the minute details and experiences are all but forgotten."

Jessie glanced over at Spencer, who was staring, slack-jawed. "I did not remember any of that."

"Wait," Jessie said, holding up her hand. "So you came to court knowing Spencer needed help?"

Louise nodded. "I am not at liberty to explain everything I know or all that I do, but suffice to say, if Cate is in danger in any realm in any time, I will be there even if I have to come from the depths of oblivion."

"Then why can't Spencer remember? If Cate was so powerful, how come he and I are…well…not the sharpest tools in the shed?"

This made Spencer toss out a quick laugh. "Jessie, your idiomatic speech is certainly entertaining."

To Louise, he said, "But she has a point. Why can we not remember independently of you?"

"We all remember as children, but no one listens. If one is not a quester or versed as we are in remembering, then the unused memories fade and eventually disappear. If you are a quester, then at around ten to thirteen years of age, when physical changes begin in our bodies, the memories begin to push through. Usually by seventeen or eighteen, if we have paid any attention at all to the vast and various memories that have crossed our mind, we begin remembering. We begin to see experiences we have had, people we have loved, and journeys we have taken. We see these in dreams, in daydreams, in still pools of water, in so much. After that, it's up to each incarnation to come to the conclusion that Catie instilled almost two millennia ago."

Jessie put her hand up to her own chest. She could barely believe that Maeve was so precise in her description of Jessie's own discovery of time and her place in it. She was seventeen when she first began remembering, and it might have been sooner had she not been so doped up during her earlier teenage years. Then, after realizing who she was and what her life could be like, she finally understood the gaping chasm in her heart and why she knew there was someone or something out there ready to fill it.

Louise gently touched Jessie. "I am out there in your time feeling the same lost, scared, empty feelings that you are experiencing and if I have remembered, then I am looking for you as well. That was the beauty of the Charm of Making; Cate wanted to always be able to connect with me, whenever and wherever we were. I am out there, Jessie. Perhaps not now, and not where you are, but eventually, I will be, and you will discover just how joyous it is to be reunited. You must always remember, both of you, that you are not alone. Not now and not ever. There are souls out there living their destiny until the time is right, but you cannot hurry one's destiny along. You must live your life secure in the knowledge that we will find each other one day."

"Like today," Spencer added.

Louise looked away. "And even then, my love, we do not always know what fate has in store for us."

He nodded. "Jessie, it may take thirty-five years or thirty-five days, but she will come."

Jessie tilted her head as she studied Maeve's new form. Something wasn't quite right, but she did not know what it was or how to articulate it. Finally, she asked, "Where is Cate, anyway?" It had seemed odd that they would all gather here except for Cate; Cate had a way of explaining everything with such clarity, yet she was absent from this soirée.

"She is doing what needs to be done. Do you have what we need?"

Jessie nodded. "I have the plans to the tower, and a bit of its history. I spent part of the day in Spencer hoping to transfer that information to him. He might have those memories if he thinks hard enough."

Louise threaded her fingers between Spencer's. "You were right, love, to have placed your faith in her. She was the key to our success in saving ourselves from the Romans, and now..." she turned to Jessie and smiled warmly. "I am very proud of you, Jessie, as is Catie."

Jessie felt herself blush. "So whose direction should I seek out at this moment?"

Louise pointed at Jessie's chest. "Why, your own, of course. For it is here and now that you will be able to transfer the information Spencer will need about the tower, about Drake and about Queen Elizabeth. Being within Spencer does not guarantee that he will remember what he needs to in order to save himself. We must transfer that piece of knowledge here. Now."

Nodding, Jessie looked in to Spencer's eyes. "Now?"

Louise nodded. "Now."

*   *   *

21st Century

When Jessie opened her eyes, she was, once again, back in the portal. Ceara was gone, which made Jessie wonder whether that meant success or failure on her part. It was always difficult to tell, since time had no real relevance from one age to the next. The fact that her own time and Cate's were paralleling had more to do with Cate's powers than coincidence.

Walking on unsteady legs, Jessie headed down the stairs to where Daniel sat reading a red leather-bound tome on ghosts and the afterlife.

Looking up from his book, he scrunched his face up. "You okay? You don't look so hot."

"Have you seen Ceara?"

He shook his head. "No, but I had to run to the store for some butter, so it's possible I missed her. You want some tea or something?"

She forced a grin. "I'm fine, just a bit tired. Can you hold down the fort until I run by Ceara's?"

"No problemo. Just remember that Mike and I are going to the seven o'clock movie. You know how I like the previews."

She looked at her watch, realizing she had been in the portal nearly two hours. "So, Sport, you still having a hard time with the ghosts?"

"I can't make out what they're saying, Jess, but I think I'm close. It's like a word on the tip of your tongue—there one minute, gone the next. But I'll get it. I'm determined to find out what they want."

"And then what?"

Daniel grinned. "Then I can help them."

Jessie grabbed the keys and started for the door. "Is that really what's driving you in all this? That you just want to help them?"

Nodding again, Daniel looked older than thirteen. "Haven't you ever wanted to help someone just because they asked?"

This made her laugh. "If you only knew. I'll be back in time for your show." With that, she started on her way down the stairs, but she didn't have to go far to find Ceara. She was sitting on the bench Jessie's father had put in at the edge of the flower garden. "I was just coming to see you."

Ceara nodded. "I know. How was your trip, my dear?"

"Excellent. We were able to give Spencer the information he needs to get himself out of there."

"We?"

Sitting down on the bench next to her, Jessie nodded. "He's found Maeve. Her name is Louise and she's one of the queen's ladies."

"Outstanding! They must be thrilled. I know I was. I mean… that brute Duncan is nothing at all like my Lachlan. He is rash and arrogant—a man who plays at life without really living it. Still, I can still see glimpses of my boy in the man."

Jessie looked at Ceara. "You sound tired."

"I may have stayed too long. It has been a long time for me and I am worn through and through. Duncan is a bit of a dichotomy. He is incredibly loyal to Spencer. I gave him the plans to the Tower, and one of his men, a huge, lumbering sort by the name of Murddoch, has agreed to sail a ship up the river. Both men will be ready to go when the time is right."

"Was it...weird? I mean, knowing his soul used to be Lachlan's?"

Ceara sighed deeply. "He is his own man in a world I know so little about. His only goal is to keep Spencer safe. Regardless of his wanton ways, it makes me very proud of the man he is. Whether or not he used to be my son, he is a good man, indeed."

Jessie put her hand on top of Ceara's. There was more. "But?"

"But nothing."

"No, there's something." Jessie stared hard into Ceara's face. "You're afraid for him, aren't you?"

Turning away and staring out at the garden, it took her several moments to respond. "I suppose that I am. Even with our combined knowledge, I just don't know if we can get them all out of this alive. It is a long shot, and Elizabeth...well...from what you've told me—"

Jessie squeezed her hand. "She's a tough nut, no doubt about it. If Queen Elizabeth wants the damn box so badly, I say we give it to her."

Ceara's eyes grew wide. "What?"

Jessie smiled. "We have the advantage, Ceara. Because of what we know about history, the ball is in our court, and I'm going to drill the sucker right at her."

*   *   *

1st Century

Lachlan found Cate in her favorite place by a creek bed that contained several waterfalls and jutting rocks that allowed the water to trickle up and over them. The water coming from the main waterfall was so loud that Cate could not hear anyone approaching. This did not mean she did not know Lachlan was nearing her. She had been expecting him.

"It was good of you to come," she told him.

Lachlan chuckled. "Does anything escape you?"

"I would hope not, Lachlan. Is it not my job to know things others miss? Come sit next to me."

After carefully making his way across, he said, "How can you hear your own thoughts out here?"

Cate tossed a pebble into the still pool of water off to one side of the falls. "I do not. My thoughts are not the ones I wish to hear when I come to this place. I have been needing some inspiration and guidance, and this is where I receive it best."

"And have you gotten any this day?"

Reaching into the calm pool nearest her, Cate pulled out a pebble exactly like the one she threw. "I have."

"And?"

"Well, Maeve's gone off to deal with Quinn in her own manner, Spencer and Duncan are attempting to escape the clutches of a Queen who rules Britannia, Jessie is retrieving information that any or all of us can utilize, and that just leaves me and you." She turned to him and smiled. "As if I didn't know. I mean, that means me. You…you've been a bit busy yourself, have you not?"

His eyes grew wide, and he looked around as if there might be someone eavesdropping among the trees. "I…I have a confession to make, Cate."

She nodded. "You warned Duncan."

He had stopped questioning Cate's wisdom and ways long ago when he realized that she was destined to become a more powerful Druid than he could ever hope to be. "I do not know what happened to me, Cate. I guess I was feeling…"

"Helpless?"

"Perhaps. When Quinn came and threatened us, I wanted to do something. I tire of standing idly by while the rest of the world in the future tries to use our ways for their own personal gain."

Cate studied Lachlan's eyes and saw a much older man behind the blue spheres looking out at the world. He had become bitter since the fires on Anglesey and the subsequent hunt for priests and priestess of the old ways.

"I know that my mother did not wish that I would ever go through, but I had to do something, Cate. Truly, I had not expected Duncan to be receptive, but he was most accommodating...appreciative, even."

"He is not quite what you expected, is he?"

Lachlan struggled to find the words to express how he felt about the whole experience. Long ago, when Ceara did not return from the forest, Lachlan had wanted to go after her, but the other Druids would not allow it. He had given his word that he would not follow in his mother's footsteps, so when the time came to send a young novitiate named Cate, Lachlan felt it should have been him. When that novitiate fell under Maeve's wing, he resigned himself to being the weakest of their triad. He was no match for Maeve, and once Cate had learned all she could from Maeve, Cate would be the most powerful of the three.

Now, three years after first sending Cate through, Lachlan had broken his word and gone through the portal. It was as spontaneous and as unplanned as anything he had ever done, and though his quest had been successful, he was unsure about how he felt about having done so. A part of him wanted Cate to reprimand him for having gone where he had sworn never to go, but here she was, as supportive of him as she had ever been. The guilt seemed to grab at his robe and wrap him up in it. "I had no preconceived notions about the man. Truly, I was just hoping I would live through the portal."

"It is a strange experience, isn't it?"

"Indeed. To be someplace one instant and then, in the blink of an eye, you are elsewhere, in another being, waiting to lose yourself in their time and their ways. It was disconcerting and upending."

"And did you accomplish what you set out to do?"

"To be honest, Cate, I was not sure what my intent was. I'm still not. I just wanted to be of some help. I was beginning to feel as if all I do is stand around watching the two of you. It was time for me to add my memories as well."

"And were you successful?"

"I can only hope."

"What was your intent, Lachlan? What on earth could send you so far away through a seam you swore never to set foot in?"

"I cannot allow Quinn to harm Maeve, Cate. Not in this life or any other. I sent him through the first time, and that makes him my responsibility."

Cate nodded. "Well, Duncan is a man capable of killing Quinn. He could do so quite easily, I suppose."

This made Lachlan tilt his head in question. "How is it you know so much about him?"

"I have spent enough time in Spencer's world to know what he is willing to die for. He has great respect for Duncan's abilities. He respects a good deal about his friend. Spencer may be nothing at all like me, but the one thing we both have in common, besides Maeve, is our loyalty to those we love. He loves Duncan deeply." Cate smiled. "Our souls are good friends there, Lachlan. We take care of each other. We protect and defend. Duncan is where he is because of the very reason you went through the portal. He may be rougher than you, but he has only the best of intentions where Spencer is concerned."

"Indeed. Brash as he may be, Duncan's heart is in the right place."

"You have done all you can do in letting him know of the danger...in reminding him of who he is. There is little more for us to do than wait and see if they can prevent Quinn from getting the box."

"We have no idea where that damned thing is by now, Cate. It could be anywhere."

Cate shook her head, her red hair floating about her face until she tucked it back in her hood. "I believe Jessie has located its general vicinity. You never give her her due, Lachlan. The girl is unbelievably resourceful."

"How sure is she?"

"Quite sure. With Jessie's knowledge, I believe we may be successful in getting the box and stopping Quinn."

"How?"

"Jessie has a most ingenious plan. It will actually be easier to facilitate now that you've been to see Duncan. Are you willing to return to him?"

Lachlan's eyebrows rose. "If that is what I need to do, then I am willing."

"Good. He needs to know what you know."

Lachlan rubbed his hands together, a gleam in his eyes. "And just what is it he needs?"

Dropping the rock back in the water, Cate leaned over to Lachlan and whispered, "He needs to know how to make a box."

*   *   *

16th Century

"No, no, no," Duncan said in exasperation. "Oak! Oak is a very specific wood. How can you not see the difference?"

"But sir—"

"I know it is hard to find in this accursed country, but you must find it and it must be oak."

The men grumbled on their way out the door, and Duncan felt a pang of guilt at their low morale. "I know it is not in your nature to lay low, but—"

"Excuse me, sir," came a very quiet English voice from the corner of the room. He had been so quiet, Duncan almost forgot he was there. The man had said nothing when his son rose from his sick bed and spoke to this tall, blond privateer. He had remained quiet when the men had eaten every bit of food his wife had cooked for them. In fact, this was the first time the man of the house had spoken in days.

Rising, the man wiped off the profuse sweat he had been shedding since Duncan had arrived. He walked over to the table. "I know where there are some larger blocks of wood down at the docks near one of Sir Charles' ships. I believe it is just the kind you are looking for."

Duncan rose and towered over the fat, sweating man. He did not want to trust this man who so quickly and easily relinquished his home to a bunch of criminals, but he did not see what harm would come if he heard the man out. "Is it oak? The wood I need must be oak."

The man nodded. "I believe so, sir."

"Can you take me there?"

The man glanced over to his wife and then nodded. "I can.

Will…will my wife be safe?"

"Have we harmed her yet? We want nothing more than to leave you as we found you. Your wife will be quite safe, I assure you. My men may look and smell like scoundrels, but they are, for the most part, honorable men."

The wife rose from her vigilant bedside of her son and took Duncan's hand. "Please, sir, whatever you did to breathe life back into my son, I—"

"Maggie! Hush, woman, at once!"

The wife turned on her husband. "I will not! Until they came, my Regginald showed not one bit of life."

"Confound it, wife, not another word! That was not my son." The man crossed his arms over his chest in defiance of the truth.

"You do not know that."

"Enough!" Duncan's word sliced through the air, stopping the combatant couple. "Madam, your son may or may not return to you from his fever, but you have my word, if there is anything I can do to assist in that return, I shall do it."

"By what means of witchcraft?" the man demanded.

"My husband may care, but I do not care by what means my son is healed. I want my son healthy, and if you can make that so, then I will do anything you ask of me."

Duncan cut a harsh glance over to the husband, who chose not to respond. "Perhaps that will happen, madam. In the meantime, to insure that your husband's health remains as it is, he will need to take me to that wood on the dock."

The wife glared at her husband. "Take him then. These men will not lay a hand on me. If they wanted to, they would already have done so."

Duncan nodded and turned back to the red-faced husband. "My men and I will leave here much sooner if we get the wood we need, sir. It is in your very best interests to help us as much as possible so that we may be on our way."

The man wiped his dripping bald head and nodded. "Aye, then. I'll take you."

Turning to the wife, Duncan bowed. "Thank you."

"Just save my son, sir."

"If all goes well, madam, he will not be the only one we save."

*   *   *

Spencer languished for the next two days in the damp darkness of his cell. Even his dreams had been empty, and for the first time in his life, he felt abandoned by those he had always counted on being there.

Except for Louise.

Every time she came to his cell, she brought with her some sort of herbal mixture that had worked wonders on his eye. The pain in his ribs had subsided considerably, and he was quickly regaining his strength. None of this surprised him now that he had remembered so much about their past together. Maeve had been a consummate healer in her day, and several other incarnations of her also carried with her an herbal knowledge so vast, it was no wonder her soul remembered.

Where was Maeve now, he wondered.

Leaning back against the cold rock wall, Spencer sighed and closed his eyes. He had tried to get to the Otherworld, in the hopes of finding Jessie or Cate, but to no avail. It was as if he was locked out, and that greatly disturbed him. It had never been easy to trust a woman, and now, it seemed his fate was in the hands of three of them.

But he trusted Louise, and that was a strange thing, indeed. Maybe it was the way her soft hands touched him, or the way her eyes said so much with but a single glance. She was worth fighting for, worth traveling through time for, and even worth dying for. She was the essence that filled his heart, empty for so long. Trusting her came easily. Waiting for her, did not.

As he listened to the sound of the water drip, drip, dripping outside his cell, he thought about the emptiness of his heart and the way he had made his mark on the world. He and Duncan had spoken of it only twice in their time together, but Duncan understood well that the soul Spencer looked for was the very one Duncan had longed for in other lives, yet never won. It was the reason Duncan went through women so fast and furiously;

hoping there was someone to fill his aching heart. But try as they may, neither of them had ever had a single memory of any love Duncan had had in his previous lives. Not ever.

Spencer felt sad for his friend; to yearn for something so deeply and yet to never touch it seemed a crueler fate than one deserved. Duncan was a good man, with the heart of a lion. He deserved to find happiness somewhere, with someone. What had happened that prevented his soul from finding that one special person?

"You are certainly deep in thought."

Spencer blinked out of his reverie. Scrambling to his feet, he began to offer his apologies. "I am so sorry...I did not—"

Louise was in his arms in a flash, covering his mouth with hers. Her hands threaded their way through his hair and she pulled him closer. The heat from their bodies warmed Spencer's chilled bones as he wrapped his arms around her thin waist and lifted her off the ground, his mouth eagerly tasting hers. They stood embracing and kissing for a long, long time, melting into one another like two drops of candle wax belonging to the same tallow.

Her breath was of apricots, and the clean scent of her made his heart pound beneath his chest and his body rigid. It was unlike any kiss he had ever shared with a tavern wench or silly village girl. This was intense, passionate, and left him longing for more. He wanted to crush her to him, to devour her and taste every part of her being. He wanted to stay just like this forever, and when Louise finally pulled away, she ran her hands through Spencer's hair and smiled, her gentle eyes brimming with tears.

"Has something happened? What upsets you so?"

She pulled him over to the stone bench and sat down with him. He could smell the food she brought with her. "I overheard Walsingham talking to the Queen about you. She has decided to grant you your freedom in exchange for the box, but she will not hand Quinn over to you."

"At least she will release me. You thought she would kill me."

Louise shook her head. "You still do not understand, do

you? She will release you, thereby wiping her hands clean of whatever happens to you after you are gone."

He nodded slowly. "Oh. Ever the diplomat, eh? She wants my blood, just not on her hands."

Louise reached for his hand. "She is not a great monarch because of her kindness or her willingness to stay true to her word."

"So your Queen believes she will get the box, a translator and the scrolls all for the low cost of my life?"

Nodding again, Louise replied, "She believes, as is usually the case, that she is in control of the play. It is time for us to go on the offensive. We have a box nearly ready that you are going to present to the Queen."

Spencer's eyebrows rose. "We?"

"Duncan has come to London and is, at this moment, carving the same sort of box Lachlan carved all those years ago."

Spencer drew back as if slapped. "What? Duncan? Here? I do not understand. How did he—"

"There is much you do not understand or know of that has taken place without you. Duncan arrived shortly after you did and has been quite busy trying to get the box carved. He…has help he never expected to receive."

Spencer blinked. "Lachlan?"

"Among others. We are going to draw Quinn out with our box. Once you get the box delivered to the Queen, Duncan and his men will—"

"No. I will not leave you."

"You must."

"I did not find you only to leave you now. There are many places we can go—"

She shook her head, causing two tears to fall. "You do not understand. It…it is not our time. I know that we both wish it was, but it is not. There is still much for us to do and—"

"What are you saying? Of course it's our time!" Spencer raised his voice. "I will not hear this."

She grabbed his hand and pulled him to her. "But you must. I know this is hard to hear, and I am so, so sorry that it hurts you, but you have a destiny to fulfill, my love, as do I. But it is not our time."

Spencer felt tears come to his eyes, but so foreign was the feeling, he did not know what to do about them. "Do not tell me I found you only to lose you again. Life cannot be this cruel."

"You will never lose me. Never. You know where I am, and when the time is right, you will return to me."

"And why can't now be that time?"

Louise took his face in her hands and kissed him so softly it hurt. "You know why. We must finish this. It is too important not to, and we cannot do so together. Do you remember our visit with Merlin long, long ago?"

He frowned, trying to bring that memory to the forefront of his mind. When he saw the image of Merlin standing before him, he nodded. "I do. Vaguely."

"Do you remember his words to us?" She lightly stroked his cheek as she peered intently into his eyes. The air around them seemed to change, almost as if it was changing colors and lightness. "Remember."

He looked into her eyes. He was remembering sitting around a huge bonfire on the coast and Merlin sat with them, breathing slowly in and out. When Merlin spoke, his voice sounded a hundred years old. "I have been watching you three these hundreds of years, and I must say you are very brave to do what you are doing."

"But?"

"But be very careful that you do not create that which should happen naturally."

"And if we did? What might happen?"

Merlin shook his head sadly. "Nothing good can ever come from such an act. Nothing. To try to manipulate time to do your bidding is a dangerous place to be. I do not recommend it."

"He warned us, Spencer, and we must heed that warning. There was no wiser Druid than he, and what he told us must be followed. Do you still believe that I am here by accident? Or worse—by coincidence?"

"It is our fate to be together, Louise. Always."

She let out a little sigh. "It is, but fate did not bring us together this time. Cate did, because she could not bear the thought of you dying trying to save Maeve." Louise caressed his brow. "If we are to exist in this life together, it must be when the time is right for us to do so…naturally, as it has in all our existences. That is the only way."

He crushed her to him. "This is torture. I do not know which is worse: not knowing who you are, but knowing that you are out there looking for me…or this…knowing who and where you are and yet not being with you."

"You shall be with me, as you always have, but only after you do all that you are supposed to do in this life. You must learn what that is, as must I."

He held her more tightly as tears ran down his cheeks. "You mean so much to me already."

Louise pulled away from him and touched his lips with her fingertips. "It is because I care for you so much that I must make you do that which you would never willingly do. You must trust that I know what I am doing and save yourself."

"And you? What of you?"

She smiled. "I have my work to do here. But you—you must find the real box and destroy it. It is what must happen, and you cannot do that from here."

Spencer nodded. He hated that he understood, but he did. So much was riding on him and his knowledge…on their combined knowledge. "Jessie came to me last night. She explained the plan you speak of." He shook his head sadly. "She omitted the part about us not being together."

"It was not hers to tell."

He bowed his head. "No. I suppose it wasn't." He gruffly wiped the tears from his face. "I am here to protect Maeve. How fares she in all of this?"

Louise laid her head on his shoulder. "Maeve knows what she must do, and it is imperative we all help her accomplish her task. That is why you must do what I ask."

"Give the Queen a fake box."

"Yes."

Spencer nodded. "I shall give her Duncan's box. You tell your Queen I am prepared to have the box delivered, but she must receive it in the courtyard. Tell her I request a horse, and that the men who help deliver the box are not to be harmed."

"Getting you all out of London alive—"

"I, too, know what I am capable of, my sweet. You just make sure the man who takes the bait is Quinn. Once he shows up, Duncan and I will go after the only place the box must be."

Louise's eyes smiled, though her lips did not. "Now, you eat. Do not forget the herbs for your eye. It is still puffy and needs tending to."

Spencer pulled her to him and kissed her long and deeply, his tongue reaching for hers as his hands roamed across her back, her shoulders, finally coming to rest at the small of her back.

She withdrew from the embrace and straightened her dress. "You need not make this any harder than it already is."

He threw his head back and laughed. "I would not have you ever forgetting what it is you are missing."

Her eyes had stopped dancing and she looked sad. "Oh, Spencer, if you truly did remember all of the things Catie would have wanted you to remember, you would know that I never forget you, and I never will. Perhaps…perhaps it is best that you do not remember as much as I would want you to. It can be…painful."

Spencer swallowed the ache he felt. "Go now, before I forget how to be a gentleman."

"You have never been anything but gentle with me, and I, too, shall look forward to the nights when you lay by my side being the sweet, gentle lover you have always been." Kissing him quickly on the lips, she headed for the gate.

"Louise?"

"Yes?"

"I do love you so."

"I know. And I, you."

*   *   *

1st Century

She had ridden along the coast for two days now, weary, saddle sore, but unrelenting in her pursuit of a man who had made the fatal mistake of threatening the person she loved most. Throughout their lives together, there had been a handful of people who had stepped into unpleasant experiences when they had threatened the body housing Catie's soul. Maeve did not like violence, but she had learned from nature itself that survival often comes at a price. Some had paid that price, while others got a glimpse of it. All knew that crossing Maeve where Cate was concerned was not a path one wanted to be on.

Riding her gray steed, Maeve thought about the last time she'd set eyes on the box. Carved from a single piece of oak, Ogham was carved into the sides along with various other symbols, the ancient language of her people which, she had discovered through Jessie, had not made it through the ages. The box was a masterpiece of Lachlan's own design. He had carved the entire thing in less than three days, determined to leave their wisdom behind for others. While he carved, Maeve, Cate and others who had made it off Anglesey wrote for long hours at a time the verses, poems, potions, laws and oral histories of their people.

Maeve now knew what had become of Quinn. He had fallen in love with soul journeying, and decided to use it to his advantage in other lives. He had turned his back on his Druid path and had chosen instead to enrich his future lives with the alchemy recipe Lachlan had foolishly placed within the box.

And it was foolish of him. She had tried to convince him that putting all of their wisdom into the box was a mistake. Some things were better left to oral tradition, and if they died, then it was meant to be. Too often, people tried to preserve that which no longer needed to exist. Life ran in cycles, and some things, including knowledge, lived and died in cycles of its own.

There was a piece of knowledge that had been plaguing Maeve for days now; questions about Quinn and the way he was slipping through time. He had come to Jessie in the body of another. In her vision, she had seen him do the same with Cate and Lachlan. So…if his spirit was inhabiting the beings of others, where was he? He had been alive when they left him in Eire, yet he had entered a man living in his own time in order to get close enough to Cate and Lachlan without losing his life.

But could one be alive in the time in which the enchantment took place? That was the question nibbling at Maeve's mind as she rode. Perhaps there was only one way in which that could happen.

"Quinn is dead," she murmured to herself. Could it be? Had he died during one of his many visits through the portal, and enchantment was now his soul's only option in this life?

"Ceara," Maeve said to the horse, who flicked his ears as she spoke. When a soul is in the portal and its originating body destroyed, she reflected, that soul cannot return to the body of that time. If it does, the soul passes on, closing the door to this time and opening a door to another. Sometimes the soul goes forward, sometimes backwards but it always goes into a newborn being. The only way that doesn't happen is if the soul, now lost in the portal without a body to return to, enters another and takes control. "Ceara did it. Is that what Quinn has done?" Maeve scratched the horse's ears and considered the possibility that Quinn was no longer alive in her time. Had he used a portal and been killed while in transit? That would explain his use of different bodies in all but Spencer's time, and even then they did not know who Quinn was or even if he was an incarnate of himself or enchanting another.

She rode for another two hours, wanting to press the already tired horse, but she dared not. If Quinn was indeed dead, she need not kill the beast in order to continue after him. Wrapped up in her cloak, Maeve wondered what she would find when she reached the portal. If he were truly dead, she would have to change her plan.

*   *   *

21st Century

Jessie was relieved that her parents were finally back from their trip. She'd needed a break from the Pit, from worrying about Daniel, from being a grown-up. She hadn't realized how the weight of the stress had been pushing against her until she was hugging her Rick and Reena. She had never been happier to see them. Now, she could get on with what she needed to do without having to take care of customers, Daniel or anything else.

Excusing herself early, Jessie made her way to her room. She needed to rest before going through the seam to see what was going on. It was imperative that she keep up with Spencer. She just needed to close her eyes for a minute…

She just needed a little rest, that was all.

Just a minute or so.

"I am so sorry for the toll this is taking on you."

Jessie's eyes popped open. She was still in her bed, but Maeve was sitting on the edge of it, her hand across Jessie's. Jessie bolted upright. "Maeve? What…?" Jessie struggled with her comforter as she tried to sit up.

Maeve smiled warmly. It was the most intimacy they had ever shared and there was something…knowing about the smile. "No, this is not real. I have entered your Dreamworld. I apologize if it frightened you."

Jessie stared at her. It all felt so real…her bed, her room, her pajamas. "Frightened? That's not the word that comes to mind."

"I had no other choice, or I would not be here. The Dreamworld is more a place for Catie than for the likes of me, I'm afraid, but what's done is done. I am here."

Maeve helped her sit all the way up and pulled the covers up around her much as her mother used to do. "It is always good to see you, Jessie, but I fear this is draining you of your energy for your life here, and that cannot happen."

"Hey, it's not like my life here is a barrel of fun. To be honest, this is the most excitement I've had since the last time I saw you. My world is a pretty dull place."

"Oh, I do doubt that, Jessie. No place could be dull with you in it." Maeve brushed a few stray hairs away from Jessie's brow, and ran a finger lightly across her eyebrow. "You are so much like my Catie, it is hard to believe." Maeve's gray eyes took on a life all their own as she studied Jessie intently. "And you do have so many…interesting phrases. It is no wonder Catie adores *you.*"

Jessie blushed. "The feelings are mutual. I would do anything to help her."

"I know, and I appreciate all you have done for her...for us, thus far."

"Has she been able to keep you abreast of our plan?"

"Yes. I believe it is a very sound strategy, indeed. If Duncan and Spencer can succeed in convincing both Quinn and the Queen that it is the true box, it may very well save their lives and allow us to protect the ancient secret." Maeve studied her. "You are worried."

"It would mean a lot to me if that silly pirate made it through. I've become quite fond of him."

Maeve nodded sagely. "Isn't it interesting how we can manage to find the goodness of the soul even though the life it is leading is not?" She sighed. "He could not be more opposite than Catie, and yet, he too has risked his life to save his past and future selves."

"I spent all day contacting people Ceara knows to get enough information to lead him to the box, and I think we're getting close."

"Is the box on Drake's ship?"

Jessie nodded.

"And do you know where he is now?"

"I'd say we're within a couple hundred miles."

Maeve nodded. "Well done. We have work to do, which is why I am here. Our dilemma is two fold: Spencer and Duncan need to destroy the box and everything in it, and Louise needs to deal with Quinn once he shows himself."

"Do you really think she can?"

Maeve grinned. "Be not afraid for that woman."

Jessie held Maeve's hand. It was surprisingly warm. "You sure know a lot about people, Maeve."

Leaning over, Maeve kissed Jessie's forehead. "I am a Druid priestess, Jessie Ferguson. It is my job to know. Now, close your eyes."

Jessie did as she was told.

tell you? I already have one who can read the ancient Druid texts."

He took a deep breath and chose his next words carefully. "I see. Then it is most fortunate you need seek no further for a translator."

"Indeed. All I need now is the chest."

Spencer nodded. Had Quinn begun his charade under the Queen's nose, or had he just shown up and presented himself? Was he already a step ahead of them all? Suddenly, Spencer realized the extent of Quinn's abilities, and it frightened him.

"My men will escort you out at midday, if that is enough time for you."

Spencer knew Duncan was somewhere in London, but he did not know exactly in what location. "I shall manage."

"Good. Then if that is all, our dealings together are nearly at an end."

He felt his chest tighten. Was Quinn right under his nose or was she bluffing? Surely, she could not afford to allow the translator to live, so why the ruse?

"Is there something else?"

Spencer stared at her blue eyes and he knew the virgin queen was likely to remain thus, for no man would be able to warm her iceberg of a heart. "No, Your Majesty. I shall see to it the box is delivered and I thank you for allowing me to continue to live."

"I trust you will keep the other bargain we made, Mr. Morgan, for surely, I am to be feared far more than this man you seek. Betrayal from you would, of course, extend to those you love as well, so do keep that in mind."

Spencer nearly gagged. Was there no end to this woman's treachery? Was she actually breaking their bargain with one hand while demanding that he keep his end of it with the other? "My days on the high seas are over, Your Majesty. All I wish to do after this is live my life farming my father's land."

"Well done. Then good luck to you, Mr. Morgan. We shall see you at dusk."

Spencer allowed the guards to take his arms as they moved down the hall. He was frantic now, wondering if he had inadvertently put Louise in more danger. Had someone heard her warning him? Had the Queen done away with her because she suspected her?

When he could stand it no longer, he turned to one of the guards. "I was hoping for one last glimpse of that lovely little tail with the blue eyes who hovers about the Queen so. I could eat her with one bite of my eyes."

Both guards laughed. The one on the right answered, "You have good taste, Irishman, but that one is all looks and no play." The guard opened several doors as they made their way to the courtyard.

Spencer's stomach churned. "Oh?"

"Aye. Some sort o' sleeping sickness possesses that one. Comes and goes, it does."

The other guard chimed in now. "One minute, she can be doing something, and the next, there is nobody home. Out like a blown candle."

Spencer's eyes scanned the area, the hallway, the courtyard, the feeling of utter dread rising from his gut. Louise was ill? Why had she not said anything? "You don't say."

"Nay. She fell asleep going down the stairs once and nearly broke her fool neck. The Queen loves her ever since she healed a scar on Her Majesty's hand. The Queen has taken good care of her and forbids anyone from meddling with her."

"But the girl…is she all right now?"

"She will always be all right as long as she has the Queen's eye. She made it clear to us all that no one was to touch the girl whenever she is in thrall, but she is something pleasurable to look at, eh Irishman?" The guard laughed as he jabbed Spencer in the ribs, making him wince.

Spencer nodded. Why hadn't she said anything?

The other guard whispered conspiratorially, "There are rumors about the court that the girl is bewitched."

Spencer stopped walking, nearly toppling the two men. "What? Are you saying the woman is a witch?"

The guards regained their balance and both shrugged. "Witch, demon, sorceress. Whatever term you use, the end result is the same: the woman just is not right."

*   *   *

21st Century

Rick and Reena were out gardening when Jessie drove Ceara up Marigold Lane. The garden had gone from gigantic weed patch to stunning English garden in just three years, and it was the Inn's crowning glory. Rows and rows of rose bushes of every color and variety were flanked by two aged wisteria nursed back to health by Reena and the local master gardener. Hedges of box elders lined either end, and a three-tiered fountain gurgled in the center.

"Hi gals," Rick said, shielding his eyes from the afternoon sun. "Feel like pulling some weeds?" He brushed soil from the knees of his gardening jeans as he stood.

Ceara chuckled. "That would be why I live on a houseboat, Rick. No weeds in the ocean."

"What about seaweed?" Rick laughed at his own joke. "Sorry. Too much sun, maybe."

"Garden looks great, Dad."

"It really popped a cork this spring, didn't it? What are you gals up to today?"

Jessie smelled a rose named Chicago Peace. "Ceara's helping me with a report for my psych class. Once I get that class out of the way, I'm home free for gen ed."

Reena wiped the dirt off her gloves onto her apron and pulled off her wide-brimmed straw hat, freeing shoulder-length auburn hair. The Oregon air had been good for her. She looked ten years younger since moving from the Bay Area. "I hated pysch in school. Big lecture hall. Impersonal. How are your latest grades?"

"Managing a B for the exact same reason." Jessie felt the grains of sand speeding through the glass. "We better scoot, though. I don't want to waste Ceara's time gabbing."

Hustling up the stairs, Jessie held onto Ceara's elbow as they made their way to the numberless door.

"Risky business with them home, my dear."

"No choice. My books and papers are spread out on my desk. If they come up, you know what to do."

Ceara nodded and squeezed Jessie's hand. "I'll follow shortly after. Everything will be set up. Don't you worry."

She added, "Now remember, my dear, if Spencer gets himself into a situation that might result in his death, you must jump out. Do not stay in him out of some morbid sense of loyalty. Do not attempt to change his fate."

Jessie nodded. She hadn't felt this nervous since her first jump through the portal. "I won't."

"You have to focus in and be very aware. Do not get so caught up in being Spencer. I know it's hard, but you must act like a flea on the dog and not the dog, otherwise, you lose your perspective, and, quite possibly, your life."

Jessie sighed. "Gotcha."

"This isn't the History Channel, and you're not Jacques Cousteau. You give Spencer everything you have about Drake… everything. You go in thinking about nothing else except Sir Francis Drake, then you replay those thoughts over and over again until they become embedded into his, and then you leave. Get. Out. No lingering out of curiosity. Out."

"Ceara…I know."

Ceara looked up, her eyes intense. "I'm sorry for overstating the obvious, my dear. I suppose I am just a bit nervous, myself. I want to make sure you don't lose sight of our objective. It is easy to get caught up in all of it."

"I understand. You be careful yourself, too. You get Duncan and the fake box to the queen and then your job is done. Come home. Don't sit around watching or waiting. We need you here in case Mom and Dad pop their heads in."

"I'll get Duncan and the box where they need to be. You just make sure Spencer finds him."

"Park Street, across from the Bull's Eye Tavern."

Ceara nodded. "At mid-day."

"Is the box finished?"

Ceara nodded. "He was putting the final carvings on it last night. It is an incredible thing of beauty and craftsmanship. My boy did good work, and Duncan has done no less."

"I can't believe Duncan managed to remember the designs. I didn't think he had it in him."

"Well, certainly not all of them, but he managed most. Duncan turned out to be a pleasant surprise. He did not want to remember anything for most of his life, but he has done remarkably well under the circumstances."

"He cares about Spencer so much, he'd eat hot coals. In the end, it's their friendship that unlocked the door for Lachlan to come through." Jessie licked her lips and turned to the wall where the door normally appeared. "This is it, then." Stepping up to Ceara, Jessie hugged her and felt a rush of emotions. It felt as if they were going off to war, each to fight her own battle until they could reunite once more.

"Good luck, my dear."

"Thank you, Ceara. See you in 1567."

*   *   *

16th Century

Duncan had just finished the latch for the box when Regginald rose from his sick bed and joined him. "The box is exquisite, Duncan," Ceara whispered, laying a hand on Duncan's shoulder.

Duncan rolled his head around, his neck making cracking sounds as he released its tension. "Your son had a very fertile imagination. There were carvings all over the place in his memory, and a few of them were quite a bit vague. I do not think I have worked so hard on anything in my entire life." Stretching his fingers, he groaned. "I hope it is worth it."

Ceara walked over to the now hollow piece of oak and stared at it. Fingers traveling over the carvings of oak trees, the moon, stars and leaves, she shook her head. "It is brilliant, though. However did you hollow it out so quickly?"

"Better tools now." Lowering his voice he whispered, "You know, you are scaring the boy's parents to death. Do you suppose there is some way to help them be less afraid?"

Ceara nodded and went to the bedroom, where the parents kept their vigil. As she approached them, they huddled together. "I know all of this is strange to you," she said to the parents as she reached out and took the mother's hand. "But in my fever, I met a…man who has told me what herbs and medicines to use that will make me better. There is no need to be afraid of me, really."

"See, wife, the boy is possessed!"

"No, Father, I am not so. Not really. I am just unwell with fever and not entirely myself. When these men and I leave, you must go and fetch the things I tell you to. I will give you very specific instructions about how to prepare it. Have the broth ready for my return. I will drink it, lie back down, and by morning, my fever will be better and so will I."

"Enchantress!" the father hissed.

"That is enough, husband." The wife turned to Ceara. "We will do as you ask, Regginald. When you…when you are better, will you…be yourself?"

Ceara brushed her hair out her eyes. "Myself, Mother, and only myself. But I need the broth, and I need you to forgive anything I have said or done while in this state. Can you do that for me?"

The mother nodded, but the father only looked away.

Regginald walked back into the room and watched Duncan now poised over a scroll. "A privateer who can write? I am impressed."

Duncan looked up, his eyes red and weary. "Actually, no. I am using the BoibeLoth to write a few notes to Quinn…in the event that our plan fails."

Ceara read the note over Duncan's shoulder and chuckled. "You are a fine man, Duncan."

"Would that were true." Duncan pinched the bridge of his nose and rubbed his eyes.

"Oh, but it is. Who else would have cared whether or not the parents were afraid of their son? You have a big heart beneath your bluster."

"In certain areas, but there are scores of women who would most assuredly disagree with you."

She put his hand on his shoulder and gave him a quick squeeze. "That will not always be the case, Duncan." She watched in silence as he picked up one scroll after another and filled it with writing barely recognizable as such. Scroll after scroll, he would write, sometimes chuckling, other times sighing, as if the weight of the words was too much for him.

"I take it your memory becomes clearer the more you write."

Duncan nodded. "I wish not to remember, yet the memories flood out like ink from the pen, out of my control and in their own shape and form."

"And you've personalized some of those memories on the scrolls?"

Ceara resisted the urge to hug him. "Good. Spencer will be ready at the noon hour. You'll then take the box to the Queen and if all goes well, you two will get out with your heads still intact."

"Murddoch will be waiting with a boat. He goes, even now, undetected by any patrols, so it should not be a problem getting away from the court unharmed. He is as decent a sailor as any man I have ever sailed with. If anyone can get us out on a boat on the Thames, it is he."

"Excellent. And what about you?"

"I am an Englishman, Ceara. No harm will come to me if the Queen believes I am merely a courier in all of this."

It had surprised her to find that she liked so much about this young man. After all, he was the antithesis of her son.

"Duncan, may I tell you something?"

"Could I stop you?"

"Not at all."

"Then proceed."

"My son was a strong, powerful priest. At some point in his life, he would have figured out that Maeve was never going to be his, not in that life or any other. He would not have pined for all of eternity. Quite the contrary. I believe Lachlan established a bond with someone long before now, and that someone is out there waiting for you, but you'll never see her, or him, as long as you fill your emptiness with tawdry women and cheap wine."

"Are you quite finished?" Duncan's tone was cold.

She smiled charmingly. "Well, I could go on, but I won't. Just ease an old woman's worries and tell me you'll think about it."

"I shall think about it. Now, would you rest your lips so I can finish a few dozen or so of these before Spencer gets here?"

Nodding, Regginald leaned back and smiled. Duncan might not be her son, but she was discovering that she loved him like one, and she would do whatever needed to be done to make sure he got out of this alive.

*   *   *

It was the first time Jessie had slipped through and felt as if Spencer knew she was there; as if he'd been waiting for her. Before long, she was repeating Drake's whereabouts over and over again like a mantra, knowing that deep within him, Spencer was listening…taking notes…paying attention.

What caught her off-guard was the sorrow emanating from him. It was so deep, so intense, she knew he was struggling with something profound.

What had happened since her last jump through time less than a day ago? Something had happened, something big.

Suddenly, as Jessie fully entered 1567, she knew what it was: he was suffering from a broken heart.

Maeve.

Spencer had lain in his cell replaying over and over again his final conversation with Louise, until the words were practically screaming at Jessie. He could not believe that he had come this far and worked this hard only to be told that this was not their time.

Not their time? How could that be?

But there was something else happening. He was calling on the goddesses of old, and reaching deep within himself to be able to go where he had never ventured before: The Land of the Sidhe.

Spencer glanced down at himself and saw the green Druid's robe he had seen Cate wearing. Was he Cate again? Was that where this awesome sense of power was coming from? Did all the beings of Cate revolve around her essence like the planets around the sun?

"You honor me with such thoughts, Spencer, but it is not

so."

Spencer glanced up through a veil of mist and realized that he was now standing in a sunny field filled with bright yellow and orange flowers. The field was surrounded by rolling hills, and the sun was warm upon his face. Cate stood among the thigh-high flowers, also clad in a green robe, a smile on her lips.

"You came," Spencer said.

"I do not truly come anywhere, Spencer. I am always here. That is what you never understood. I am not a thing of the past. I am very much a part of every present...if you allow it, if you listen, if you are willing."

Spencer walked toward her. The flowers seemed to part before him as he strode up the slight incline. "Where am I? What is this place?"

"What do you think it is?"

Spencer looked around, feeling watched, sensing the presence of others who chose to remain out of sight. They were not alone; on this he would stake his life. "The Faerie Realm?"

Cate glanced around at the flowers, the butterflies and other creatures inhabiting this realm. "Well done. We are in the Land of the Sidhe. You brought yourself here, Spencer, for the first time in your life. Truly, you must be confused to have summoned me to here of all places."

"I did not know where I was going or even what I was doing. I just know that my heart aches and I know not what to do."

"Some day, if you ever truly trust that you know what you know, all of our incarnations could actually appear before you, filled with wisdom, guidance, kind words and even advice, if you needed such."

"Is Jessie—"

Cate shook her head. "Though she is presently with you now, she is not a strong enough priestess to know how to separate herself from you even here in this realm. Like you, Jessie has not grasped the full measure of her spiritual nature. The Land of the Sidhe is not for novitiates or novices. It is a powerful place that can lure you into oblivion if you are not careful."

"But I am less than a novice."

Cate raised an eyebrow as she moved down the slope toward Spencer. "Are you? Jessie has only been remembering for three years now but you...you have remembered for almost half of your life. The difference is that you heard the call but did not heed the message."

He nodded. The sun felt good on his face and shoulders, lulling him into a sense that this place was real. "Tell me about this place."

Cate shook her head. "See? You are still doing it. You have all of the answers you seek but you refuse to listen. Most of life's answers are within you, yet you would rather find them outside of you. How did you know when you first arrived here that this was the Land of the Sidhe?"

Spencer frowned. "I...I do not know."

"Of course you do. You always have known so many things that still manage to elude you. You are one of those people who know so much, yet you do not trust that you know anything at all."

Spencer stared at her in awe. Slowly, as if the skies were parting and he was able to see for the first time, he saw some of her truth. "I know this place because you know this place."

"You know more than you realize."

"What I know is that my greatest joy, our greatest joy is Maeve and the bond we share. She is the rays of sun, the stars in the sky, the breeze of spring. She is—"

"Yes, she is, yet, you came here because you believe you lost her."

Spencer nodded and bowed his head. "I do not understand how she could release me. How could she come into my life only to leave, tearing me in two?"

Cate shaped her hands into the form of a ball and then opened them up revealing a glowing blue sphere. Entranced, Spencer stepped closer to the sphere that hovered at eye level. "You are powerful, indeed, Cate."

"It is the faerie world, Spencer. One can do many otherworldly acts here. It is not necessarily power. Look. Look inside and see possibilities. See the truth. But see."

Spencer saw himself in the cell with Louise. She was treating his ribs and his eye with her herbs and ointments.

"She has such a gentle touch."

Cate lifted an eyebrow. "Interesting choice of words, Spencer."

Spencer looked up from the sphere. "I do not understand. Why are you showing me this?"

"You came here for answers only you can provide. The answer to all of your questions lies not in what Louise said or did, but in what you did not do."

The sphere popped like a bubble and disappeared.

"You have the wisdom, Spencer. I and our lives between us made sure our knowledge was passed on, that we would be able to remember, to find each other, to reconnect. When you return to the task at hand, when you go back to your life, I want you to remember these words: Action Follows Thought. Meditate on them, for it is those words and their wisdom that will help you find the answers you seek."

"Why? Why can't you simply tell me?"

"Because that would be taking your power away and cripple you. To be powerful, one must embrace the power within. When you embrace it, fully accepting who you are and can be, you will be able to find all you need, be all you must and discover all your heart desires."

"I came wanting answers, and now I only have more questions. There is so much that I need to do, and yet I feel so unprepared."

"You are more prepared than you think and you are not alone. That is the beauty of us, Spencer: we are never alone."

He looked at Cate and saw strength and wisdom he had not thought a woman could possess. "And Louise?"

"Remember my words to you, Spencer, and you will understand everything that is happening around you. Go now. Jessie is with you and so are the others who can help you wield your courage and power. Go, and fulfill your destiny."

As if blasted out of the Land of the Sidhe by a great wind, Spencer found himself leaning against a wall in his cell. He had wanted…needed answers and all Cate had given him was riddles. "Damn that little Druid." Rising, Spencer straightened his clothes and breathed in one last stale stench of his cell. He would not be returning to this place alive whether or not it was his goddamned destiny.

"Well, ladies," he said as he heard the guards approaching. "If we're all in this together, then how can we possibly fail?"

And then, ever so quietly, he thought he heard a woman's voice whisper, "We can't."

*   *   *

16th Century

Outside the tavern, Duncan saw Spencer walking ahead of six armed guards. "Remember," he ordered his men, "there will be no fighting this day regardless of what they say or do. We get the box to the Queen and that is that. Understood?"

His men all nodded and responded, "Aye."

Spencer ran to Duncan and wrapped his arms around his friend. "I ought to kick your tail for following me here," he whispered.

Duncan clapped him soundly on the back. "What, and let you have all the fun? I think not, old friend. I had it under good advisement the sort of plan you'd concocted for yourself, so I came forthwith to pull your burning breeches out of the fire."

The guards that had surrounded him caught up to Spencer, but Duncan's men would not let them through. "I have what the Queen seeks," Duncan announced loudly.

Spencer sauntered over to the box that sat on the table. Before he glanced down, he closed his eyes, took several deep breaths and called on the memory of Cate.

Then, Spencer squatted down and looked at the box. It was exactly as she remembered it. The carvings were accurate and detailed, the box was the right shape and color, and the wood was flawless. It even looked old. "You aged it," he said in Gaelic.

Duncan put his arm around Regginald. "She knew of ways to age wood so that it has a more…ancient feel to it." Duncan's reply was also in Gaelic, but it did not flow nearly as easily as Spencer's words as it was not a language he knew in this life.

Rising, Spencer looked at the boy. Peering deeply into

Regginald's eyes, Spencer whispered. "Ceara?"

Regginald's eyes softened as she touched Spencer's face. The English guards reacted with disgust and stepped farther away from Duncan and his men. The word bugger was uttered by some.

"Jessie."

Spencer squatted down so they were face-to-face. "Of all the memories of hers, yours is like a beacon, Ceara. She must have known you were here."

Ceara nodded. "We came together."

"And a damn good thing," Duncan added, enjoying the discomfort of the guards, who were now well out of earshot. "The box looked newly carved when I finished, and Quinn would have known it for what it was within seconds. Ceara told my men what to get for it and we rubbed it in and gave it a more aged appearance. What do you think?"

"I think…that I am not the only one who has an army ready to help the cause."

"Nor are you the only one to draw them forth," Duncan replied. "I have much to learn from Lachlan. I could have been more help had I listened."

"We all reach the beginning of our path in our own time."

"Come now, my friend. Let's get this accursed box to the Queen and be done with it." Spencer motioned to one of Duncan's men to carry it.

As they walked in front of the English soldiers, Duncan elbowed Spencer. "They do not quite know what to make of us, eh?"

"Nor do I, for that matter. This is quite an odd mixture of sorts. "

"We're going to have to make quite a run for it, my friend," Duncan said in Gaelic. "I hope you're up for it. You look like you tangled with a jilted lover's husband. Can you run?"

Spencer nodded. "I have no choice."

Duncan shook his head. "Whether or not they expect us to run is irrelevant. We are ready. Murddoch will be waiting for us. If we can make it to the water before the soldiers find us, then—"

"Then what?"

"Finding Sir Drake, of course, and the real box."

Spencer glanced over at Duncan, seeing the light play off his golden hair. "I must say that I do so like the sound of that."

*   *   *

When at last they reached the Queen's courtyard, the men were drenched in sweat, and the soldiers retreated to the basins for a quick drink before forming a half circle behind Spencer and his men. Then they waited nearly an hour for the Queen. When she did finally arrive in full retinue, everyone bowed, including Duncan and his men. Spencer did not. He was looking for someone in particular, tradition be damned.

As the women entered, the swooshing of the fabric of their dresses drowned out all other sounds as a rainbow of gowns progressed to the center of the court. The Queen was a wearing a gold silk gown that gripped her bodice tightly before spanning out in a six foot diameter. Light yellow jewels dotted the gown on either side and were woven into a lace that rested on her collarbone. Her hair was swept up and away from her face, held there by a clip with the same yellow jewels.

While all eyes were on the Queen, Spencer's were glued to Louise, who wore a lavender gown of a shiny fabric he had never seen. Lace protruded from her collar, her sleeves and along the bottom of her dress. Her hair hung longer than that of the others, and Spencer estimated that she was the youngest of the ladies.

As they walked out, the very air itself seemed to part as they made their way. Together, the Queen, her ladies and Lord Walsingham made a grand entrance as if this were some sort of special ceremony. When the Queen's eyes fell on the box, Spencer could see her excitement and trepidation, but more strongly, he felt her greed.

"Her Majesty, the Queen."

The Queen walked around the box once, her gold dress swishing as she moved. She paused once to run her fingertips lightly over the carvings. She studied the box for some time before turning her gaze to Spencer. Her eyes narrowed as she assessed him. "It appears, Mr. Morgan, that you have, indeed, kept your end of the bargain."

Spencer nodded. "I am a man of my word, Your Majesty."

His implication did not go unnoticed by Queen Elizabeth, whose eyes became tiny slits. "I said appears, Mr. Morgan. The box could be the one in question, or it could be something not genuine. Fortunately, there is one who has the capacity to enlighten all of us here."

"By what sort of witchcraft is it that he would know an ancient tongue of another culture whose major tradition of passing wisdom on lay in the oral tradition?" Spencer cast a glance at Louise, whose eyes grew wide at his words. It was well-known that the Queen forbade the use of the word witch in her presence, even though she, herself often sought the advice of astronomers and other such magicians.

"No magic necessary, Mr. Morgan. We English leave the magic to your people."

Everyone in her court snickered as if what she had said had been truly funny or even slightly witty. "My man has his means, Mr. Morgan, as I am sure you have yours. The important thing for you to understand is that you and your men's lives depend upon whether or not this chest contains authentic materials. If it does not, if you have tried to fool this Crown, you all will be hanged before sundown."

Spencer bowed slightly. "I have nothing to fear. Bring your man in and let him tell you so."

A guard walked to a second larger door and waited for the Queen to offer a command, then he opened the door and out walked a short, dumpy man wearing clothing only a nobleman could afford: the fluffy lace and frilly undergarments of a fop, a dandy, a man who wished all who met him to understand he was a man of wealth and means.

The man glanced over at Spencer and Duncan and his malicious grin hung between them like a dark cloud. Something ominous hovered near him, making Spencer cut his eyes over to Duncan, his thoughts willing Duncan to stay his normally fast fists.

So sure was the Queen how this would play out, she was allowing Spencer and Duncan to actually see who Quinn was. Did Quinn not understand that he, too, was slated for slaughter the moment he gave this woman what she needed?

"Gentlemen, this is Lord Baltimore. He is going to examine the chest as well as the scrolls within. Your fate rests in his hands."

Spencer felt his stomach tighten. So, she had managed to lure him in with her pronouncement spread throughout London that she needed a BoibeLoth reader. Quinn must have made a straight line for the court when he heard the call. All the what-ifs came flooding into Spencer's head, and he realized, perhaps too late, just how precarious their safety was.

Panic seized him roughly by the throat, but fortunately, he felt he was not alone, and a sudden wave of calm came as quickly as the panic.

"Jessie—" he uttered, sensing the calm coming from deep within where Jessie lingered. Yes, she had come. She was bringing him the gift of her knowledge, but there was so much more than that.

Suddenly, Duncan stepped out of line and bowed. "Your Majesty, allow me to introduce myself. I am Duncan Parnell of West Sussex."

"An Englishman," the Queen said, trying to keep an eye on Lord Baltimore who was carefully kneeling in front of the box. "How did an Englishman come to be involved with an Irish privateer?"

Duncan looked over at Lord Baltimore who glanced up to hear the answer.

"I am not. He merely hired me and my men to retrieve the box from his ship. I came as protector of my men."

The Queen nodded once. "Then these are not his men?"

"Oh no, Your Majesty. His men mutinied when he landed. He hired us to pull this box out and keep it with us until such time as he came to retrieve it. His ship has sat empty for days."

The Queen looked to Lord Walsingham. He nodded in confirmation. "There is a ship that has been docked and has remained empty for some time."

"Very well. Then you have done your duty to the Crown and we are grateful. You and your men may go."

Duncan bowed. "Thank you, your Grace." But Duncan locked eyes with Lord Baltimore. For a long time, the two men glared openly at each other.

"Is there something else?" the Queen asked testily.

Duncan turned to her. "I was raised by Protestant parents who taught me the importance of fair play." Pausing, Duncan inhaled sharply. "And it seems to me, as an outsider of the Court, that you have given Lord Baltimore all the power to crush this Irishman, whether the chest is genuine or not. If he says it is not, the Irishman hangs, but you shall still have a box which only that man can tell you is real." Duncan shrugged. "He has the power of life and death over the Irishman. That's a heavy burden, indeed."

The Queen weighed this. "And what would your good Protestant parents have advised?"

"They would advise, Your Majesty, that if the box is labeled a fake by Lord Baltimore, that you burn it before everyone's eyes right here. That way, this interpreter must be very careful before making his determination. If he lies about its authenticity, then it will burn, taking whatever it is you seek with it."

"Burn it?"

"Aye. What good would it be to you if he deems it is not the box you seek? If this man has intentions of perhaps keeping some of the secrets solely with himself, then burning the box will prevent him from doing so." Duncan shrugged again and spread his hands like he did not care in the slightest. "I am just a humble servant of Your Majesty who trusts no one."

Queen Elizabeth pondered his words. Then slowly, she turned to Lord Baltimore and sized him up. "Have you an issue with this?"

Lord Baltimore glared at Duncan, who was grinning like a fool. "No, Your Majesty, I do not, but I would advise that you let me translate a few of the writings before allowing the Irishman and his men to depart."

She flicked her wrist at him. "I do not require your advice, Lord Baltimore. Everyone will remain here until you tell us whether or not the scrolls are authentic." She gestured to Duncan. "That includes you, Mr. Parnell. I am intrigued that you would offer such a strange notion as burning this beautifully crafted chest. It makes me wonder if you know more than you let on." She turned to Lord Baltimore. "Continue with your examination of the chest and its contents."

Lord Baltimore tore his seething gaze from Duncan's face, composing himself enough to act as if he did not care that condemning the box as fake meant watching it go up in flames. Duncan had played a shifty card, and Quinn had no way of counterbalancing it without losing everything within.

Finally, when Quinn had gathered himself together, he spent several long, quiet minutes examining all sides of the box. He ran his hands over it like a man would a woman he was seducing. At last, he turned to the Queen and bowed. "This chest is the one."

The Queen could not hide her pleasure, and Spencer suspected this would be one of the few times in her illustrious reign where emotions not only overcame her, but were revealed by her. "Excellent. And now the scrolls. What of the scrolls?"

Lord Baltimore meticulously unfastened the leather and metal clasp and opened the chest. Dozens of scrolls lay side-by-side. With trembling hands, he reached in and carefully extracted one scroll from the pile. As he unrolled it, he scanned the old writing before handing it to the Queen, who took it and looked at it, and then handed it back to him. "Well?"

Lord Baltimore swallowed audibly. "It—is them, Your Majesty."

Inhaling slowly and deeply, she nodded. "Excellent."

"But there are many scrolls within, I sugg—"

Once more, she flicked her wrist at him. "I need not your counsel, only your talent at deciphering and translating." To Spencer she said, "I would normally offer gold or some sort of reward, Mr. Morgan, but you have relieved my ships of enough that we can call us even. You and your men are free to go, Mr. Morgan, as per our agreement."

But Spencer was not listening to the Queen. Instead, he was looking at Louise and thinking about Cate's words. If it wasn't what he did, but what he didn't do, what was it he hadn't done?

"Come along, sir," Duncan said, pulling Spencer roughly toward his men. "My Queen bade us to leave, and I'll show you and your men out. You have overstayed your welcome." Shoving Spencer roughly toward his men, Duncan turned one last time toward Lord Baltimore, who stood protectively by the box glaring at them.

"Amazing talent, old boy," Duncan tossed out. Wherever did you learn to read such a peculiar language?"

"I serve my Queen."

"Of course you do. Don't we all. Well then...best of luck to you." Duncan laughed and motioned for his men to move forward. "Come now. We must be off."

As the eight men hastily made their way through the streets outside the palace, Spencer saw four horses being held by Regginald, whose face reflected the light from his torch.

"Ceara!"

Spencer cast a suspicious eye to Duncan as they ran. "Your doing?"

"I wish I could take credit, Spencer, but I cannot. Ceara arranged for the horses knowing how limited our time would be. We will have a better chance of reaching Murddoch on horse than on foot."

Spencer nodded and ran harder. "A brilliant plan is afoot?" he asked the sickly young boy as they reached him.

"We'll get out of this alive, Spencer Morgan, if that is what you mean." Ceara smiled. "So, the Queen really did let you go after all." Handing the reins to Spencer, she backed away from the horses. "I half-expected her to toss you into the Tower while the scaffolding was being prepared."

"She let us go, but her men are close behind, to be sure."

"The soldiers will never catch you. Remember, they suspect you are on foot with no help and will be searching for you in either a tavern or an inn. They will expect you to stay together since you have no reason to fear being chased."

Duncan mounted the black horse and pulled Spencer up after him. "Well done, Ceara." The other men mounted their horses as well.

"How long before Quinn knows he has been duped?"

Duncan shrugged. "That, my friend, depends upon the scrolls. He could figure it out in the first five or not until the last five." He reached down from his place in the saddle and took Ceara's hand. "I have much to learn from your son. Thank you for all you've done."

"You're both welcome. Now go. Time's a-wasting."

Spencer clung to Duncan as he spurred his horse into the darkness.

When all eight riders were out of sight, Ceara sighed. Her job was done here. All she could do now was return to the portal and wait for Jessie.

But first, there was a young boy with a fever who needed her help.

*　　*　　*

With the box now in her private chambers, Elizabeth could barely contain her excitement. Her blue eyes danced wildly as she walked slowly around the box trailing her fingertips lightly over the rough edges. She stroked the top of the lid like a lover, sighing loudly in anticipation. She placed her cheek against the top of the chest as if listening for something no one else could hear.

"Lord Baltimore," she whispered, caressing the box.

"Yes, Your Majesty?" Lord Baltimore was at her side in an instant.

"It is time. Read through every scroll until you come to the word for gold. Do not linger upon words long forgotten. Get to that scroll…that precise word. Do you understand?"

Lord Baltimore nodded. "I am looking for the word gold. Anything else?"

"That will be all for the moment. Once you find that, you may cease your reading and focus solely upon the correct translation of that scroll. I need the exact and proper wording from that scroll. You need to be precise and flawless."

"I understand."

Lord Baltimore waited for the Queen to step aside before

opening the chest. Scores upon scores of scrolls lay atop each other. "I need a cloth or something where I may lay the scrolls when I am finished."

Louise scurried away, returning with an empty chest. "Will this do?"

Lord Baltimore glanced at it. "That is fine." His eyes locked onto Louise's as he took the empty box from her. For a protracted moment, he looked over the box at her, eyes aflame. "Set it there."

"Yes, sir." Setting the box down, Louise stepped closer to him. He could smell her fragrance. "Will there be anything else?"

Lord Baltimore studied her, his eyes roaming from her chest to her feet and back again, finally lighting upon her ample bosom bursting from her bodice. "Perhaps later," he said, returning his gaze to the chest at hand.

Dozens of scrolls were in the box, and it was his task to go through as many as he could before the Queen lost patience. She wanted results and she wanted them when she wanted them and not a second later.

"Will you be reading them before the end of this century, Lord Baltimore?"

"Your Majesty, my apologies." Lord Baltimore gently pulled out two scrolls and quickly read them. His BoibeLoth abilities were better than he had hoped. He was able to read through them quickly, putting aside four useless scrolls immediately.

Reading several more, Lord Baltimore could feel the Queen's eyes at his back. "What is upon those you have discarded?"

"Someone's trite pearls of magic wisdom, Your Majesty. Druid mish-mash. Nothing much of interest."

Then he unrolled the next one, and felt the blood drain from his face. For a long time, he stared at it, reading it three times before gritting his teeth and tossing the scroll into the second chest. Pulling out the next scroll, not reading it, but still seeing the words from the last scroll, Lord Baltimore fought the anger rising in his throat.

"Lord Baltimore, is there something the matter?"

Rolling the scroll back up, he tossed it into the second

box. "Nothing, Your Majesty. It's just...er...the handwriting is difficult to read at times. It is, after all, quite ancient."

"Louise, bring me one."

Louise reached for the scroll beneath the last scroll, the one that had caught his breath in his throat, and she handed it to the Queen, who unrolled it and looked at it with but a cursory glance. "Such odd and mysterious writing. Were these intelligent people? I wonder."

"It is strange and bizarre writing, Your Majesty. It does not even appear legible," Louise said, setting the scroll in the second box.

Lord Baltimore eyed her suspiciously for a moment before returning to his task. When he was halfway through, he knew what he needed to do next. Turning to the Queen, Lord Baltimore shook his head. "I am terribly sorry, Your Majesty, but I believe we have been duped."

The Queen rose from her chair and looked even whiter than the lead-filled powder she had plastered on her face. "Duped? I thought you said the box was real."

"The box is, Your Majesty, but the scrolls...they...are replicas, probably replaced by the very Irishman you released."

Queen Elizabeth turned to Louise and said in an icy tone, "Get Walsingham in here."

In an instant, Lord Walsingham was at her side. "Your Majesty?"

"Did you send the soldiers?"

Lord Walsingham bowed. "I did as you bade me, as always."

"Send more, and tell them I want the Irishman alive."

Lord Walsingham appeared struck. "Alive, Your Majesty? I fear it might be too late for th—"

"Alive! I want him alive!"

Lord Walsingham scurried from the chambers, leaving Lord Baltimore, the Queen, and her ladies. "Explain this to me, Lord Baltimore. How was it we were duped?"

Lord Baltimore picked up a scroll. He did not open it. "The first scrolls I read did have the ancient writings on them, but the deeper I got, well, the scrolls no longer had ancient wisdom and stories on them."

"What did they have?"

"Well…my Queen…they said…not so pretty things about… you."

"Me?" The blush of anger rose around her cheeks. "What did they say?"

Lord Baltimore swallowed loudly. "What a fool you were and that you were too easily deceived by your greed and lust for power."

The Queen's eyes narrowed. "Is that so?"

"Should I continue reading them anyway?"

"There will be no need of that. You may finish reading the scrolls in front of the prisoners when they are returned."

"I do so apologize, Your Majesty."

"He will account for his actions, as well as his words, and in a manner most unpleasant."

Lord Baltimore nodded and tried to suppress a smile. "They must have the real scrolls, Your Majesty. Of that, you can be sure."

"Louise, please show Lord Baltimore to his quarters. I will send for you, sir, when the Irishman has been brought to me. That is all."

Louise curtsied. "Shall I dispose of these?" she asked, pointing to the scrolls in the second box.

"Yes. Burn them, but bring the ashes to me."

Picking up the second box, Louise escorted Lord Baltimore to his chambers.

"That was an embarrassing moment, wouldn't you say?" Lord Baltimore said, running his fingers across her arm.

"You are too great a man to be humiliated by the likes of that Irishman, my Lord."

He inched closer, putting his hand on her lower back. "You are an astute young woman. Perhaps when you have finished burning the Queen's embarrassments, you would like to come back and show me what other skills you possess." He licked his fat lips.

Louise blushed and backed slightly out of his grasp. "Why sir, you do so flatter me, but the Queen—"

"Has an empty, lonely bed, sweet girl. That does not mean the rest of us must follow suit." Brushing his lips over her ear, Lord Baltimore whispered, "I saw how you looked at me. Do not be coy, my girl, for passion is a gift from God himself."

"God, maybe, but I am quite sure the Queen would say otherwise." Louise smiled seductively. "I shall bring you some wine this evening before bed. Perhaps then you can open God's gift to me."

Lord Baltimore grinned lasciviously. "Very good. I shall be waiting. Do not disappoint me. I would hate to have to tell the Queen you refused to make me...comfortable."

Forcing her sweetest smile, Louise nodded. "I shall return shortly with your wine, sir." With that, Louise took the box to the kitchen where she opened the one scroll she had read.

Quinn—you are an ass in fool's clothing. While you read this, we are getting the true box and will have destroyed it before you can explain to the Queen how it was you were so fooled. By then, we will all be safe and sound and out of your reach forever. Cate, Jessie, Spencer, Duncan, Lachlan, Ceara...and, of course, Maeve.

Louise smiled as she tossed the scroll onto the fire. They had planned their parts and played them exquisitely, even without being fully aware of what she herself had in store for Quinn.

*   *   *

They were well out to sea by the time the Queen's men were sent the opposite way by an sixteen-year-old blond boy who pointed them in the wrong direction. Not long after the soldiers rode away, Ceara returned Regginald to his parents, where his mother mixed up the herbal broth Ceara had given them and then watched in silent anticipation as Ceara drank it. After explaining to his mother how often to administer the potion and how to cool down the fever with cold water, Ceara lay down on the bed and closed her eyes. Her soul lingered with him for a moment longer before returning through the portal.

It was up to Jessie and Spencer now.

"It's up to us now," Spencer said to Duncan as they sailed

toward the northern coast of Spain. "If we can wrest that box from Drake, then this is over and Quinn will be rendered powerless, regardless of the life that bastard chooses to live." Spencer waited for a response from Duncan, then patted him on the shoulder. "Are you not well?"

"Much has changed within me, Spencer." Only the moon and a flickering lantern illuminated Duncan's face, casting shadows to one side.

"Oh?"

Duncan stared at the stars and sighed. "I have spent a lifetime pushing Lachlan's memories from me, as if they were some sort of poison. I have blocked them with drink, with sleep and even using my own mind. I never truly understood why they were such a threat to me until all this started." He turned to face Spencer. The wind pushed his hair into his face so he tucked it behind his ears. "In many lives, Lachlan was in love with Maeve. For some reason, there was always some hope within him that she might someday return his affections. I don't believe she ever did. I think it has taken him this long to realize...she never will."

Spencer still said nothing, though his thoughts were many.

"She never will, Spencer, because long ago, even before Cate, there was someone else Maeve loved...someone who became Cate, and you, and Jessie and all the souls betwixt. Maeve consigned her life's eternal fate to that soul which is now yours." Duncan shook his head. "Do you have any idea how fortunate you are? Do you realize how singular it is to go from life to life knowing you will eventually be loved by the right person?"

Spencer nodded slowly.

"Well then, my lucky friend, your destiny awaits you, while mine...mine is as elusive as a cloud. Still, I refuse to be as stubborn or as foolish as Lachlan has been. I'll not wait and wonder if Maeve might or might not choose me in this life, for the answer is as plain to me as my own name. I will not let another man's obsession keep me from being happy in my life. Instead, I am going in search of the one I have always managed to dismiss, or even miss altogether. In this life, Spencer, I will be loved."

Spencer's eyes grew wider. "What are you saying?"

"I am saying that when this is over, I shall return to England where my soul was released at the beginning of this life, and I will live the life I was meant to live."

"England?" Spencer felt his stomach lurch. "Are you certain?"

"I have given it a great deal of thought, and I realized one very important thing: I was not born to the sea like you were. I was born to the land and I will never find love as long as I am on the wrong path. Ships, I am afraid, are not my path."

"The sea is not your path."

Duncan nodded. "I have loved the sea with you, Spencer, and enjoyed our adventures immensely, but this is not my way. As much as it pains me, my way is no longer with you...out here. For as long as I am out here," Duncan waved at the sea, "I will never be whole in here." He smacked his chest with his hand. "You are my greatest friend, my best companion, but not even adventures with you can replace what's been missing in this soul for a very long time. She is out there, Spencer, looking for me. She shall never find me as long as I stay on this ship or any other. She will never find me if I am on the wrong path. I hope you understand. This is something I must do for me."

Spencer nodded, turning away from his friend's pain. How could life be so cruel that he would lose Louise and Duncan all in one grand motion? "I do understand, my friend, though I will be painfully sorry to see you go. If there is a wisdom within you giving you direction and pointing the way, then you must follow it wherever it takes you."

For a long time, the two men stood side-by-side leaning on the railing and watching as the dark green sea washed by. Spencer's thoughts were clouded by a sadness that cut deep. He wondered if Jessie could feel it as well.

At last, when Duncan spoke, his words barely rose above the sound of the sea. "Will you be going back for her?"

Spencer swallowed the knot in his throat and shook his head. "No."

Duncan looked sideways at Spencer. "No?"

Spencer shook his head again. "No. She said it was not our

time and that I had a destiny to fulfill."

Duncan turned his face back to the water. "Ouch."

"Aye. She could not be swayed. In this life, she is as stubborn as she has ever been."

Duncan chuckled. "That's Maeve's spirit through and through. There are some things that never change regardless of the age. So, what will you do?"

"What I do best, I suppose. Sail the oceans and relieve that damned British Queen of yours of much of her wealth."

"Really?"

"Yes, well…that, and keep my eyes on Sir Drake and his exploits."

"That will not please the Queen. She will want to see you hanged."

"Or worse. Jessie tells me Elizabeth reigns for forty years, so it is not likely I will outlive the bitch."

Duncan chuckled. "No wonder it's better that we forget most of our past lives. Forty years, eh? I wonder…does she remain the virgin queen?"

Both men laughed.

"So, you plan on being the gnat that buzzes around her ear?"

Spencer nodded. "That, I do."

For several minutes, neither man said a word. Finally, Duncan turned to Spencer and clapped him on the back. "Well, if this is to be our last voyage together, let's start it out with a bottle of whiskey and remembrances of tales of old."

Spencer pointed toward the cabin. "Then lead the way, old friend, lead the way."

*　　*　　*

Louise stood at the door to Lord Baltimore's chamber. She could feel the clamminess of her own palms. Bearing a tray of wine and fruit, she knocked.

"Do come in."

She was not surprised to see Lord Baltimore lounging on

the bed. "I brought you the wine you requested, my Lord."

He grinned a wolf's grin. "Very good, young lady. You were quicker than I hoped. Come."

Louise entered his chamber and closed the door. "The wine, I am told, is especially good this evening. The Queen had it prepared for a celebration that…well…was not to be." Setting the wine down on the table, Louise poured two goblets. She felt Lord Baltimore's gaze cover her buttocks as surely as if it were his hands.

"Yes, well, the Queen will have her celebration, but first, we shall have ours."

Louise handed him the goblet which he took while reaching out and cupping her breast. "Oh yes. You'll do quite nicely."

"What is it we are celebrating, my Lord?" Sitting on the edge of the bed, Louise allowed Lord Baltimore to pull her bodice down so he could fondle her.

"The death of that accursed Irishman." At the last word, Lord Baltimore squeezed her breast so that it pained her. "Come now, girl, off with your clothes."

Louise sipped her wine, but did not do as he bid her. "I heard the Queen talking."

Lord Baltimore removed his hand and sat up, sloshing a bit of his wine on his nightgown. "About what, dear girl?" "About how glad she was to have such a trusted advisor as you. She intends to keep you on in the eventuality that the Irishman confesses as to the true whereabouts of the scrolls."

This pleased Lord Baltimore, who tossed back his wine. "Excellent. I was afraid she might be…disappointed in my performance, such as it was."

"Quite the contrary. She intends to tell you come morning how she appreciates you so." Louise delicately sipped her wine, watching as he eagerly finished his.

"Then perhaps you will do me the honor of keeping me occupied until morning, my sweet, tender girl." Tossing the goblet to the floor, Lord Baltimore planted his face in Louise's chest, where he inhaled her scent before kissing a nipple. "You are so delectable to behold that my head is swimming with delight."

Smiling, Louise held his face to her bosom.

*   *   *

Spencer was enormously happy to see Jessie waiting for him in his Dreamworld. He had known she was with him because of the bits and pieces of her memories that kept floating in his mind's eye as he tried to drift off to sleep, trying to forget the words Duncan had said to him.

"I knew you were here," he said, as he walked toward her.

He was surprised to find himself standing before a fire not unlike the one of the stone circle. He was also surprised to find Jessie wearing a sky blue robe. She carried on her face the same look of surprise…or was it delight?

"So, this is how you see me, eh? As some robe-wearing Druid priestess?"

Spencer ran his hand over his face. "I suppose I do."

She walked over to the fire and stared into it. "It is a nice compliment, but I'm afraid she is a whole lot wiser than I ever could hope to be. Still, it is flattering to be seen in that light. Thank you."

"I do not mean to flatter, Jessie, and you are wrong in assuming you will never be as wise as Cate. Without your wisdom and guidance, who knows what might have happened?"

"Yeah, well, you came to me in order to get to Cate. I'm just happy I didn't let you down."

"Quite the contrary. We all owe you a great deal."

Jessie turned from the fire and motioned for Spencer to join her at the log that lay before it. "I will always come for you or Cate, or any of us, if you call. I can't imagine not coming."

"Just the same, thank you. I wanted you to hear me say it before…well…before this is all over."

Sitting next to Spencer on the log, she saw the flames dancing in his eyes. "You're afraid."

Spencer looked over her head and at the fire. "Indeed."

"Of Drake?"

"Him, too, I suppose. It would seem my life will never be the same after all this. I found Maeve only to lose her again. I have lost Duncan to a love he is sure is out there. Perhaps I have even lost a bit of myself now that the two souls I have loved most will no longer be here in this life with me. So yes, Jessie, I am afraid. I am afraid of my life without them."

Jessie rose, turned to the fire, remembering how Cate and Maeve had parted it to reveal special things. Did she still have the power buried deep within her?

"This will be a bitter victory for me in many ways, Jessie, for even if I can defeat Drake, I have to destroy something that would forever alter the way future generations see the Druids and Celtic society."

Jessie studied the fire, felt the heat from the flames, and felt the raw energy from the living fire as it leaped out at her. Within that energy were glimpses to be shared...if only she could remember...

"Perhaps it is best that the Druid path of long ago remains a mystery, Spencer. Albert Einstein, the most brilliant man of my time, once said, 'The most beautiful thing we can experience is the mysterious. It is the source of all true art and science.' He to whom the emotion is a stranger, who can no longer pause to wonder and stand wrapped in awe, is as good as dead."

Spencer stared into the fire. "It appears that Cate's mysteries will remain just that, then."

Jessie smiled. "Maybe, maybe not."

"My guess is they will, for I have hardly any recollection of the Druid ways, whether or not they are a mystery. I may have remembered many of her memories with Maeve in various incarnations, but Cate's powers are all but lost to me."

Jessie turned to him. "Fortunately, I do not give up as easily as you, for they are not lost to me." Instinctively reaching into her robe, Jessie pulled out the same two colored powders Cate had used. She cast a handful of the powder into the flames. "Mangashar Daianshura Thurnung Uiscumok." Suddenly, the flames broke apart, revealing Francis Drake at his desk in his cabin.

Spencer leapt to his feet. "How on earth—"

"Watch. Watch not with your eyes, but with your soul. Know what you cannot see. See what is really there...and consider

Cate's words to you."

"Cate's words?"

"Just watch. I promise you will not regret it."

The image in the fire changed. Spencer breathed hard as he watched Louise struggle to get Lord Baltimore under the covers. Then, pulling her bodice back up, she picked up the goblet he had tossed to the floor and placed it back on the tray, which she slid near the door.

"What is she doing?" Spencer whispered, as if Louise might hear him.

"Just watch…and remember the words Cate told you."

Louise straightened up the room before pushing a large chair over to the bed. Then, she reached under the bed and pulled out a book, which she placed on her lap as she sat down in the chair.

"I do not understand."

"Because you are seeing with your eyes. See with your soul Spencer, with our soul, with Cate's soul, and if you do, you will know there is no need for you to be in such pain."

Spencer nodded, unsure of what it was Jessie wanted from him, but he concentrated on not what his eyes interpreted for him, but on what his soul felt as it looked.

Louise leaned back in the big chair and closed her eyes. "Annal Nathrak, Uthvas Bethud, Dochial Dienvay." She said this three times, and after the third round, her body slumped into the cushions, her hands on the book in her lap.

"Louise!"

"Spencer," Jessie said softly. "What did you just see?"

"I…I don't know. What happened to her? What was it she was saying?"

Jessie closed the flames with a slight movement of her hands, and then smiled at how quickly Cate's memories were becoming a part of her. "What were Cate's words to you? Do you remember?"

Spencer thought for a moment and then nodded. "She said it wasn't something that I did, but something that I didn't do that would tell me all I needed to know. Damn it to hell, Jessie, I do not like riddles and do not know what she was getting at! I just do not remember like you do!"

"You need to. It would make your life better."

"What happened to her Jessie?"

Jessie shook her head. "It is not my place to say. It is a mystery you must solve, Spencer. Perhaps in the solution, you will remember more."

"But—"

"No. Enough about that for now. In a few days, you will face Drake, and he is a force to be reckoned with. You and Duncan will need to be at your best, so no more pints of whiskey. It dulls your senses and you are going to need to be sharp if you're going to best a man like Drake."

Spencer kept staring at the fire. "You won't tell me?"

Jessie shook her head. "If Cate had wanted you to know, she would have told you. Until you remember on your own, there is nothing more I can do for you except help keep you from getting yourself killed. So pay attention here, because this thing isn't over until you get the box."

"Can't I just kill the bastard?"

"You can't. He has much to do yet, but you will certainly become a very rich man when you take his three ships from him. What you do with that wealth is entirely up to you."

"What good is wealth if I've no one to share it?"

"For today, for now, you have a job to do and it is going to require every ounce of cunning you possess."

With that, Jessie disappeared into a mist that seemed to come out of nowhere and disappear as quickly as it came, leaving Spencer with sagging shoulders and too many questions to ponder.

*   *   *

16th Century

Quinn, looking like Lord Baltimore, was glancing around as if lost. All around him were forests filled with ferns, white flowers and evergreens of all sorts. The sun's rays caressed various parts of the forest floor, and bees could be heard along with an occasional frog and cricket. A creature ducked behind a tree, but he wasn't quick enough to see what or who it was.

"Come out, Maeve. There's only one person who could have made this happen."

Maeve came out from behind a wisteria vine that could have been a hundred years old. "I am right here, Quinn."

Quinn whirled around, then looked back over his shoulder at the shadow that disappeared back behind an enormous cedar. "Then who—"

"The inhabitants of this realm, of course. Do you not know it?"

"I know more than you realize, Maeve. This is the faery realm. I know that. You would be making a mistake in underestimating me. Still, I am curious to know why we're here."

Maeve laughed. "Underestimate you? I would never presume to do such a thing."

"You are too late. The Queen will first torture then kill Spencer, and there is nothing you can do to stop it."

"Oh, really?"

"The fool overplayed his hand. He does not have the scrolls but I am quite sure he knows where they are. It's going to be a long, slow death for the Irishman."

Maeve tilted her head in question. "You believe the box is still in play?"

"Of course it is. He gave us the box, now he has to give over the scrolls. That is all I need, and once we get them, your man Spencer will serve no other purpose. You can watch him beg for mercy that will never come."

Maeve crossed her arms and shook her head. "You truly believe you are still controlling this?"

"I am."

Maeve laughed. "You were a silly man in the first century, but now, you are simply a blind, arrogant fool."

Quinn studied her eyes, and suddenly he backed away from her. "Just watch it from wherever you perch, Maeve. Spencer will go out in a great deal of pain."

Maeve narrowed her eyes as she closed the gap between them. "What perch was I on when you drank my wine?"

Quinn's eyes bulged. "W-what?"

"There is no perch, Quinn." Maeve's voice held a razor edge. "That would assume that I am stationary, when in fact, I am often in transition. So the question I ask you is what do you think happened after the wine?"

"You bitch! You poisoned my wine?"

Maeve said pityingly, "See how limited your knowledge and wisdom are? If I poisoned it, you would be dead, and the dead do not come here…" Maeve spread her arms out, "…to the faerie realm. So I ask you once more…what do you think happened after you drank the wine?"

Quinn glared at her. "I should have known that tart was you."

"Oh, you think so? You seem to believe that traveling through time makes you omniscient. If that were truly the case, you would have known that Louise was not who she appeared to be."

"That was always your greatest weakness, Maeve: you gave up the power too easily. You had it in the palm of your hand when you first sent Cate across, but you foolishly walked away just when you could have turned it to your advantage."

"What happened to you, Quinn? We sent you out with our trust to keep some of our people alive, and this is what you chose to do with it? To further your own purse? To wreak havoc with those in your life?"

Quinn waved her off. "Please. Do you not think your altruism helped destroy our people? Give, give, give. Help the chiefs lead, heal people, remember laws, and still, no one protected us, no one made sure we lived. What good were the Druids if we could not even protect ourselves?"

"But we could. We are. We—"

"You are wasting your breath, Maeve, not to mention my time."

Maeve's lips twitched. "Time is an interesting concept, Quinn. On one hand, we cannot control it, and on the other, there is so much within it that we can."

"You are wrong, Maeve. I will control my destiny."

"That is where you are seriously mistaken, Quinn. Any

control you thought you had over your destiny was lost the moment you threatened Catie. I thought you would have known that by now."

Maeve made a single slight motion with her hand, and out of the woods walked four female inhabitants of the Land of the Sidhe. Quinn looked around at each one as they surrounded him.

"What is this, Maeve?" he sneered. "Reinforcements?"

One long stride brought Maeve right up to him. Her gray eyes narrowed. For a long moment, she just stared with an intensity that made Quinn try to step away.

"You have no control here, Quinn. No control, no power, and soon, no access to the living beings you have so arrogantly taken over."

The four females tightened their grasp on Quinn and he struggled with both the truth of Maeve's words as well as her intentions.

"You are finished with slipping through time and moving in and around the Land of the Living. From now on, I consign you to oblivion, where you can think upon what you have become and consider the many mistakes you've made in your first century life."

Quinn's eyes grew wide as he tried first pulling, then pushing against the faeries restraining him. "No! Maeve, wait!"

"From this day forth, your soul will be chained here in the Land of the Sidhe, where they will make sure it stays so it can do no harm. You will never use the portals, possess human beings, or otherwise engage in any earthbound activity again. You are, in essence, cancelled."

"Wait!"

"You have used your Druid wisdom for evil, used the portal for personal gain, and used human beings to further your own journey, and for those transgressions, you must forfeit the gift of life itself. I consign you to oblivion."

Quinn frantically looked about him.

"You continue to underestimate the Druidic powers that dwell in the cosmos. What do you think the Queen's men will find when they enter your chambers? They will find poor Lord

Baltimore deeply asleep in his bed. She will send for her healer, who will announce that you have fallen into a stupor from which you will never recover. Your body will languish like that for years, until it finally lets go, and Lord Baltimore will die. His body will be buried, he will be forgotten, and you...you will see it all from here."

Quinn knew it was futile, so he changed tack as the faeries began dragging him away from Maeve. "What of my other lives?"

Maeve shook her head. "There are no other lives for you Quinn. Wherever you are, whoever you were is now soulless, soon to die. Oblivion, Quinn, means there is no you in any age."

"You haven't seen the last of me, Maeve!" he screamed as the faeries pulled him deeper into the forest.

"Yes I have," she said quietly.

*   *   *

Cate woke so quickly she was standing in the middle of the field before she was fully aware of what she was doing. She'd been dreaming...of Spencer, of Maeve, of a world she knew nothing about.

Ah, yes...Jessie. Jessie was beginning to remember. She was starting to accept the power within her.

There had been several others along the way who had fought Cate's eternal presence, but eventually, most acceded and allowed her memories to come through. She knew it was only a short wait while Jessie figured it all out. She was young, eager and desperately in love with the idea of having someone to love her in the life she was living.

Weren't we all?

Cate held her face to the sun and closed her eyes. Life was such an incredible gift, yet people were invariably miserable in it, always searching for that elusive something to fill the gaping void in their lives.

Sensing his approach before seeing or hearing him, Cate turned to find Lachlan approaching her.

"You slept here last night?" he asked, pulling a flower from her hair.

"I needed some clarity, yes."

Lachlan nodded. "It is happening."

"Yes, it is."

"What if they are not successful? What then?"

Cate sighed and shrugged. "I do not think like that, Lachlan, you know that. Spencer knows what needs to be done, and he will do it because of who he is."

"You may have put too much faith in him, Cate. The man is a pirate and a killer, after all."

"And a very successful one at that," she said tartly. "Do you think he would have been able to reach Drake if he had been born a farmer?"

This made Lachlan laugh. "You are a far better Druid than I, Catie. I can barely handle Duncan's residue in my soul. He is an empty, morose being with nothing to live for and even less to offer. His existence saddens me greatly."

"Then perhaps you ought to help him."

"No. He must find his way in that life. I would not presume to meddle."

Cate lifted an eyebrow. "What are you implying?"

Chuckling, Lachlan shook his head. "Oh, I believe you know. You allow them to get beneath your skin. You care too much about their life outcomes. Quite simply, little priestess, you care too much."

She could not deny it and didn't even try.

"But then, you have always loved deeply, my friend, and for that, no one can fault you."

"Love? Is that what it is?"

"Isn't it? Is that not what you feel toward young Jessie?"

Cate frowned as she thought about it. "I imagine it is. How very interesting."

"Indeed."

Cate bent down to retrieve her walking stick. Ogham symbols were scrawled along the lower half of the stick. "She exists for me, Lachlan. In here as well as here." Cate pointed to her head and placed her hand over her heart. "I want her to be happy, to be loved, to experience the joys of being alive. I want her to be fulfilled."

Lachlan studied her a moment. "And Spencer? What would you wish for our pirate friend?"

Cate glanced across the field of yellow and blue wildflowers swaying in the breeze. As she refocused her gaze, the flowers transformed into waves of ocean. "I would wish that Spencer lives through his encounter with Drake and finds happiness on a new path."

Lachlan tilted his head at her. "So that he, too, can experience the joys of life?"

Cate refocused her eyes and the flowers were flowers once again. "That, and that he is still alive when Maeve needs him."

A confused look crossed Lachlan's face. "Needs him? Will she need him soon?"

Cate smiled as she started to walk back to the village. "Not soon, no, but she will."

Lachlan hurried to catch up to her. "Because of Queen Elizabeth?"

"Perhaps."

"That woman knows what Maeve is up to, is that it?"

Shaking her head, Cate picked up her pace. "No, Lachlan. The Queen has no idea what Maeve is up to because she is not up to anything."

"What do you mean? Maeve—"

Cate stopped and smiled warmly into his perplexed gaze. "Maeve is not up to anything, Lachlan. She does as she has always done: prepare the way."

*   *   *

The Queen seldom followed her men into the guest chambers, but when one of her ladies came bawling to her about Lord Baltimore and Louise, she had to see for herself.

Walking into the chambers, she was taken aback by the scene before her. On the bed before her lay Lord Baltimore.

Sitting in a chair with a book open in her lap, sat Louise, either dead or asleep. The Queen had seen her asleep often enough to know one from the other, and sure enough, as the Queen slowly approached her lady-in-waiting, she could discern the slow in and out movement of her chest.

"Louise has had one of her episodes, James. Please see to it that she is placed comfortably in her bed with a cool cloth across her eyes."

James nodded and proceeded to gather the sleeping Louise in his arms.

Not one to miss the hubbub, Lord Walsingham came up next to the Queen and shook his head. "This does not bode well." He gestured to the figure on the bed.

"Dead?"

Lord Walsingham nodded to one of his men who bent over the still figure and listened to his chest. "He lives."

"Is he asleep as well?" the Queen asked, knowing full well that her maid had come in babbling that she had been unable to wake either of them.

Lord Walsingham stroked his chin. "Alive, but not alive."

"This is no time to wax poetic, Walsingham. I need this man alive and in possession of his senses! Get someone in here to help or take him outside to a cold pool, but get him awake!"

Lord Walsingham motioned for one of his men to do as the Queen bade, as he was loath to leave her side. He was dying to know what skills this man possessed that would make the Queen care so much about his health—for everyone knew there were few men in Elizabeth's world she cared for at all. Was there more to this translator than he at first thought? He had known the Queen long enough to know she valued few things above her place on the throne, and one of those was money for the Crown. If she could make England richer by any means, she sought out that means. Had this man promised her something he could no longer deliver, or was he just another pawn in one of the many games she played?

Walsingham would never find out. A confused and befuddled Louise awoke the next day with wild tales of her bizarre and outlandish dreams. Lord Baltimore never regained consciousness, and slipped away a few months later in the room that had become his final resting place.

*   *   *

1st Century
"What did you see?" Lachlan asked.
"Maeve. She is returning."
"Then she is well?"
Cate shrugged. "She is unharmed physically, if that is what you ask."
"And what of Quinn?"
Cate shrugged again. She was exhausted from using the sight, tired from her travel, and empty from not having Maeve at her side. This affair had gone on long enough and she would be glad to have Maeve home. "I do not see that, I see her on the bow of a ship with her eyes closed and her hair trailing behind her. She is at peace."
Lachlan tossed a log onto the bonfire and paced across the grass. "She must have been successful, otherwise why would she be returning? Has she not come to you?"
"She has, but not recently. Lachlan, Maeve went to Eire to take care of Quinn. If she returns, then she has done just that."
"You truly believe Maeve has it in her to destroy one of her own kind?"
Cate stared at the fire. Her eyes burned from being open too long. "That is not her way. Whatever Maeve did, she did it the only way she knew how. She did whatever she believed was best."
Sitting next to Cate, Lachlan stared up at the stars. He wondered if the stars were still as bright when Duncan looked at them. "What is best for you, Cate?"
Cate turned from the fire and stared at him. "What do you mean?"
"The portal has changed everything now. Now, you care about the life of a young woman who will not be born for two thousand years. You care about a man who kills people for profit. These people are not yet alive, yet on some strange level you

connect to them as if they were. It must make you see the world differently."

Cate rubbed her eyes. "Life is about nothing else except change. It changes daily. Those of us who adapt to those changes have better lives than those who do not. The portal has not changed me, Lachlan. Life has changed me, as it is supposed to."

Lachlan took her hand and gave it a quick squeeze. "You are wiser every day, Cate. Still, the portal has created…issues for us. I was just wondering where it will end."

Cate turned to fully face Lachlan. "You should never have gone to Duncan. That is why you have all these questions and concerns. You went through when you were not ready and now you know what it is like. Now you know him, and no matter how you look at it, he is part of you. That can never be undone."

Lachlan said nothing.

"You experienced the fullness of life in another time, and it is alluring, isn't it? You can see now why your mother did not ever want you to go through. It is temptation to you now—a temptation that did not exist for you until you went. Did it thrill you or scare you?"

"A little of both, I suppose," he admitted.

Cate nodded. "And why was that?"

For a few moments, Lachlan stared at the stars. "It is not right, Cate, for us to meddle in the lives of others, even if those people have our soul."

"Meddle? Is that what you think we do?"

"Is it not?"

Cate rose and stood with her back to Lachlan as she stared into the fire. "Oh, Lachlan, are you still so hurt by your mother's death at the hands of the portal that you cannot still see the value in it?"

"I see danger, Cate, for all of us."

Cate pulled herbs out from her pouch and crumbled them into the fire, which sputtered and sparked and leapt before parting. "How is the portal any different than having the sight, being able to read omens or hearing the spirits when they whisper to you? We are born as gatherers of knowledge and collectors of wisdom, Lachlan. It is who and what we are. Surely you know this."

"What I know, Cate, what I realized the moment I slipped into Duncan, is how discontented I am. In one brief moment, I felt his emptiness, his sorrow, his incompleteness, and I knew those feelings are also mine. He was mirroring what I feel like in this life, and I am not sure what I ought to do about it."

Cate closed the flames with a wave of her hand and turned to Lachlan. "Go on."

Sighing, Lachlan shook his head. "Poor Duncan—without roots, without heart, without connection to anything except Spencer. Through his eyes, I saw my life, the huge hollow place in my heart, and…well, I am ashamed to admit it, but I am no different from he."

"Of course you are."

"No, Cate, I am not. I am in love with a woman I will never have, and yet, I linger on the edge of her life hoping that some day, she will look at me the way she looks at you."

"Lachl—"

"Let me finish. I know now, in my heart, she never will, and though I will love her always, in this life, I must make my journey away from her…and you."

"Away? Are you—"

"I am leaving for Wales before she returns. I have heard there is a tribe there that needs a teacher and a Chief Druid and I am going to see if they will accept me."

Cate's head swirled. The idea of Lachlan leaving them had never, ever entered her mind. "England?"

Lachlan nodded. "I am a good teacher, with a sound head, a strong body and an honorable heart. You no longer need me… perhaps you never did. What you need to know you will learn from Maeve, for she is a far more powerful Druid than I could ever hope to be. It is time for me to go, lest I wind up living the same kind of hopeless existence as Duncan."

"Will you at least wait until Maeve returns? She may yet need us to do something about Quinn."

Lachlan shook his head. "I cannot. It would be too hard to say goodbye to her, and I do not wish to have any more dealings with the portal. You and Maeve opened it up and it is for you to do what needs to be done. As for me, I am through with it."

Cate sat next to him and slipped her hand into his. "This isn't just about the portal, though, is it?"

"It is. I do not want it in my life, and in a matter of three years, it has managed to seduce even me. I do not wish to live in either the past or in the future. I want to live this life to its fullest measure. Surely, you can understand that."

She did, though it pained her to admit it. "She will be upset that you did not wait to say goodbye to her."

"She will." Rising, Lachlan pulled Cate up with him and crushed her to his chest. "Your time travel the first time saved our lives, Catie. This time, it revealed a life unlived. Thank you, my sweet friend, for giving my life back to me not once but twice. I swear to you I will not waste a moment if it."

Hugging him tightly, Cate wasn't sure she could let go.

"I cannot remember my life without you, Lach."

Lachlan chuckled as a single tear rolled down his cheek. "And I will not forget what my life was like with you, my friend."

They stood embracing for a very long time, and when Lachlan saw a star streak across the sky, he knew it was time to leave, and released her.

*   *   *

"You're going back?" Cate asked as she and Jessie stood near a tall waterfall just outside the stone circle that was their Dreamworld. Jessie had always thought the mist curtain between the stone circle and the forest was fog. This was the first time Cate had led her away from the circle with its never-dimming bonfire and three foot high stones. They'd silently walked down a path that ran into a pool of water pounded by the water as it roared on by. It was the most incredible waterfall Jessie had ever seen, but then, why wouldn't it be? It was her Dreamworld.

Watching the mist rise off the rocks and water, Jessie nodded. "I have to see this one through to the end, Cate. It was really very difficult having to wait until Ceara and I could go to Wales before finding out if you'd made it off the island. Those were the longest days of my life, and I really do not want to go through that again."

Cate knelt beside the water and tickled it with her fingertips. "I am sorry it was so hard on you. I guess...I never expected you to care so much."

"Well, I do."

"Even for Spencer?"

Jessie smiled, as she seemed to do whenever someone said his name. "Even for him, yes. Maybe especially for him because he needs it the most."

This made Cate smile as well. "Perhaps you are right. It is odd to care so much, though, is it not?"

Jessie nodded. "Totally weird, but then, what isn't anymore? I know that my life will never be the same."

"Nor will mine. Lachlan has decided to go out on his own. I have felt his absence more than I could ever believe."

"Really? Wow. Duncan is doing the same. He needs a quest of his own."

This seemed to surprise Cate, who glanced up from her place by the water's edge. "Truly?"

"Yeah. Time to go on with his real life, away from Spencer, away from...well...the sea. Perhaps something happened when Lachlan went to Duncan."

Cate rose. "Perhaps, like all things, our time together had come to an end."

"Where will he go?"

"Londinium, or a village nearby. He believes Britain is calling him...though, I do find it odd he kept calling it England."

"That would be Duncan's influence. It's called England now, though if you put Ireland, Scotland and Wales with it, we call it Great Britain."

Cate grinned. "Great is it? Well, that is interesting."

"You know, at one point in history, England owned five-sevenths of the known world."

"Then it sounds like the perfect place for him."

Jessie patted Cate's shoulder. "I know it must be hard. You two were finally learning how to be friends, weren't you?"

"In a manner of speaking. I know how he felt about Maeve,

and I think he often saw me as a rival for her affections."

"Tough draw."

Cate looked at Jessie and smiled widely. "Indeed."

"Can I ask you something?"

"Of course."

"Would it have bothered you if Maeve returned his affections?"

Cate scrunched up her face as she thought. "She does love him, just not how he would like. But no, it would not bother me. Maeve is her own person. She comes when she comes and goes when she goes, and that is one of the aspects I love most about her."

Jessie shook her head. "You have got to be kidding. Her loving someone else as much as she loves you would not bother you?"

Cate shook her head. "I have always known my place in her heart, but Jessie, my place is not the only place."

"Then what the hell is a soul mate?"

"A Soul. Mate? Oh. You mean an Anam Cara." Cate bent back down to the water and flicked water onto an orange flower protruding from a rock. "One has many Anam Cara, Jessie. With all the souls out there changing shells, finding one would be nigh impossible, don't you think? That is why Maeve and I continue to practice our remembering. I want to be able to find her."

"I think I get it. So, there's more than one soulm...Anam Cara out there for everyone. I find that very comforting."

This made Cate frown. "Why comforting?"

"People in my time are looking for Mr. Right. You know... the one person who is right for you."

"One? That would be very difficult with the thousands of people in the world."

Jessie grinned. "Uh, Cate, there are over six billion people now."

Cate's eyes grew wide. "Is there such a number?"

"There is."

"Is there room for trees?"

"Barely."

"Hmm. Your world sounds in dire need of your Druid skills, Jessie. If you use them, if you stay on your path, then Maeve will find you or you will find her. It is straying from the path that prevents us from finding the ones we are connected to. So you stay on your journey, and your heart will stay in a good place. Just be patient."

"I want to become a Druid priestess."

"Then you need only ask Ceara to train you if you truly believe you are ready."

"Don't you think I'm ready?"

This made Cate laugh outright. "Oh, Jessie, I am sorry. I am not really laughing at you. You will know when you are ready. It will come."

"It's come," Jessie said with stubborn insistence.

"Excellent. Then tell Ceara. She will train you. Just understand that Ceara's ways are the old ways. You'll not become a Druid priestess overnight."

"I have the time."

"You will need it."

"I'll make you proud."

"I already am."

Jessie blushed. "Really?"

"It cannot be easy to live in such a joyless place, isolated from nature, from the spirits, and yet...you do."

They sat in silence for a long, long time, watching the waterfall, listening to the water as it crashed into the surface below. The mist rose off the water, filling the forest above them.

Then Jessie swung her legs over the rock and hopped off to the soft ground below. "Drake is near and I want to be there when Spencer finally gets him."

"Very well. You be careful Jessie Ferguson. Your world may be a dark, scary place, but it is far brighter with you in it."

As Jessie started up the path to the circle, she turned one last time. "Cate?"

"Yes?"

"Did Maeve kill Quinn?"

"You know, Jessie, I honestly do not know."

Jessie pondered this a moment. "Do you think she killed him?"

Cate shook her head. "I am sure that she found some other way to render him harmless."

"I sure hope so, because as it stands now, Spencer is certainly going to have his hands full with Drake."

"Is there anything more I can do to help?"

Jessie shook her head. "I got him to Drake. It's up to Spencer to finish the job."

*   *   *

16th Century

"I do not understand at all," Duncan said, lowering the telescope. "All three ships are heavy-laden, yet he does not appear worried in the least that we are sharing his waters."

Spencer laughed and clapped Duncan on the back. "Is that why you've been staring through that thing for so bloody long? Duncan, we are on a British ship, remember?"

Duncan shook his head. "See what I mean? I am getting too old for the likes of this. I had forgotten where we got this vessel."

"And besides, we are but one ship, Duncan, and he is but one arrogant man. He'll not flee or even prepare arms...that's how confident the man is."

"It appears that that might very well be what costs him his life."

"Perhaps, but not this day. This day, he will remain alive; embarrassed perhaps, but very much alive."

Duncan handed the telescope to Spencer. "And you truly believe our crew can take three ships."

Spencer nodded. "Once we wrest hold of the first one, then it will be a fair fight, and you know how well our men do when the fighting's fair."

"Why do you suppose he has stayed so close to the shore?"

"He may have taken down a galleon or two in these waters. She sits so low, he has come quite close to overloading the back ship."

"Which one is he on?"

Spencer pointed to the second ship. "Jessie said he was in the Seagull prior to having lost his ships."

Duncan snatched the telescope back from Spencer and raised it back to his face. "The Seagull is it? Well, there's a wooden gull on the bow of the second ship, so it appears you did not misplace your trust when you put it on the girl."

"You gave her too little credit."

"And you gave her too much. You still do! How is it we've not heard what has become of Quinn? For all we know, he could be one of our own!"

Spencer frowned. "You are being ridiculous. You well know that he was Lord Baltimore."

"Do I? How do we really know that? Maybe it was just another clever possession. Did you ever stop to think of that? That maybe Quinn has duped us all?"

Spencer said nothing.

"See? We've left our fate in the hands of people long dead and a young girl not yet born."

"I trust that Maeve took care of him, Duncan, and so should you. That faith is really all I have at the moment."

Duncan shook his head. "It is a damn good thing you never got involved with women because you are a fool where they are concerned. I only hope we don't live to regret the trust you place in the weaker sex."

"Enough of your maudlin sentiments, my friend. Go one last time and prepare our men for battle. You, Captain Duncan, are about to commandeer your first vessel."

Duncan went below, and Spencer studied the row of British ships they were bearing down on. Destiny was at hand.

Once he destroyed the contents of the box, what would he do? Would his own pirating days be over? Destiny was at hand. Would he join ranks against the English Elizabeth who had the clear intention of ruling all of the islands? And how would he find Maeve? When would he find her? Had she even been born yet?

And what of Jessie? What would become of her? Would he see her again, or would she be like Cate, a vague memory that walked through his dreams?

Spencer discovered that he was smiling. She was a plucky one, that girl; picking up for him when he should have been run through. She had internal fortitude and he liked that in a woman. He liked that young woman, and was not at all bothered by the memories they now shared.

Perhaps, in the end, what he liked most about Jessie was that she was proof of the good in him. She carried within her the wisdom Cate had collected, yet, there was an innocence about her that he loved.

Loved.

Yes, he supposed he did love her; like a friend one grows up with. He'd have killed Quinn with his bare hands in order to keep him from hurting Jessie. If that wasn't love, he didn't know what was.

Suddenly, he puffed his chest out and straightened his spine. She had come through for him when he needed her most. Now, he would do the same for her by defeating Sir Francis Drake and putting an end to that damned box once and for all. It was the least he could do, and he would do it.

"The men are ready." Duncan was dressed as the captain of the vessel.

"You could pass for an Englishman," Spencer replied.

"I am an Englishman."

"And I forgive you, nonetheless."

Duncan grinned. "You are certain you do not wish to salvage the treasures on that ship before sinking her?"

"Quite sure. We are after the box, Duncan. Nothing more, nothing less."

"Very well. Wish me luck, my friend, as it appears this is our final curtain together." Duncan hugged Spencer to him. "You will always be my greatest friend." And with that, Duncan pushed him away and started for the port side of the ship, where he began waving to the men aboard the other ship.

"I've a message from the Queen!" Duncan shouted to the captain who stood tall on his deck.

"Let me hear it then," the captain shouted back.

Duncan shook his head. "It is intended for your ears only.

May I come aboard?"

The captain gestured over at the near empty deck. "Where is the rest of your crew?"

"She would give me only a skeleton crew since I am just delivering a message to you. You know how tight fisted she can be with gold."

The captain laughed. "Drop plank then and deliver your message. If it's good news, I'll share a spot of my favorite ale with you."

Duncan nodded to his men, who dropped plank over to the British ship. As Duncan started across the board, he whispered, "Lachlan, if you're in there, give me all the wisdom you can, or surely I am a dead man."

*   *   *

"Welcome aboard, gentlemen," Francis Drake announced when the last of Spencer's men left the rowboat and boarded the Seagull.

Spencer knew immediately that the man before him was Drake. Whether it was his long, arrogant stride, his helmet or just the way his eyes had that piercing look about them, Francis Drake had the bearing of a young captain who was all-too-familiar with getting what he wanted.

"You are from that vessel that was about yesterday, are you not? As you can see, one of my ships was lost and the other appears to be listing as well. I believe I must have overloaded them." Drake surveyed Spencer's crew, who knew enough to keep their Irish mouths shut. Spencer looked to Duncan, who did the talking. "My men and I were fortunate to escape with our lives, sir. What demon ran afoul of us, I know not, but down our ship went without so much as a sound or warning."

Drake raised a skeptical eyebrow. "Your ship sank as well? Isn't that peculiar?"

"Indeed. It was dark. Too dark to see, and we are all that is left of Her Majesty's crew."

Drake seemed to flinch. Stepping closer to Duncan, Drake appeared to be carefully choosing his next words. "You are on a mission from the Queen?"

Duncan nodded. "She sent us to find you, sir. You are, are you not, Francis Drake?"

Drake straightened his shoulders as if he were in Her Majesty's presence. "I am. And what good wishes have you brought me from the Queen, Captain..."

"Duncan, sir. I am Captain Duncan of the now sleeping beauty called the Phantom."

Drake stepped back as if slapped. "Phantom? Your ship was called the Phantom?"

"Aye, she was. T'was the Queen's own bidding, sir. She... fancied the name so she bade me to christen it such."

Drake turned to his second. "How is it the Queen has never bid me to name a ship?"

Duncan cleared his throat. "Sir, the Phantom is her name because she intended us to move about the oceans unseen, whereas you, sir, are her golden boy that she holds up to the rest of us. Just one look at my crew, sir, and you'll see that I may have named the ship, but the crew, well, she skimped quite a bit on them."

Appeased by the flattery, Drake threw his head back and laughed heartily. "Of course. Of course. But you do wrong by your men, Captain Duncan. They did manage to survive rough waters that the crew in my last ship seemed incapable of doing."

"Too true, sir, but only because I owe them wages!"

The men all laughed and as the tension slowly eased off the deck, Spencer calculated close to forty men of Drake's to his thirteen. If they needed to attack, the only advantage they would have was the element of surprise. So far, Duncan had been a far smoother talker than Spencer had ever seen, managing to disarm the egotistical Drake with words instead of swords. Spencer glanced over at his friend, still in conversation with Drake and suddenly ached at the loss of him.

"So, the Queen sent you to find me, did she? Should I be flattered or worried?"

"The former, sir. She believed you were elsewhere, but she spread a little coin about, found out where you were, and gathered us together as quickly as possible."

"Lucky you to have been favorably chosen by Her Majesty. Now, what is it that could be so important that she could not wait?"

Duncan reached into his jerkin and pulled out the scroll with the Queen's seal. "I know not what or why, other than she bade me give this to you and not leave your ship until you did as commanded."

"She commands easily for a female," Drake muttered, opening the scroll. His face became pale as he read it, and his jaw set. Then, with a quick flick of the wrist, he tossed it over the side of the ship.

Spencer looked over at Duncan, but Duncan would not return his gaze. Instead, Duncan was studying Drake's second-in-command. Spencer knew exactly what he was doing, so he waited.

Drake sauntered back over to Duncan. The quizzical and arrogant look on his face had transformed to something more like wariness. "Do you know what it is that the Queen has sent you to retrieve?"

Duncan shook his head. "She does not share her wishes with me, Drake. My only job was to—"

"I know, I know, to deliver the message and not leave here without a...certain item."

"I trust you to follow her orders, as she has nothing but wondrous words about you."

Drake nodded as he walked around the deck in a distracted manner. "Of course, of course. Unfortunately, I do not possess the item in question, and I wonder what it was that made Her Majesty believe I do."

Duncan took a breath and cut his eyes over to Spencer. "She strongly believes you do, sir."

"Well, for once, our great lady is wrong."

"Then my men and I would appreciate you returning us to England, where we will deliver your message."

Spencer felt his muscles tense. Duncan again glanced quickly at the second, knowing by the man's change in posture that they were going to have to fight their way out of it, because there was no way Drake was going to return to England. He couldn't. History would not allow it. He would fail here. Jessie had guaranteed it to be so.

Of course, whether or not Spencer and Duncan made it out alive was another story altogether.

"If you will not cooperate, the Queen has ordered us to force your hand." Duncan withdrew his cutlass and clipped Drake's chin, narrowly missing his neck. The blow sent Drake backward, but not before he could withdraw his sword.

"Is the box truly worth dying for?" Duncan asked as metal clanged sharply against metal. All around them, the clash of swords rang out as Spencer's men turned a surprised crew into half a crew as quickly as that. Duncan's voice rose above a cacophony of noise as he struck his second blow against Drake.

Drake shouted, "I thought you did not know what you came for? Well, my friend, you shall not get it."

Drake fought well, but even he could see the efficiency of Spencer's men in dispatching Drake's crew. They had been caught off-guard and it showed as their blood continued spilling across the deck.

"Her Majesty trusts me, Drake, as she trusts you." Duncan made several well-timed maneuvers, eventually dislodging the sword from Drake's hand. With the tip of his sword pressed against Drake's Adam's apple, Duncan smiled. "You may be a match for any man on sea, but your swordsmanship needs work."

"You have me at a disadvantage, sir."

Duncan leaned in. "Tell your men to cease their fighting or I'll remove your head from your shoulders."

Drake cocked his head. "You do not mean to kill me then?"

"I do not go about killing my fellow Englishmen. If you do as requested, I shall forget this moment of weakness and let you and the remainder of your men live."

Calling out to his men, Drake managed to be heard, and one by one his men ceased fighting, surprised that Spencer's men did not run them through the moment they did so.

Spencer glanced around at the carnage. He estimated fifteen of Drake's men were dead or dying, and only two of his were wounded. How this man would become a legend was beyond Spencer's comprehension.

Joining Duncan, Spencer kept his sword drawn and at the ready.

Duncan lowered his sword so that the point now lay in the hollow of Drake's neck. "I would have killed you without another thought, but my friend here seems to believe there is much still for you to do in this life. Now he may believe in your destiny, but I have neither the time nor the patience for any more of your silly games. Get that damned box up here, and be sure the one they bring is the right one. You may send two of your men to bring it on deck. If they try anything, I will disappoint my friend by permanently removing your head from your body and feeding it to the sharks below. Do we understand one another, sir?"

"It is in the hold."

Duncan pressed the tip into Drake's neck. "I think not."

"What?"

Duncan shook his head and Spencer barked at his men to check Drake's quarters. "You never would have left the box in the hold. I am quite sure we'll find it in your cabin, won't we?"

Drake tried to back away but was caught in the mast rigging. "How does she know that I have it?"

"She is the Queen. It is her job to know these things. You underestimate her by believing you could keep something this important from her. You knew how important it was to her, yet, you have kept it from her for this long. Why?"

Drake shrugged. "I have no idea why it is so damned vital to her. As a matter of fact I am not so sure that the chest in my quarters is the one she seeks."

"And why would that be?"

Drake shook his head. "There is nothing in it but old paper scrolls with what looks like children's drawings on them. I had expected gold, even gems, but worthless paper? Perhaps her Majesty ought to consult her Magus again."

Spencer inched closer, no longer able or willing to remain quiet. "Ahh, I see now. You were afraid to show up with what you believed was the wrong chest. And all this time, we thought you knew how valuable it was."

Drake frowned at Spencer. "I do not understand. You're Irish...and...and..."

Spencer grinned. "That I am. Perhaps you have heard of me and my crew. Captain Spencer Morgan at your service." Spencer bowed low and deep. When he rose, he saw the look of disdain in Drake's eyes.

"You!" Turning to Duncan, he asked, "Why are you working with this...this—"

"Scallywag? I have asked myself that several hundred times in our years together, but I never get a good answer."

"You're the man who has stolen booty from me, from my ships, from—"

Spencer laughed. "It was not yours for the taking. Just like the box. It is not yours and never will be."

Drake rubbed his face with one hand. "If you believe that chest is what Her Majesty is truly after, you are a bigger fool than I. I nearly tossed the damn thing overboard on several occasions."

"But you kept it."

Drake nodded. "It fits her description, but the contents... well...she never told me what was inside, but I cannot imagine for the life of me why she would send me around the seas in search of a bunch of old scrolls with illegible writing on them. You'll see for yourself." Drake glanced over at his men as they brought the chest up the stairs.

Duncan did not take his eyes off Drake. "Well?" he said to Spencer, who knelt on the deck and lightly caressed the carvings on the lid. A flood of memories careened through his mind. Suddenly, there was Cate's hand, carving a delicate vine that had been too small for Lachlan's large hands to reach. Her hands moved with love and devotion.

Love and devotion.

Spencer caught Duncan's eyes as he, too, recognized the box. "It is."

Nodding, Spencer watched Duncan as he reverently fluttered his fingertips over the lid, perhaps more gently than he'd ever touched any woman. "My God, Spencer, I'd have known it even without Lachlan's memories." Duncan slowly, lightly ran his fingers over every carving. "She's weathered some, but does not appear to have been molested."

"Molested?" Drake said indignantly. "I am no barbarian."

To Murddoch, Duncan said, "If he makes a sound, take his nose first, then his sword arm. After that, do what you will, but keep him quiet." Duncan knelt at the chest again and avoided Spencer's gaze. "Future be damned, Spencer. The man is a twit."

Spencer grinned and knelt beside his friend. They lowered their voices to barely audible whispers. "I am too nervous to open it, Duncan."

Duncan reached for the clasp. "Damned good craftsmanship, if I do say so myself."

"Lachlan was no slouch. Had you not spent so much time pushing him away, you might have learned something."

Duncan nodded. Laying both hands on the lid, he carefully opened it to reveal less than two dozen aged scrolls.

Spencer looked over at Drake. "Where are the rest?"

"The rest? That's all there was! I swear!"

This time, it was Spencer who was on his feet, dagger drawn and now inches from Drake's face. "Do not lie to us, Drake, or it will surely be the last thing you do in this life! Where are the others?"

Before Drake could speak, his second-in-command spoke. "He tells the truth. I was with him when he first opened the chest. It was only half full of scrolls."

Spencer lowered the dagger. "If he lies—" Spencer's voice was so low it sounded more like a growl, "I will deliver that chest to your Queen with both of your heads in it."

Drake shook his head. "He speaks the truth. I opened it, rummaged around looking for anything of value, but that's all there was. As I said, I had contemplated tossing it overboard, but we decided to keep it on the chance it might be the one she spoke of."

Lowering the dagger, Spencer glared into Drake's wide eyes. "Duncan, have the men signal the ship. I cannot stand to be on this deck a moment longer."

Duncan gave the order and three of their crew held up lanterns on the starboard side, waving them back and forth.

"Very clever, Spencer. You do still have a ship in these waters."

"Fear not, Drake. I got what I came for and will allow you and your men to live." Spencer stared at the scrolls. Had Quinn managed to get to the chest after all? Or had someone else removed them before Drake found the chest? Or maybe his memory wasn't exact. Perhaps these were all they had written.

"This is less than half of what was entombed," Duncan whispered as they stared into the chest.

"I know."

"What now?"

Spencer knelt beside Duncan. All the scrolls were still neatly tied with twine except for one. One on the top had been tied with a purple ribbon.

Purple.

Maeve's favorite color.

"Duncan…"

"I see it."

"How's your BoibeLoth these days?"

Duncan grinned. "Did you forget who it was who wrote the forgeries?"

Spencer grinned back.

"What about yours?"

"Like I was there yesterday."

"Then open it, Spencer."

Spencer picked up the scroll tied with the purple ribbon. Carefully untying it, he unrolled it. The paper was clearly different than he recalled, and lighter than the others, but the writing…the writing he recognized. Ten thousand years could go by and he would always remember the slant of her hand, the delicate curves and lines of the ink. He had no doubt who wrote this. What he didn't know was when.

"Well?"

Spencer rose, took one warning look at Drake, and walked across the deck away from him. Spencer closed his eyes and pictured the ancient writing of his ancestors. Then he read the letter.

My Eternal Love–

No, these are not our scrolls. I returned to Ireland and replaced the ones we wrote with these. As you can see, they are filled with some of Catie's herbal recipes as well as some poetry, but nothing that Quinn could ever use or want. I have destroyed the originals, though it made my heart ache to do so. We worked so hard, after all, to get them all ready.

Quinn has been taken care of, and we need never fear him again. I did what had to be done, and that is all I will say of it now. Just know we are safe from him forever.

I am sorry it took so long and hope you are in no mortal danger. It took me several days to get to the chest, as the cavern where we buried it had a rock slide and many large boulders were blocking the entrance. I hope I have gotten those scrolls out in time.

I know you wanted something from Louise, but it was not our time. Do not worry...the time will come when you and I will, once again, be reunited. Until that time, my love, you have a life to live, lessons to learn, and a heart to fill. Stay alive and I will call for you when the time is right. Stay alive, Spencer, for Louise does not wish to be in this world without you.

I am now, and shall always remain,

Yours, Maeve.

Spencer could barely read her name through his suddenly blurred vision. There it was. Maeve.

Lowering the letter, he and Duncan stared at each other a moment before they both burst into laughter.

"My word, Spencer, but that woman has always been more than a step ahead of us!"

Drake strained to see what the two men could possibly be laughing about.

"Leave it to Maeve to take care of our business for us," Spencer said, clapping Duncan hard on the back. "She is nothing if not presumptuous!"

"Oh she of little faith."

Spencer shrugged and started back across the deck. "She's a Druid, Duncan, and it is her way to go and her right to know. Suffice it to say, she made sure we could not fail while changing nothing in history. Drake will lose his three ships here, just as Jessie said he would, and the secret to the transmutation of gold will be lost for all of eternity."

Francis Drake turned to Murddoch and asked, "Who are they talking about? I heard them mention a woman! Are they discussing the Queen?"

Murddoch chuckled. "Hardly. More like their Queen."

"You both must be mad," Drake muttered when Spencer and Duncan approached him.

Spencer grinned. "You might very well get to be right about that, Drake, especially once you hear your outcome in this little parlor game."

Drake stiffened. "I, sir, am not afraid. I have faced death before and—"

"Who said anything about death?" Spencer smiled broadly now. "Were you not listening when I told you that you had a destiny to fulfill? The forces that be want you to live a good long life, and I, for one, am not about to trifle with those forces."

Drake tilted his head. "You're still going to let me live?"

"You and your crew, yes."

Drake's eyes left Spencer's face and glanced at something over his shoulder. "Perhaps it is I who will let you and your crew survive, Captain, for here comes an English ship as we speak."

Spencer did not bother to turn and look at the ship he knew to be his very own "borrowed" ship. Instead, he moved closer to Drake and leaned in. "You will live, and you will serve the Queen well, but in order to do so, here is what you are going to do…"

*   *   *

As the highest mast of Drake's ship dipped into the water, Spencer and Duncan quietly studied the heads bobbing in the water.

"You're sure they'll be able to make it in from here?"

Spencer nodded. "Trust me, Duncan. He will tell some incredibly tall tale about the outcome of his three ships, and it will go down in history as fact. He'll be fine. Believe me."

Duncan sighed. "And the chest? Are you sure it was so wise letting him have it?"

Watching Drake cling to the chest, Spencer nodded. "Once the Queen has the box, she will end her quest for the elusive alchemy of transformation She can move on with her monarchy, and our friend Drake can continue plundering the high seas."

Duncan raised an eyebrow. "What did you say to him before he jumped into the water?"

"Just a little helpful advice. I told him if he were smart, he would fill the chest with gold, hand it over to his Queen, and tell her he lost three ships trying to wrestle the box away from the Spanish."

"What did he say?"

"That he needed not my help in telling her exactly what happened."

"So he'll make up his own lie."

"Exactly."

"May I ask why you destroyed the scrolls? They were, after all, forgeries."

"Regardless, I do not want the BoibeLoth in her hands. She is an...enterprising monarch, your queen, who hates Scots, tolerates the Irish and plays with the Spanish and French. I'd rather she turn her attention completely away from our people. If that man is smart, he'll fill that chest with gold knowing it will be a salve on her wound for not getting what she wanted."

"Please stop referring to her as my queen. She is not my queen."

"If she is not your queen, then England cannot be your land. Where would you like me to deposit your sorry ass?"

Duncan thought for a half second and then smiled. "Scotland."

"Scotland?"

"They're hearty adventurers. I think I will start my new life there, in the sun, with the sea at my back and the vineyards in the foreground."

Spencer laughed, though his heart grieved. "Then Scotland it is."

Duncan walked up to Spencer and laid his hand on his friend's shoulder. "Do not grieve for me, Spencer. It is just this life. There will surely be many others because I intend to remember as much as I can."

"Truly?"

"That Lachlan sure as hell did not let up. He wants me to remember and so I shall."

Spencer sighed and turned away. Yes, there would be other lives, other adventures, other memories to make and to remember. In the meantime, there was plenty of time to fill waiting for Louise to call him.

Plenty of time.

*   *   *

21st Century

Jessie and Ceara trudged up Marigold Street arm-in-arm. It had been three days since Jessie had returned. Her trip to the sixteenth century had taken so much out of her she had slept for two solid days. Her mother kept asking her if she was sick, but Jessie knew that tone well enough to know she was worried that Jessie had fallen back into the drug habit. She did not blame her mother for worrying that she had fallen off the wagon. Off her rocker was more like it.

She had gotten so involved with Spencer, she'd forgotten her less-than-fascinating life.

And then last night, the dream had come.

Well, it wasn't really a dream. It was the Dreamworld she hadn't yet learned to control or master, or even understand. It came to her when she least expected it, and though she had fallen asleep before the lights went out, she found herself, once again, in that strange time.

"So what did she say?" Ceara demanded. "Wait. It's a nice day, my dear. Let's sit on the bench over there."

Jessie helped Ceara to the bench and sat next to her.

"That's much better. Now go on."

"Well, we were at the stone circle when Maeve appeared. She motioned for Cate to finish telling me her story." Jessie leaned back and smelled the aging wisteria vines behind her. "So, Maeve took my hands, pulled me to her and hugged me." She closed her eyes, briefly, remembering.

"I cannot thank you enough, Jessie, for keeping Catie safe once more."

"Me? It was you. I didn't do much at all."

Maeve's eyes danced with the flames. "What I did, you made possible, and in doing so, you helped prevent Quinn from painting the world dark colors."

"Is he dead?"

Maeve shook her head. "Death is not a containment for evil, Jessie, I had to imprison his soul."

"Whoa. You're more powerful than I realized."

"Power is only as good as the wielder. That is why you must learn to control yours, for as strong as I am, Catie will be a far greater Druid than I. You possess a kind heart and a pure spirit. You are what is good in humankind, Jessie, and it is time you accept the helm Catie and others have prepared for you."

"I think I am ready, Maeve."

Maeve smiled and touched Jessie's cheek. "I know you are."

Jessie nodded. "Did you leave Quinn in oblivion then?"

Maeve shook her head. "His memory of the scrolls, of the chest, of our time together in this life could hurt us if he ever got out, so I had to remove him for all time. I will not spend eternity worrying about him showing up. He is and shall remain in the Land of the Sidhe."

Cate reached out and brushed her fingertips along Jessie's cheek. "We may share the same soul, Jessie, but in our hearts, you and I are separate beings. What you have done for all of us is a bravery I am proud to be a part of. I want to leave here today knowing that you believe us to be friends as well."

Jessie nodded quickly. "I'd really like that, Cate. You feel so—"

"Alive?"

"Yeah."

"I am alive, and though I am not with you, there is one who is and she knows it is her turn to become the teacher. Go and learn from Ceara, Jessie."

Jessie opened her eyes and saw Ceara smiling at her. "You brought everyone together to make it happen, Jessie. Once again, you have saved lives."

"For the first time in my life, I am ready to assume the mantle of power handed down through the ages. I am more than ready, Ceara."

Ceara rose and took Jessie's hand. "Cate was right about one thing, my dear. It is time for us to begin your lessons in earnest. Are you ready for the next level in your education?"

Jessie quickly came to her feet. "You bet."

"Good, because there is someone in this life who is going to need you soon and you must be ready. You will need every bit of Druid magic and wisdom at your disposal to get him through this trying time."

Jessie felt her stomach lurch. "In this life? Oh God, please don't tell me it's Tanner."

Ceara shook her head. "It's not Tanner. It's Daniel."

"What?"

"Deep peril is gathering all around him. Profound danger."

"I'll do anything to protect him. You know that."

"I do," said Ceara in the same firm tone. "And this time, we will prepare you for the fight of our lives."

Publications from Spinsters Ink
P.O. Box 242
Midway, Florida 32343
Phone: 800-301-6860
www.spinstersink.com

ACROSS TIME by Linda Kay Silva. If you believe in soul mates, if you know you've had a past life, then join Jessie in the first of a series of adventures that takes her *Across Time*.
ISBN 978-1883523-91-6 $14.95

SELECTIVE MEMORY by Jennifer L. Jordan. A Kristin Ashe Mystery. A classical pianist, who is experiencing profound memory loss after a near-fatal accident, hires private investigator Kristin Ashe to reconstruct her life in the months leading up to the crash. ISBN 978-1-883523-88-6 $14.95

HARD TIMES by Blayne Cooper. Together, Kellie and Lorna navigate through an oppressive, hidden world where lines between right and wrong blur, sexual passion is forbidden but explosive, and love is the biggest risk of all.
ISBN 978-1-883523-90-9 $14.95

THE KIND OF GIRL I AM by Julia Watts. Spanning decades, *The Kind of Girl I Am* humorously depicts an extraordinary woman's experiences of triumph, heartbreak, friendship and forbidden love.
ISBN 978-1-883523-89-3 $14.95

PIPER'S SOMEDAY by Ruth Perkinson. It seemed as though life couldn't get any worse for feisty, young Piper Leigh Cliff and her three-legged dog, Someday.
ISBN 978-1-883523-87-9 $14.95

MERMAID by Michelene Esposito. When May unearths a box in her missing sister's closet she is taken on a journey through her mother's past that leads her not only to Kate but to the choices and compromises, emptiness and fullness, the beauty and jagged pain of love that all women must face.
ISBN 978-1-883523-85-5 $14.95

ASSISTED LIVING by Sheila Ortiz-Taylor. Violet March, an eighty-two-year-old resident of Casa de los Sueños, finally has the opportunity to put years of mystery reading to practical use. One by one her comrades, the Bingos, are dying. Is this natural attrition, or is there a sinister plot afoot?
ISBN 978-1-883523-84-2 $14.95

NIGHT DIVING by Michelene Esposito. *Night Diving* is both a young woman's coming-out story and a thirty-something coming-of-age journey that proves you can go home again.
ISBN 978-1-883523-52-7 $14.95

FURTHEST FROM THE GATE by Ann Roberts. *Furthest from the Gate* is a humorous chronicle of a woman's coming of age, her complicated relationship with her mother and the responsibilities to family that last a lifetime.
ISBN 978-1-883523-81-7 $14.95

EYES OF GRAY by Dani O'Connor. Grayson Thomas was the typical college senior with typical friends, a typical job and typical insecurities about her future. One Sunday morning, Gray's life became a little less typical, she saw a man clad in black, and started doubting her own sanity.
ISBN 978-1-883523-82-4 $14.95

ORDINARY FURIES by Linda Morgenstein. Tired of hiding, exhausted by her grief after her husband's death, Alexis Pope plunges into the refreshingly frantic world of restaurant resort cooking and dining in the funky chic town of Guerneville, California. ISBN 978-1-883523-83-1 $14.95

A POEM FOR WHAT'S HER NAME by Dani O'Connor. Professor Dani O'Connor had pretty much resigned herself to the fact that there was no such thing as a complete woman. Then out of nowhere, along comes a woman who blows Dani's theory right out of the water.
ISBN 1-883523-78-8 $14.95

WOMEN'S STUDIES by Julia Watts. With humor and heart, *Women's Studies* follows one school year in the lives of three young women and shows that in college, one's extracurricular activities are often much more educational than what goes on in the classroom. ISBN 1-883523-75-3 $14.95

DISORDERLY ATTACHMENTS by Jennifer L. Jordan. The fifth Kristin Ashe Mystery. Kris investigates whether a mansion someone wants to convert into condos is haunted.
ISBN 1-883523-74-5 $14.95

VERA'S STILL POINT by Ruth Perkinson. Vera is reminded of exactly what it is that she has been missing in life.
ISBN 1-883523-73-7 $14.95

OUTRAGEOUS by Sheila Ortiz-Taylor. Arden Benbow, a motorcycle riding, lesbian Latina poet from LA is hired to teach poetry in a small liberal arts college in northwest Florida.
ISBN 1-883523-72-9 $14.95

UNBREAKABLE by Blayne Cooper. The bonds of love and friendship can be as strong as steel. But are they unbreakable?
ISBN 1-883523-76-1 $14.95

ALL BETS OFF by Jaime Clevenger. Bette Lawrence is about to find out how hard life can be for someone of low society standing in the 1900s.
ISBN 1-883523-71-0 $14.95

UNBEARABLE LOSSES by Jennifer L. Jordan. The fourth Kristin Ashe Mystery. Two elderly sisters have hired Kris to discover who is pilfering from their award-winning holiday display. ISBN 1-883523-68-0 $14.95

EXISTING SOLUTIONS by Jennifer L. Jordan. The second Kristin Ashe Mystery. When Kris is hired to find an activist's biological father, things get complicated when she finds herself falling for her client. ISBN 1-883523-69-9 $14.95

A SAFE PLACE TO SLEEP by Jennifer L. Jordan. The first Kristin Ashe Mystery. Kris is approached by well-known lesbian Destiny Greaves with an unusual request. One that will lead Kris to hunt for her own missing childhood pieces. ISBN 1-883523-70-2 $14.95

Visit
Spinsters Ink
at
SpinstersInk.
com
or call our toll-free number
1-800-301-6860